BLOOD RUN EAST

Detective Chief Superintendent Simon Shard found himself lumbered with the job of seeing Katie Farrell, the Belfast bomber, out of the country. Not that he minded too much until he lost her and word came of a threat to blow up the Chemical Defence Establishment at Porton Down. The trouble was, that the CDE had been having second thoughts about bad eggs in one basket and its lethal germ cargoes were being spread out along the west and south coast of England. One cache was not far behind Worthing, up on the South Downs under Chanctonbury Ring, and that was where something very nasty was found in an abandoned water-tank.

BLOOD RUN EAST

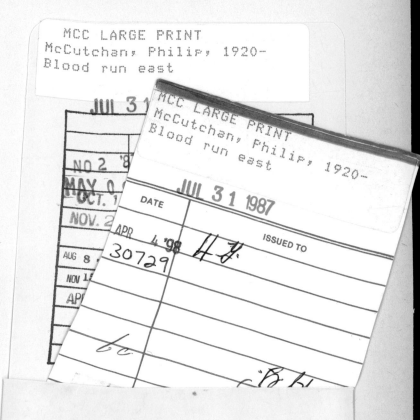

BLOOD RUN EAST

by
PHILIP McCUTCHAN

MAGNA PRINT BOOKS
Long Preston, North Yorkshire,
England.

British Library Cataloguing in Publication Data.

McCutchan, Philip
  Blood run east.
  I. Title
  823'.914(F)   PR6063.A167

  ISBN 1-85057-062-0
  ISBN 1-85057-063-9 Pbk

First Published in Great Britain by Hodder & Stoughton Ltd, 1976.

Published in Large Print 1987 by arrangement with the copyright holder.

Printed and bound in Great Britain by
Redwood Burn Limited, Trowbridge, Wiltshire.

CHAPTER ONE

One of the signs read CHEMICAL DEFENCE ESTABLISHMENT; others, many others, read simply: DANGER KEEP OUT. At times red flags flew. The buildings themselves were unremarkable, just one more group to add to the various defence establishments on Salisbury Plain. Their remarkability lay strictly within the walls, and the security clamp was heavy. Apart from the men who worked there, admittance was for the élite, and needed much high authorisation and examination of documents. The drivers of the two container transporters were heavily screened men from the Ministry of Defence security staff. Each day for the past three weeks they had brought their vehicles to Porton Down, each day they had unloaded nondescript items of equipment: non-chemical stores and office furniture in the main. Each night they had taken aboard the loads for which they had come: packed cases of slides, containers very carefully handled, glass vessels protected by wicker frames and much padding and filled with bacteria-growing materials, jars of liquids similarly protected. The transporters themselves and their drivers and drivers' mates were given other protection: the protection of cars, plain cars filled with armed security men and police officers in plain clothes. In the early hours of each morning they left Porton Down under a strong cloak of security, turned left out of the gates along a gated roadway that led to the main A-30 road connecting London with the west through Salisbury: on this road they turned left again, lumbering night-shrouded through Stockbridge, Winchester, Petersfield; heading east to reach their destination in the dark hours, unloading beneath a similar security screen in the countryside south of the Downs before returning west.

★ ★ ★ ★

Shard was always an early riser: today he got up extra early, waking Beth as he did so. He drew back the bedroom curtains, letting in the sun of a bright, crisp day. Beth protested: 'Simon darling, it's only half past six!'

'I know that. I feel like walking.'

'Not all the way to your office?'

'Not all the way. As far as I feel like. After that, the nearest tube station.' Shard stretched:

he was tall and well-built. Beth, idly staring at his silhouette, thought pleasurably of the latent strength of a healthy, active body. 'Can you get breakfast early, Beth?'

'I suppose so. Mother won't get up for it.'

Shard just stopped himself saying, 'Exactly.' Instead he grinned out of the window, looking down into the quiet Ealing road with the gardens freshly dew-sparkled and responding to the sun. A walk today would not just be exercise: it would be an avoiding action. Mrs Micklam, staying a week, was all the better for avoidance, especially at breakfast. Momentarily, Shard's face darkened into a frown: he'd heard it said that in the fullness of time all daughters grew like their mothers, which was a thought better discarded. The frown vanished: Beth would be the exception, and Shard had no time for disloyalty, especially in himself. He turned away from the window, ripped off his pyjama jacket, advanced on the bed and pulled Beth out and up and into his arms. He kissed her on the lips, then pushed her away, turned her round, and gave her bare behind a light smack. 'Breakfast!' he said. 'Out there, people are being born and dying and committing crimes—and you're delaying the law in the execution of its duty by lying in bed and—'

'Shut up, Simon, it's too early.'

11

★ ★ ★ ★

Work, for Simon Shard, lay basically in the crummy office in Seddon's Way off the Charing Cross Road where the legend on the door said he was a dealer in stamps—a Commercial Philatelist, precisely. The cover irritated Shard: by training and past experience he was a copper and until a year or so ago he had been of the Met and proud of it. He could see the need for a degree of anonymity where the Foreign Office was concerned, but fancied that ninety per cent of it was sheer bull resulting from a love of play-acting, self-dramatisation, not to mention self-aggrandisement, and a dislike of ever getting vulgarly involved—especially on the part of his immediate boss, the man known to the Department as, simply, Hedge. A very thorny, prickly Hedge, standing aloof guard between the Head of Department, who was never mentioned by any name at all, and his underlings, in which term Hedge always managed by his manner to include the whole of the British public. Shard was frequently visited by an uncomfortable suspicion that a kind of Parkinson's Law operated in Security: cover, anonymity, intrigue and poppycock increased in direct proportion to the decline of British authority in the wider world. Reaching his office, having taken the tube ultimately from Ealing Common, and feeling slightly ashamed of his subterfuge, Shard glanced up the stairs leading to the next landing. Seddon's Way he shared with others, some of them as anonymous as he: upstairs lived and worked Elsie, her name inscribed in red felt-tip on a piece of card above a redly glowing bell-push. From her direction there was silence: her working hours were chiefly nocturnal and now she was enjoying repose. Shard let himself into his office, a sleazy room the walls of which were hung with foreign and colonial stamps upon squared paper and shelves filled with Stanley Gibbons catalogues. In one corner stood a massive steel safe in which, though more stamps there were as literal cover, were stored yet more precious scraps of paper, the files that formed the life-blood of Shard's particular niche in Security; these being chiefly in microdot form and thus unobtrusive to the eye, casual or otherwise: Shard's experience in CID had taught him how to make the best use of hiding places. He sat in the swivel chair behind his desk; the moment he did so one of his telephones burred at him softly, the closed line from the FO. A sixth sense warned him of Hedge. He took up the handset, eyes rolling in mute appeal to heaven. 'Shard.'

'At last!' The voice snapped and bit. 'I've tried *three* times to get you—'

'I walked, Hedge.'

'Walked! Why?'

'Reasons,' Shard said equably, 'which would take too long to go into now, Hedge, since I gather you're being urgent about something. Are you?'

There was a sound of fuming. 'You know I detest flippancy. Yes, the matter's urgent. Can you come over right away?'

'To your—'

'No, no, no! I'll be walking along the Embankment. Pick me up...that is *contact* me since you haven't your car with you, near the *President*. All right? Fifteen minutes, Shard.'

'I'll be there,' Shard said, and rang off. He got up, tried the handle of the safe from force of habit, found it secure, and left the office. Going down the stairs, he sent up a prayer of thanksgiving that Hedge didn't go in for physical disguise: had he done so, his flair for dreaming up obstacles would have immeasurably complicated life. Shard would have spent his time searching out Red Indian chiefs, bog Irishmen wearing caubeens, poufs in pearls and earrings, off-duty dustmen and God alone knew what. As it was, fifteen minutes later, Hedge was unmistakable in his Whitehall garb, all

14

black coat, striped trousers and bowler hat with umbrella: Hedge, perhaps because he was too old, had never gone for the with-it image. There was a light wind now, blowing up the dust and discarded scraps of paper, and Hedge was clutching the bowler hat as he leaned over the wall of the Embankment, a little downstream from the RNR drill-ship, staring out over the river and the hurrying strings of barges behind their tugs. The clothes apart there was something vaguely Drake-ish about Hedge's back view, as though he were staring towards some armada sailing through the mists of time, and regretting the absence of a set of bowls.

Shard, after a dash through traffic, leaned over beside him. Hedge glanced sideways and grunted. 'Well, you've got here, praise be.'

'You look tired. You sound it, too.'

'I've been up all night, that's why! Not a chance to get home since first thing yesterday morning.'

'Oh, dear,' Shard said solicitously. 'What have you been up to, Hedge?'

Hedge glared, snapped, 'You're not indispensable. Don't think for a moment you are.'

'What's that supposed to mean?'

'You know very well...this blasted frivolity! Just a word to Assistant Commissioner Hesseltine, and back you go to the Yard.'

15

For the second time that morning, and for related reasons, Shard bit off an indiscreet reply. The Yard called him back strongly, in fact, and Hesseltine, who happened to loathe Hedge's guts, had been a boss he liked to work for. But to Beth, or more precisely to Mrs Micklam, the FO had immense cachet. Mrs Micklam, who, when thwarted tended to take it out on Beth, thought there was something a little common about having a son-in-law who was a policeman and never mind the rank of Detective Chief Superintendent. The last thing Shard wanted to do was to hurt Beth; so he said, 'I apologise, Hedge. No more frivolity. What is it you want?'

'Blood run,' Hedge said briefly.

'Where and who?' The Departmental term "blood run" was used, inter alia, to cover the export from the UK of embarrassing persons; it customarily involved a good deal of work and travel, but Shard was not too displeased: when he got back to London, mother-in-law might well have folded her tents. 'Also when?'

'I'll take that in reverse order,' Hedge said, staring gloomily at a tarnished seagull doing its best to pretend the filthy London river was the deep ocean. 'When—tonight. Who—does the name Katie Farrell mean anything, or not?'

Shard's lips framed a silent whistle. 'Belfast?'

16

'Right. Shall I summarise?'

'I'll do it for you: six murders personally, involvement in dozens more by way of indiscriminate explosions. Wanted here, and in Belfast, and in Dublin. Anything else, Hedge?'

Hedge nodded. 'Plenty! There's a Middle Eastern involvement. An involvement of an oil-producing country—I can't be more precise than that.' Hedge paused, took out a linen handkerchief, and blew his nose: the signal was now at go for exposition. Hedge went on, after making a casual 360-degree turn to assure himself of no unwanted audience, and then re-aligning his view over the river. 'We, that is the Department, Shard—we know where Katie Farrell is.'

'Where's that?'

'On ice.'

'You mean in custody?'

Hedge shifted his feet irritably. 'Of course I mean that, Shard—'

'And where's the blood run to? Belfast, Dublin—which presupposes we're not charging her here, and I'd like to know why not, Hedge. We know she was responsible for—'

'Outrages in England, yes, we know all right!' Hedge paused, frowning. 'I'm not saying I like this, but I have my orders, and so, now, have you.' Another pause, another nose

17

blow. 'She's to be let through, Shard. She's too hot to hold and Government won't take the risk.'

'Of retaliation?'

Hedge nodded glumly. 'But not the *obvious* retaliation. I mentioned the Middle East. We have to protect our oil supplies or we collapse immediately—I needn't tell you—'

'How are they involved, Hedge?'

Hedge spread his hands. 'The supply line's under threat if we don't go along with what these people want—'

'These people? Who are "these people", do we know?'

'Not with exactness, no. But we do know what they want—and that's Katie Farrell.'

'But for God's sake, why Katie Farrell?' Shard was puzzled. 'What the bloody hell... Look, Hedge, you're saying the Middle East is behind some of the terrorist moves in Britain, aren't you?'

'I didn't say that!' Hedge snapped.

Shard stared across the water, seeing nothing. He said, 'This stinks to heaven, Hedge. Letting her go...we'll be breaking faith with all sorts of people, selling them down the river! Our own troops and civilians who've died as a result of what the Farrell woman's done...' He paused, feeling sick in the guts. 'And what

18

about her? What happens to her, when she gets where she's going?'

Hedge grimaced. 'Riches, I shouldn't wonder. Her friends out there will do her much honour, I fear.'

'But *why*?'

'We don't know why they want her, if that's what you mean. It could be a case of standing by their friends—'

'Which means the Middle East *has* been behind the terrorists, doesn't it? So why the cave-in? What about North Sea oil?'

Hedge made a contemptuous noise, dismissive of the North Sea. 'Dreams, dreams! Costs escalating fast, the tax position not helping. There are even rumours that some of the companies are finding each other's fields, would you believe it? Oh, it's coming through now, certainly, but the bulk still comes, and will continue to come hopefully, from the Middle East. We shall always need their oil for the right mix. It's a *vital* supply line.'

'So decency—all right, it's an old-fashioned word—goes overboard.' Shard sent a long breath hissing out through set teeth. 'God, what bastards we've all become!'

'Don't blame me,' Hedge said testily. 'I've said I don't like it. We must consider all that's at stake, though.'

'Which means you're asking me to be the stooge.'

'Not asking, Shard, telling. I'm sorry, but you'll operate the blood run in person. Obviously, no such hand-over can be made in this country and in fact our Middle Eastern friends have expressly ruled it out. They've been precise as to the route in the first stages: no private, clandestine flights, no doubt in case we attempt a double-cross by, as it were, *losing* the woman. You'll accompany her through the normal exit formalities, and the officials immediately concerned, that is, the Home Office people and no others, will be briefed and she'll have full clearance and assistance. You'll stay with her to the handover point, which'll be made known later—'

'Suppose I—'

'Shard, you'll have a full briefing on procedures this afternoon. I'm only giving you the outline at this moment—and it includes this: you'll not go out by air at all. It appears that our...shall I call them our *principals*, don't wish the woman to be in close proximity to other passengers in the confines of an aircraft. So you go out by sea—Townsend Thoresen, Southampton to Cherbourg, with car and cabin to ensure privacy. Ship crowds, I suppose, are of themselves cover. I can't indicate your onward movements from Cherbourg—'

'Don't bother!' Shard interrupted. 'I don't want this job, Hedge. It's too dirty.'

'Someone has to do it, and you've been chosen.' Hedge sounded patronising and pompous to the point of here endeth the first lesson. 'As of now, you're under orders emanating from *very* high up indeed. You would be *most* unwise to make difficulties.' He gave a small cough, almost one of embarrassment. 'The woman...Katie Farrell. Er...you're very happily married, of course...'

Shard stared at him. 'Very. Why d'you ask?'

'Because,' Hedge said ominously, 'there are dangers.'

'To my life?'

'Oh, certainly,' Hedge said, sounding infuriatingly offhand. 'But there's always that, isn't there? I'm referring to something else. The woman's said to be immensely attractive...and you'll be travelling as man and wife. She's really quite something—I've seen her for myself. You'll have to take a very firm grip, Shard, a *very* firm grip.'

★ ★ ★ ★

Shard left Hedge to make his way home at last; Shard went off under orders to make his private arrangements and report at 1400 hours at an address in Knightsbridge, ready in all respects for an indefinite period of field duty. He went off seething with anger: it had been, he considered, bloody impertinent of Hedge to appear to hint that he might be amenable to his sex urges to the point of allowing them to come between himself and his duty: Shard could and would put up his defences as securely as any other experienced officer. Besides, the woman was known to be a multiple killer: his whole instinct was against her...he grinned a little at his thoughts as once again he unlocked the door of his office in Seddon's Way. Sex was sex: when you were engaged in its practice you didn't normally run through the crime lists. He was about to call Beth and invent a trip to Scotland or some such when his security lined burred: again, Hedge.

'Shard!' The voice was high, shaking. 'Oh my God...'

'Steady, Hedge! What's up now?'

Hedge babbled. 'My wife, Shard. My wife, she—she's gone—*gone*, d'you hear? There's blood all over the hall, and my man's dead. Get here, will you? Get here right away!'

★ ★ ★ ★

Hedge's manservant, Morton, was dead all right: open-eyed, open-mouthed, in a dressing-gown pulled over pale pink pyjamas. The face was blood drained but at the same time blood soaked: the head was stove in like an eggshell, and its fragile pieces reposed in a bloody mess, sticky on the hall's parquet. More blood spattered the parquet in a line of drops leading to the massive front door. At the rear end a green-baize door stood open, showing stairs leading down to the basement: Hedge lived now in an upstairs-downstairs kind of house: having raised a mortgage which he continually complained was crippling him, he had extended his flat to the entire house, buying back what once his family had owned. Now it not only crippled Hedge financially but crippled Mrs Hedge in running it; but Hedge was too important to live in a flat. He had, in fact, been nudged by the Head of Department on account of the security aspect. In such an upstairs-downstairs establishment, therefore, the open door betrayed, to Shard, a pre-death urgency in the movements of a well-trained servant. The drops of blood stopped at a point four feet from the front door, as though someone had taken precautions before emerging into the public view. Hedge, poor Hedge, was in a terrible state, shaking like a leaf and slopping neat whisky from a crystal

23

tumbler, carelessly allowing it to mix with the blood until Shard took the tumbler away from him. Shard put it down on a silver salver resting on a mahogany chest shining with polish, and squatted beside Hedge's manservant: clearly a blunt instrument and thus far conventional. He stood up and looked around the hall, at the open green-baize door.

'What about the rest of the staff, Hedge?'

'Staff?'

'You have a cook,' Shard said remindingly.

'Oh—yes. Mrs Morton, the wife.' Hedge gestured down towards the corpse on the floor. 'She's away...a sick sister in Leeds.'

'Due back when?'

'I don't know—tomorrow, I think. My wife—' Hedge broke off. 'My wife's gone, Shard. And she's hurt—that blood near the front door.' He covered his puffy fat face with his hands and his shoulders shook more than ever. Shard murmured words of comfort and reassurance, but thought his own thoughts. The man, Morton, was in pyjamas: forensic would give the time of death in due course, but for now sometime during the night would have to suffice. During the night, Hedge's wife could be presumed to have been in bed—at any rate, not out and about and unaccounted for. Hedge's wife wasn't the sort for night-life while

Hedge was working. If this had happened, within, say, the last couple of hours, then she might well have gone out for some early shopping—but since Morton was wearing pyjamas it hadn't: so something rather nasty had happened to Hedge's wife. Shard asked, 'Any ideas, Hedge?'

'Nothing specific. My job—this sort of thing has always been on the cards.'

Shard nodded absently, murmuring half to himself, 'Someone who came in—right in, was admitted...someone known to your wife and to Morton?'

'I don't see—'

'I could be wrong, Hedge, the door to the servants' quarters: it's open. Did you open it?'

'I went down to look for my wife, of course. But the door was open when I went down and naturally I left it as it was. Nothing's been touched—'

'Fine. Where do the Mortons sleep—not in the basement?'

'Attic.'

'Sure. Well, the front door bell rings and Morton comes down in pyjamas. He doesn't go down below first—or I presume he doesn't —he goes straight to the front door and answers it. He lets someone in and calls your wife. *Then* he goes down to the kitchen to wait till

25

this visitor leaves. For some reason—maybe when he hears sounds of departure—he comes up to the hall again.'

'And is killed.'

'Yes. Think hard, Hedge. Someone known, trusted, but with a reason to...do what he, or she, has done.'

'I can't. I'm not in a fit state.' True enough, Hedge's usually pink face looked ghastly, a sort of dead white around the gills with a high flush over the cheek-bones. Suddenly, he slumped into a chair by the side of the mahogany chest. 'You could be all wrong, Shard. There could be plenty of reasons for Morton going to the basement before answering the door...he could have been down there already, couldn't he?'

'He could, I suppose. A cup of tea—anything. But I'd say a well-trained servant usually shuts doors behind him, wouldn't you, Hedge?'

'Is it important?'

Shard said quietly, 'It could be, for the reasons I've given. It could narrow the field. But after forensic's been, we'll have more to go on time-wise. I suggest you call Assistant Commissioner Hesseltine, Hedge.'

'I'm not having that man here, poking and prying.'

'But—'

Hedge got violently to his feet, shaking, his face more than ever livid and his voice high again. 'You heard what I said, Shard. This stays with us. We have more know-how...more finesse than Hesseltine's people when it comes to this sort of thing—'

'You mean you think there's a Security aspect, Hedge?'

'Of course!' Hedge snapped.

Shard shrugged. 'I'm not saying you're wrong, but it could still be wiser to let the Yard cope from the start. We're going to need their network anyway before it goes much farther.' He hesitated. 'Tell me how your mind's shaping on this, Hedge.'

Hedge stared, licked his lips, swallowed, then sat down again, looking huddled and old. 'All right. I've no idea *who*, none at all—I can't say if you're right or wrong about someone *trusted* in my house. But I believe it could connect with—'

'With the blood run—Katie Farrell?'

Wordlessly, Hedge nodded.

'A hostage, by Christ,' Shard said between his teeth. 'Your wife, to guarantee nothing untoward happens on passage?'

'That's what I'm afraid of, yes.'

Shard turned away, feeling sickened afresh as he looked at the dead man and at the drops of blood leading towards the front door. Maybe he was too soft for his job, but he had never got used to the idea of the suffering innocents who had become a feature of the day and age— the day and age of varying kinds of terrorism and hatred. When troops or police got hurt, it was bad enough, but at least their involvement was of a different kind, and they knew what they faced: not so the hijacked, the kidnapped, the peaceful beer-drinkers in the pubs, the commuters at the railway stations. And now Hedge's wife: she brought it closer home even though she had always been a shadowy figure in Hedge's background, seldom met in the flesh and seeming timid in company, well-connected and a little bovine—an aristocratic cow...Shard caught himself up: God knew what the poor woman was facing now! He turned back to Hedge.

'Do you want me to take charge?'

Hedge looked up, staring bleakly. 'You've a job to do already. I want you to stay with it more than ever—I'll be relying on you absolutely now, Shard.'

'I'll not let you down.'

'I know. You're a good man, Shard. We haven't always seen eye to eye, but—' Hedge broke off, seemed to make an effort. 'I'll speak to the Head of Department myself. In the meantime, I'd be grateful if you'd...put things in motion, you know what I mean.'

Shard nodded, thinking about ambulances and fingerprints and, more importantly perhaps, overall discretion. 'My detective inspector's on leave, but Kenwood's a first-rate DS. I'll get him round at once. I'll use your closed line if you don't mind.'

★ ★ ★ ★

Back in Seddon's Way Shard cleared his desk for what could be a longish absence and then rang Beth, feeling on edge as he did so. What Hedge believed had happened to his wife could also happen to Beth. When his home telephone was answered it wasn't Beth, it was Mrs Micklam.

'Oh—Mother-in-law. Where's Beth?'

'She's gone out, Simon.'

'Where?'

'I don't cross-examine her. I'm not a policeman.'

Shard held onto his temper. 'I may not be able to call again. I have to go north this afternoon and I expect to be away some days, a week, maybe longer—Beth'll understand.' He hesitated. 'Gone shopping—has she?'

'That's what she said.'

29

'Well—give her my love.' He added, before ringing off, 'And tell her to take care of herself. Don't forget that.' He cut the call on the beginnings of a long rattle from Mrs Micklam: the only way to preserve discretion with Mrs Micklam was to be decisive and then face the music later. After he had rung off, Shard sat for a few moments in thought, frowning, then with a sudden movement of determination took up his security line and called the Head of Department direct without going through the normal Hedge-screen.

'Shard, sir. Do I take it Hedge has been in touch by now?'

The cold voice, cold like gunmetal, said, 'You do. What's this about?'

'*My* wife, sir. I'm asking for protection in my absence on duty.'

'A little extreme?' The voice was colder than ever.

'I don't think so, sir. I think she could be at risk. I stress the word, *risk*. Personal considerations apart, we don't want to be hamstrung twice over.'

There was a pause, then: 'Point taken. She'll be under surveillance, if that sets your mind at rest.'

'It does. Thank you, sir.' The call was cut; Shard's face lightened a little. He checked

30

through the hand-case that always stood ready in his office for sudden journeys, opened his safe and took out an automatic. He checked the slide, removed his jacket and pulled on a shoulder holster. Then he went out for a pub lunch in the Strand, an early snack; at 1355 hours a taxi dropped him and his hand-case in Knightsbridge, one street away from his notified destination. Lighting a cigarette as the taxi pulled back into the traffic, he looked around, sharp-eyed but casual, and moved off. No tail that he could identify, but no amount of experience could ever absolutely guarantee safety against good tails. At 1400 hours on the dot he rang a bell in a block of flats in Hans Crescent, feeling curiously glad, never mind the address, of the hard shape of the automatic beneath his arm-pit.

CHAPTER TWO

Shard was admitted by an elderly man, straight-backed and moustached like an ex-sergeant-major. He was taken along a thickly-carpeted hall, moving soundlessly on the pile, and

31

ushered into a large room, a drawing-room furnished in leaf green with immense, comfortable arm-chairs, and heavy velvet curtains of a darker green beside two tall windows, double-glazed: nothing of London's traffic could be heard in this gracious, elegant apartment. Three men were seated, talking in low voices: all got up when Shard was announced. The first man to greet him underlined the military aspect initiated by the doorkeeper: small and perky, bright-eyed, clipped moustache, soldierly bearing, grey hair cut short back and sides.

'Colonel Smith,' this man said briefly. 'So you're Shard. I don't envy you your job, I must say, but we'll go into all that shortly. Meanwhile let me introduce these gentlemen.' He waved a hand at a tall, thin man, clean shaven and bald, with a face that was vaguely familiar to Shard. 'Mr Jones,' he said.

Shard took Mr Jones's hand, just familiar enough with the face to know that he was no Mr Jones; and his suspicion that Colonel Smith was also using cover was confirmed when the third man was introduced as Mr Brown. Smith, Jones and Brown: he, Shard, was clearly to know no more than that. It intrigued him: three nameless men, men of an obvious if quiet authority, the men of power and decision who normally lurked, faceless as well as nameless, behind the scenes of Whitehall.

Smith gave a small cough, and gestured to one of the chairs. 'Sit down. Relax. Drink?'

Shard nodded. 'I could do with a whisky, thanks.'

'Coming up.' Smith went over to a walnut table, on which stood decanters, tumblers and a soda siphon on a silver tray. Shard sat, sinking into the chair's enfolding comfort, the last comfort, probably, he would know for some time—if things should go wrong. He met Smith's eye as the Colonel came across with the whisky. Smith seemed to be a mind-reader—or just a man of much experience.

'Worried, Shard?' he asked, lifting an eyebrow.

'No more than usual, I'd say.'

'Good! I must warn you, we expect opposition. Strong opposition.'

'Not surprising,' Shard said. 'May I ask who from, in particular?'

'You may indeed.' Smith stood with a straight back, one hand behind his rump. 'We expect opposition from certain gentlemen who've formed themselves into one of these private armies we hear so much about—and because they disapprove most strongly of what we're about to do with Miss Farrell.'

'As a matter of fact,' Shard said bluntly,

'so do I!'

'And so say all of us,' Smith murmured, his eyes glinting a little. 'But what has to be done, has to be done, and that's all about it. The facts of life have undergone a change, Shard. The country cannot, I repeat *cannot*, do without oil and expediency is king. My heart bleeds for all our consciences, but there it is. Oh, I know we're all bastards, no point in denying it! The opposing gentry have their heads well and truly in the sand as regards our oil position and that's no help to anybody, is it?'

Shard didn't respond; he said, 'So there's been a leak already, has there?'

'I'm afraid so.'

'D'you know where from?'

'If we did, the long knives would be out by now. No, of course we don't. Nor—although they've contacted us—do we know who's involved in this private army. All I can say is, it's not the *known* ones, they've been checked out.'

'Is there an Ulster overtone?'

Smith shook his head, brought out a pipe and began to stuff it with Three Nuns, dribbling curly fragments onto his trouser-knees. 'We think not. That is, we *know* not—the various set-ups there are among those checked out. But I wouldn't entirely rule out some unofficial connexions—some splinter groups acting independently perhaps, although I've no evidence that points that way. *Any* way, come to that!'

'But it would add up, wouldn't it?'

'Very much so, which is why I'm keeping an open mind. You'll need to do the same, Shard. And a sharp lookout as well. I'm afraid it's going to be a case of enemies on every hand. You won't be able to let up until you make the hand-over—there could be an attempted snatch at any time. 'By the way—your friend Hedge.'

'What about him?'

'His wife.'

'You know about that?'

'We know more than you do, currently. A telephone message, anonymous and from a call-box, reached his office on the stroke of 1300 hours, and I was informed. They've got her, Shard.'

'Which side?'

'The oil interests. The ones we're in effect working for, God damn 'em! If anything stops our woman reaching the hand-over point, which by the way is yet to be announced, then Hedge is a widower. His good lady is the oil men's safeguard.'

'Unless she can be cut out.'

'She can't be.'

'You're not going to try?'

'No.' The Colonel's voice was crisp. 'Don't be ridiculous. You know better than that. Risks have to be calculated, and this one's not on. Your success is the only guarantee.'

Shard took a gulp at the whisky: he felt a sinking sensation in his guts, one that the whisky failed to assuage. Less and less did he like the sound of this job. Danger was around him always, everywhere—danger to himself: this, with a natural degree of reluctance, he could accept. He'd known the score when he'd accepted secondment from the factory, as the Yard was known in his circles. But the knowledge that any slip on his part could kill off Hedge's wife was a big load in itself and could result in over-reaction, in over-edginess: Hedge was a strain at the best of times... Shard put Hedge from his mind as Colonel Smith, speaking with a quiet emphasis, passed his route and pick-up orders. The route orders were incomplete, adding little to what he had already been told by Hedge: Southampton-Cherbourg and at Cherbourg a man would make contact in the Hotel Sofitel, a man named Paul Legrain, a Frenchman. Shard's guess was that the Cherbourg contact would merely hand him on down the line to the next check-point as it were. He said, 'I suppose a Cherbourg

36

hand-over's been tried out on them, Colonel?'

'Of course. They insist that's not on. One can see their logic, one must admit. They're not naïve.'

Shard gave a sardonic smile: they would be far from naïve! Britain was Britain; but France was France and while the French—and anyone else whose territory was to be crossed by the blood run—might choose to wink at what the British Government was doing, they could conceivably decide to block the crossing of frontiers once Katie Farrell was no longer a British liability but their own. When that happened, they would have their own problems. Shard accepted another whisky while Smith, with occasional comment from Messrs Jones and Brown, went on talking. Katie Farrell's past, or such of it as was known, was filled in—the bombings and shootings and political affiliations that had led to her recent and unpublicised arrest by the security forces inside Britain. Her mother had died some five years earlier—she had been an Irishwoman living in Birmingham and a staunch IRA supporter. There were no other living relatives. The mother had been unmarried, and there was no information as to the identity of Katie's father: Farrell was her mother's maiden name. She maintained that she had never known her father and had no idea who he had been.

'It doesn't really matter now, does it,' Shard said bleakly. 'We'll be rid of her—for a while, anyway—and she'll be richly rewarded by the oil sheikhs, as I gather from Hedge.' He lifted an eyebrow at Smith. 'I accept that I'm just the blood-run operator this time, but I'd like to know a little more about the Eastern involvement, Colonel.'

Smith glanced across at Mr Brown: Brown gave a nod. Smith said, 'Petrodollars, to use a convenient phrase. Recycling.'

'But not through the banking system?'

'No. To subversive elements—*any* elements subversive to Britain's interests. The oil revenue surpluses are right behind Katie Farrell, Shard, and in broad basis, I'm ashamed to say, it's those surpluses, plus of course the threat of tap-turning, that's getting her out now.' Smith used a phrase that Hedge had used earlier. 'I'd prefer to be no more precise than that, Shard. I'm sure you understand.'

★ ★ ★ ★

The sergeant-majorly man came in with China tea and biscuits: after partaking, Brown and Jones left. Shard knew that their anonymity was safe, that the flat would be equally anonymous, totally unconnected, and would after his own departure be vacated by all the cloak-and-dagger brigade. A passport was produced by Colonel Smith, a double passport in the names of Mr and Mrs Garrett—Andrew and Jill. Shard stared at his photograph, at Katie Farrell's. Passport photographs were passport photographs, but she looked sexy just the same. Her life had been a waste of natural talent, Shard thought, she was built more for bed than for the bullet and the bomb. He scrawled his signature in the space provided, then studied the signature of his temporary wife: it was bold and vigorous and full of character. He was going to have his hands full...he looked up at Colonel Smith.

'Where do I take over, and when?'

Smith glanced at his watch. 'Not yet. Patience! Later there'll be a car outside—'

'With her in it?'

'No, no. Empty and waiting for you. Before you go down, I'll hand you the keys and documentation, all correct for the continent—green card, AA five-star, the lot.'

'And the woman?'

'You'll drive towards Knightsbridge, and turn along the Brompton Road. Keep in the near-side lane. There's a bus stop outside Harrod's. Katie Farrell will be in the queue, with two officers from my department. She'll be wearing a light blue head scarf and dark glasses and carrying a yellow hand-case, zipped. One of my chaps will give her the tip when you approach, slow. She'll recognise you, wave, and call your name—Andrew. You'll lean across and push your passenger door open. She gets in, full of gratitude. You drive off smartly and head for Southampton. The Townsend Thoresen *Viking 1* leaves from the Old Docks at 2100 hours.' Smith added, 'You shouldn't have any trouble with the woman, Shard. She's only too anxious to get out!'

★ ★ ★ ★

At half past six, with full documentation in his wallet, plus passage tickets, Shard went down alone and put his case in the boot of an unobtrusive dark green Ford Escort. He drove into Knightsbridge, and into the Brompton Road, moving slowly in a stream of homeward-bound traffic, stop-start-stop, eyes watching the kerb closely. The passers-by looked drab and full of worries; they mostly had pinched faces, faces that reflected the day and age, the age of austerity and shortages and hardships for which Katie Farrell's paymasters, his mission's initiators, had been primarily responsible when they had shaken the West's prosperity back in 1973: Shard reckoned he would face a lynching from the crowds if they got a whisper of what he was doing. He edged along the near-side lane, began to approach the bus stop: a bus was just pulling away. Four places back in the remaining queue was a girl between two men, a girl in dark glasses and blue head scarf, carrying a zipped grip: Shard caught her eye, and reached towards his passenger door.

She waved, called something, smiling.

He pushed the door open.

'Andrew, how lovely!'

'Get in.'

She got in, slammed the door. Shard rejoined the traffic, hooting angrily behind him. The two men showed no reaction, stared as vacantly as anyone else awaiting the advent of a London Transport bus. Shard glanced sideways: the dark glasses and head scarf remained *in situ*, unrevealingly, but perfume stole out, not too obtrusive but very, very heady. Shard felt irritation: the bloody woman, he thought, could almost have *known*...known that he was susceptible to scent discreetly used! It did things, as Beth had discovered early on. He couldn't help the way he was made, but neither could he drive through London's traffic, nor sail the night seas to Cherbourg, with his nostrils finger-clasped. He drove in silence, a silence that Katie Farrell didn't break any more than he, and thrust his thoughts dutywards, towards Mr Brown and Britain and oil shortages and petrodollar surpluses, towards Hedge's wife and Hedge himself and the shadowy men who would be waiting somewhere along the track from now on out to snatch Katie Farrell away to their own concepts of justice. Driving west, he joined the M-3, still silent. However sexy the girl was, this was no holiday trip; he hated all she stood for, all she believed in. That stopped any desire to fraternise. All the same, he felt something in the air later when the motorway signs showed the slip road for Camberley: he thought of the Royal Military Academy at Sandhurst. There was a kind of tension emanating from Katie Farrell and, guessing why, he let something snap.

He said savagely, 'You're scared, aren't you!'

Her voice was cool; tension or no, she scored a point for self-possession. 'Am I?'

'You know you are.'

'Why should I be?'

He snapped at her. 'Military area.' He pointed left. 'Over there is Aldershot. And Guildford.'

'I had nothing to do with that.'

'Oh, no?'

'No.'

'You're all part of the outfit. Don't try to shift the responsibility.'

She laughed. 'All the English are oppressors. Don't you try to shift *that* responsibility... Andrew, my love!'

He looked sideways in the fading daylight, feeling cold anger well up. 'Now just you listen. You can drop the endearments—when we're alone. Tonight aboard the *Viking*, we have a shared cabin booked. That's for obvious security reasons. Don't provoke me. If I have to be a bastard, a bastard I can be, and with much pleasure. I have to deliver you. I've been given no instructions to deliver you unmarked, and we shan't be disturbed in the cabin. Do you get me?'

There was a hint of a smile, and she shifted a little in the seat, brushing her body close to Shard's. 'Is that a threat?'

'Yes.'

'Maybe I like big, strong men.'

'Shut up,' he said. 'You talk like a poor man's Mae West.'

She laughed, lightly: more scent wafted. Shrugging her shoulders she said, 'Don't worry, I'll behave. I want to get where I'm going, don't I?' She said no more. Shard drove on fast towards Basingstoke and Win-

43

chester and the A-33 that would carry him down to Southampton. Past Basingstoke the light went: Shard looked at his watch, and as he did so he heard the bleat of a siren coming up fast from behind: in his rear-view mirror he saw the flashing blue lights, two of them. Instinctively he slowed; one of the police cars swept past, flashing on its stop sign, waving him down onto the hard shoulder. The second car pulled in behind as Shard obeyed. From the lead car a uniformed constable approached and Shard wound his window down.

'What is it?'

'Mr Garrett?' The man crouched on his haunches.

'Right.'

'I have orders to intercept, sir.'

Shard looked blank. 'Intercept what, Constable?'

'You, sir.'

'You know my orders?'

'Not in detail, sir. I'm merely following instructions—'

'From whom?'

'From the Chief Constable, sir.'

'I see. And your force?'

'Hants Police, sir.'

Shard nodded. 'All right. Now—what do you want me to do?'

'Follow me, sir, please.'

Shard smiled. 'All right,' he said, 'but I'd like to know why?'

The police officer gave a jerk of his head, indicating the route South and West. 'It seems there's the likelihood of a hijack on the A-33, sir. We're going to escort you along an alternative route.'

'All right,' Shard said again, nodding. 'Just as you say.'

The constable straightened, saluted, walked back to his car. Shard said, 'Keep your head down, Miss Farrell,' and let in his clutch. With his foot hard down, the Escort responded beautifully: they shot ahead, skimming past the lead car before the uniformed man had got in. Bullets followed them as the cars got on the move. Katie Farrell, the dark glasses off now, stared at Shard.

'What's the idea?' she asked.

Shard grinned tightly through his windscreen as he sent the Escort hurtling ahead. 'Sixth sense, plus two other things.'

'What things?'

'I saw the way that man looked at you: hate's an under-statement. And the accent wasn't cop. It was retired army officer. These people aren't professionals when it comes to the crunch. You can consider that as attempt number one, Miss Farrell, now past.'

'Past?'

Shard grinned again. 'No follow-up. Too risky for them to keep shooting on the move. They'll live to fight another day. I didn't expect them to be on to us quite so soon, that's all. We'll take this as a warning—they're better organised than I'd expected, what with mobiles and all. And I'll tell you something else for free.'

'What's that?'

With deliberation Shard said, 'I'm glad we got away without my having to damage them. Because, whatever my job says, I happen to think they're right.'

'That's not friendly,' she said, pouting.

'Nor am I. I happen to think, Miss Katie Farrell, that you should be spending the rest of your life in prison, preferably guarded by women who've lost husbands because of your activities. No—don't come back on that, or I might react. Just shut up, right?' She shut up; Shard kept the speed going: the night-dark countryside rushed into his headlights, the trees silvered ghostlike, air streaming cool through his driving window. Into Southampton and its crowds and lights, slow now; Shard deviated into police headquarters and called the FO, making a report of the attempted interception.

46

Then down to the Old Docks, over the railway sidings, past a filling station, down to the check-point and the scrutiny of officialdom. Shard handed the passport through, was given a searching glance and a nod and, without comment, his embarkation card. He drove on through, turned for the great ramp of the car ferry, was beckoned into an echoing cavern of steel and paintwork and the smell of oil and petrol. They were among the last few to embark: as they got out of the car with their hand-cases, the drive-on doors were already coming up to slot into position for the outward passage to Cherbourg. They shut with a clang of steel, a final sound. Shard, not normally a man of nerves in the plural, gave a sudden shiver: the shutting of that door left him with the feeling of a coffin-lid, the workaday car deck becoming the coffin itself. They were shut into it...with what, with whom? Too much was known of their movements already: the opposition was scarcely likely to leave them in their anonymity for long, now the first assault had been made.

Shard shook himself free of such fantasies as coffins. He put a hand on Katie Farrell's arm. 'Come on,' he said. 'We'll find that cabin.' As he spoke there was a crescendo of sound from somewhere below and the deck started shaking as though it must part company with the vessel's hull as the screws right below them began to thrash the water, propelling the car ferry off the stern-on berth. Again the coffin-image: it was a doomful sound, a thud of earth magnified a millionfold.

CHAPTER THREE

In self-defence Shard closed his mind against naked flesh: Katie Farrell, in the privacy of the cabin, without dark glasses and head scarf, with long fair hair falling about her shoulders, was enough to stir cast iron. Her eyes were Irish blue, her clear skin had a light tan, she had an attractive smile...Shard had to face the fact that terrorists were not all of the criminal classes, that some of them could be ordinarily nice people who took an utterly detached view of the bestial and criminal content of their activities. Hence it was possible for them to appear, like this Katie Farrell, as fresh flowers of youth with pretty faces, disarming smiles, and simple charm. You had to keep telling yourself the lady was a killer, and that made the job harder.

In addition, this one was naked: Katie Farrell had stripped right off.

Behind his mental shut-off Shard reflected. She hadn't wanted to go to the cabin, he had to give her that; she'd said, 'I'd like a drink, Andrew. The bar looks nice.'

'We're going to the cabin.'

'Well, if not a drink—maybe it's too public —why not stay on deck and watch the lights of England fade?'

'We're going to the cabin. I'm giving you an order.'

'Ah, you're a hard husband—'

'Shut up.' He took her arm in a policeman's grip, hurting her. 'You're a martyr to sea-sickness—'

'I'm *not*—'

The pressure of fingers increased. 'This deck, port side. Number 24. *Get there.*'

She got. Once inside with the door closed and curtains drawn over windows that gave onto a deck furnished with couchettes, he had told her to open up her hand-case.

'What for? You don't imagine I have a bomb, do you?'

'You've had them before. Do as you're told.'

She glared. 'Look, mate! You're not the first. It's been checked already.'

'I'm sure it has, but I like to do my own

49

checking too. I'm kind of personally involved.'

'You're a bloody perfectionist, are you?'

He shook his head. 'No. Just a self-preservationist who takes no chances at all, which is a fact you'd best bear in mind, Miss Farrell. Now—do as you're told.'

'I will not!'

'All right.' He took the case and unzipped it. He turned it upside down, spilling femininity and intimacy but no bombs. That was when she'd shrugged, smiled, and said flippantly, 'Well now, you may as well do the job thoroughly and see if I have explosives tucked away where no explosive should ever be,' and she had undressed and stood stark naked before him with her upraised arms lifting small, tight breasts into pinnacled mounds, provocative and sensuous. The abdomen, he noticed, showed considerable operation scarring: an appendectomy low down, and elsewhere what could have been the result of a caesarian section: abortion? She was not known to have any children. On the fringe of the pubic hair was a birthmark, a red double moon, very distinctive. 'Go on, then,' she said.

Even in his own ears he sounded prim and unctuous. 'There will be,' he said, 'no personal examination.'

'Why deny yourself a pleasure, Mr Detective?'

'Look,' he said heavily, 'I'm not a nude-struck youth. I've seen it all before, many times. It fails to thrill.'

'Like hell it does,' she jeered. 'Aren't you just being faithful, or something?'

'Faithful?'

'To your wife, Mrs Detective. I suppose you're married?'

'Yes.'

'You're married again now, bigamist!' Her eyes mocked. 'What would Mrs Detective say?' She laughed. 'Does she know?'

He said, 'Get dressed. That's another order.'

'You're full of orders.'

'Which you're going to obey,' he said harshly. 'Look. Miss Farrell. We have a long way to go, and we're never going to be out of each other's company en route. I have a job to do and the sooner it's done the better. Meanwhile we both have a vested interest in success, right?'

She shrugged, turned aside and reached for a packet of cigarettes. Shard flicked his lighter and held it out; as she bent towards the flame the long fair hair, tumbling about her face, fell across his hand like spun silk. Answering his question she said on an outblown cloud of smoke, 'I want to get there, yes.'

'Then please co-operate. Trouble could come

at any moment. If our friends get hold of you, you're a dead duck, as though I need to tell you that.'

She blew more smoke, eyes narrowed. 'You don't really care, do you?'

'Not for you,' he said brutally. 'But I obey orders as well as give them. I might point out that my life's at risk too. I aim to protect that as well as yours. I may be prejudiced, but I reckon it's a more valuable thing, Miss Farrell.'

She laughed. 'I call that unpolicemanlike.'

'Call it what you want,' he said indifferently. 'Just get dressed, that's all.'

This time, she obeyed: Shard watched as long slim legs stepped into briefs and creamy breasts vanished beneath a jumper. No bra; maybe she'd burned that somewhere back along the lib line. Skirtless, she lay on the lower of the two bunks, reading a paperback that she had taken from the feminine mêlée in her hand-case. One thing—she was still cool. In her line of business, she had to be; but he would have expected a little more overt awareness of the thin rope she was treading. She hadn't even referred back to the abortive cutting-out attempt back on the M-3. Shard, sitting on a hard chair alongside the bunk, deciding to remain wakeful throughout the passage, did some circumspect probing as to Hedge's missing wife:

Katie Farrell had nothing to offer. The chances were, she genuinely didn't know: the principle that the less you knew the less you could give away was not confined to the establishment forces. Shard, listening to the beat of engines, feeling the roll and pitch as later the car ferry met a strong wind south of the Needles, thought of other things: of failure principally, and its results. Death for Hedge's wife and a vengefulness on the part of the men of power in the Middle East that could turn off the oil taps and cause another kind of death, a quick throttling of western industry that would leave Europe gasping for its life's breath. He switched these thoughts off: like Katie Farrell's naked body, they were better disregarded. While switching off, he reflected glumly that once the world's most viable protection had been a British passport; now it was an oil well. The Middle East had overtaken with a vengeance, guaranteeing sanctuary and sanctity for its friends...

★ ★ ★ ★

'No breakfast. I'm sorry.'
'Why not?'
'Too much risk.'
She said angrily, 'Oh, God, they must know

53

I'm aboard after last night. Those phoney cops knew our route...and Southampton's the fairly obvious end of the A-33.'

'Sure. But this isn't the only ship sailing out of Southampton. In any case, it's not them I have in mind right now.'

She glared, blue eyes hard. 'Who, then?'

'The passengers, who happen to be mainly British.'

'My face isn't that well known—'

'There have been photographs. Even so, it's not just the general public. There could be others...soldiers on leave, troops who've served in Belfast—or security men and other official people. Men who know of you but are not in the present picture—get me? We don't want scenes.'

'Aren't you over-reacting?'

'Yes,' he said, 'perhaps I am, but it's safer that way, so that's the way it's going to be.'

'Don't we ever eat again?'

He shrugged, smiled. 'Once we're off the ferry, we can choose our places to suit ourselves. In the meantime, we stay in here till they announce the car deck's ready for disembarkation. Then, in a nice intent crowd, and with head scarf and glasses—we go, all right?'

★ ★ ★ ★

The car deck came alive with sound: voices, footsteps, engines in a smell of exhaust smoke. Following the queue they rolled out into bright sunshine, inching along towards the check-point inside the port area. No trouble: a scrutiny of their passport and they were waved through. Outside the gate in the wire barrier Shard turned right.

'Now will you tell me where we're going?' the girl asked.

'The Sofitel, not far.' Shard waved a hand towards the tall green building alongside the sea approach to the commercial port and yacht harbour.

'Breakfast?'

'I don't know yet.'

'Do we check in?'

'I don't know that yet either.'

She gave him a shrewd look. 'You mean we have a contact to make.'

'*You* have, Miss Farrell.'

'Me?' She sounded surprised.

'You identify, then I talk.'

She nodded slowly. 'So that's how it is. We're out from under now, are we? Out from officialdom's umbrella?'

'Correct.' Shard turned right again, heading in for the Sofitel's car park: away across the old Cunard terminal, a vast tanker loomed, a half-million tonner, its superstructure and funnel in clear view above the building, a powerful reminder of where the world's centre of gravity lay. 'We're in the hands of your people as of now.'

'British Government no longer interested?'

'Only in success, that's all.'

'No more help?'

He shook his head. 'None at all. It's up to us.' He drove on, stopped and parked in a space between a Renault and a Simca, both with French registrations. They walked past a fountain playing into an ornamental pool, and into the hotel foyer. Shard led the way to a table for two with comfortable chairs set in a recess. 'Coffee?' he asked.

'Yes, black.'

Shard went across to reception. *'Bonjour, mam'selle*...my name is Garrett. Are there any messages?'

The girl checked a board behind her. *'Non, m'sieur.'*

'May we have coffee...*café?'*

'Oui, m'sieur, I will ring.' She did so; Shard went back to the table and brought out a packet of cigarettes, offered Katie Farrell one. They lit up; a waitress appeared and Shard ordered the coffee and biscuits. The foyer was very quiet, very peaceful: they drowsed. The advent

56

of coffee brought them back to life. Shard looked at his watch: contact was to be made at 0830 hours. It was now 0825. He drank coffee: 0830 came and went. Nothing happened: some people were never punctual and this was France. There was an air of slow motion, except on the roads; but Shard felt a surge of worry, envied Katie Farrell her apparent lack of concern. She seemed to trust him completely, which was odd when you came to think about it: she fought the British, she blew them up, but to her they still represented what they had for so long represented to the world, solidity and dependability—or at any rate, *he* did since she was trusting her life to him in a highly positive way...

A voice called: 'M'sieur Garrett?'

'Yes—' He was on his feet in a trice.

'There is a telephone call, m'sieur.'

'Thank you.' He signalled to Katie Farrell: together they went across and took the call. She listened, then put her hand over the mouthpiece and spoke to Shard.

'It's Paul Legrain. Does that check?'

'That checks. *Is* he?'

She said, 'Yes. I identify the voice. Here.' She handed him the receiver.

Shard said, 'Garrett,' and then listened to a brief message in poor English. As soon as it had

57

been passed, the call was cut. Shard replaced the handset, thanked the girl in reception, and paid for his coffee. Then, taking Katie Farrell's arm, he led her out of the hotel.

'Well?' she asked.

'14 rue Benjamin Carot. And we walk.'

'Why?'

'Ask Paul Legrain,' he said. 'Anyway, it's a nice day.'

'Do you know the way?'

'Legrain's route instructions were adequate.'

They walked towards the town, along the sea-crusted wall of the yacht harbour. There were still men with money enough to burn: the boats, some sail, some motor, were of all nationalities and included plenty of British. Even the White Ensign was there, to indicate the exclusiveness of the Royal Yacht Squadron. There was a sharp tangy smell of the sea overlaid with petrol and oil fuel. Elderly Frenchmen sat around on seats and bollards, grizzled men in blue jeans and berets, dreaming perhaps of a past when Cherbourg was a simple fishing and naval port primarily, a past less gaudy and more truly salty. They turned right at the end of the *avant-port*, waited to cross the railway line while truck after truck of Japanese Datsun cars went past in a huge trail of import, then across the swing-bridge and another right turn down the other side of the harbour. Across the road were bars and cafes, even at this early hour with their patrons drinking coffee or cognac at the pavement tables. They crossed the road into a spider's-web of side streets leading from the waterfront, still pervaded by the sea and fuel smells but now with the smells of food added: fruit, baking bread, meats and garlic. Soon the streets became narrow, dirtier, smelling more of drains; and the passers-by somehow more furtive and sinister. The shopping crowds were gone now, so, except for the odd sleazy front, were the pavement cafes. The atmosphere was quite different.

Katie Farrell said suddenly, 'This I don't like.'

'I don't see you,' Shard said, 'as chickening. So why? Or is it just that you haven't a bomb handy?'

'Don't be funny!' she snapped.

'I'm not. But Belfast has its back streets, as don't we all know—'

'This is different. It's just a feeling.'

'You'll get used to it. Come on.' He took her arm. 'It's not far now, if I'm following Legrain's instructions right, which I am.'

They walked on: the bright day had gone and cloud was rolling up ahead of a wind that blew fragments of paper scudding through the dirt. The streets seemed to close in, suddenly unfriendly, suddenly menacing: a brooding sullenness brought about by the unheralded disappearance of the sun, perhaps by the change in Katie Farrell's manner. Keeping close to the girl, Shard studied her face obliquely: she was reacting badly, seeming nervous and fearful, on edge maybe as to the next stage of the journey and what it might bring forth. She might, even now, be untrustful of the British Government or of Shard himself. As they came to the turn into the rue Benjamin Carot, she asked, 'Are you sure it's okay?'

'Yes. Aren't you? You know Legrain, I don't.'

After a brief hesitation she said, 'Yes, it's all right, I suppose I'm worrying about nothing.'

'Then stop h'm?' Checking numbers they went on. Number 14 was not immediately obvious; Shard found it after a search up a dark alleyway off the street: a mouldering door with heaps of débris close by, builder's leavings it looked like, added to by both dogs and humans: the smell was powerful. Shard bunched a fist and knocked on the door: on the other side of it lay knowledge of the next step, the next contact-point, and such knowledge was vital, never mind the filth that he was fairly obviously about to enter. There was no answer to his knock immediately: he banged again, then heard sounds from within. A moment later he heard the movement of rusty bolts and the door went inwards, creakily, protesting its age.

With darkness behind him, a man showed.

'Paul Legrain?'

There was a nod. Shard glanced at Katie Farrell: she, also, nodded.

'Garrett and wife.'

'*Entrez, m'sieur.*' Paul Legrain, a man of around thirty years of age by Shard's information, though he looked older, stepped back, opening the door a little wider. Katie Farrell went in, with Shard close behind her, a hand inside his jacket, fingers round the butt of the automatic. Ahead in the gloom he saw, but saw too late, the loom of more men. As an electric light came on overhead and he saw black hoods and guns pointing, his arms were suddenly grabbed and pinioned from behind. His automatic was removed. Twisting as far as he could, he looked into a heavy face beneath a totally bald head, a face set virtually neckless upon immense shoulders. His arms, pressed to his sides, felt in a fair way to cracking through his ribs. Katie Farrell backed up against him, trying to get away from the guns, panting like a stag at bay. The man behind him pushed forward and he moved like a child, willy-nilly, half carried by the monstrous bald man's ferocious grip, with Katie Farrell being propelled before him. There were stairs ahead, leading steeply upward. With no word said, they were forced up the stairs, the front door now shut and bolted behind them. Reaching a landing, still with the guns pointing, they were pushed through a doorway opening left. They went into darkness, but when Shard was inside another light was flicked on and he saw five more men, all sitting in chairs, all to a point lifelike and all dead. Each man's throat had been cut, each man's head lolled sideways from a gaping red neck, each body sat in an attitude of ease. It didn't look like the work of ex-Army Officers.

CHAPTER FOUR

Katie Farrell's face was as white as a shroud: it wasn't just the fact of death—as much as Shard, she'd seen plenty. It was the macabre quality, the deliberate arrangement, the pose of the corpses. The room was a spread of blood:

it could be smelt.

Shard looked at the hooded men with the guns. 'All right,' he said. 'You've succeeded in impressing us. Now let's hear why.'

'You don't need any explanation, Mr Shard. Look at their faces.' The man who had spoken, Shard fancied, could have been an Ulsterman. 'What do you see?'

'A Middle East aspect on two of them,' Shard answered. 'On the others, European. All right, so you're the other side. And Paul Legrain?'

'Legrain did what he was told. He got you here.'

'And now?'

The speaker's eyes flashed behind the slits, briefly. 'We don't want him any more. As for you, Mr Shard, we don't intend you any harm, but you'll have to stay here for the time being, I'm afraid.'

'While you—'

'While we make certain arrangements for Miss Farrell.'

'What arrangements?'

Another concealed grin: 'As if you need to ask. I'm not saying more than that. Something tells me you're not all that unhappy anyway.'

'My feelings don't come into it. I have a job to do. I intend to do it.'

There was a jeering note. 'Like how, Mr Shard?'

No answer from Shard: with those guns on him, ready to kill Katie Farrell at least, it was a clear case for biding time. He looked again at the dead representatives of the oil power block and their European lickspittles, wondering if his part in the blood run had been planned to end, after all, in this sleazy Cherbourg house...not that it made any odds now. As the gunmen closed in around him, separating him from Katie Farrell who so far had not uttered, he made an appeal.

He said, 'Miss Farrell's is not the only life in the balance.'

'Well? Go on, Mr Shard.'

'Her people have a hostage. Maybe you knew that.'

There was a pause. 'I'm not saying whether we did or not, but it makes no difference.'

'If I fail, that hostage dies.'

'I'm sorry, believe me.' Was there a kind of sincerity in the tone? Shard wondered.

He asked, 'But you won't take it into account?' He added, 'She's an innocent woman, nothing to do with any of this, no connexion with your politics or those of your opponents. She's someone's wife and to that extent unique. There are plenty of Katie

Farrells. What, exactly, do you achieve?'

Behind the black hood, the eyes glinted: Shard had the feeling the hidden lips were smiling, even laughing at him. 'No comment,' the man said, and jerked his gun. 'And nothing of what you said taken into account. Now turn round and face the door.'

Bitterly Shard said, 'You're all a lot of bastards, on both sides,' and turned away as ordered.

★ ★ ★ ★

Three gunmen had remained in the death room with Katie Farrell: two, plus the heavy bald man, went down the stairs with Shard. From the ground floor level they went down again, to a cellar, stone-built and damp, with a bare electric light bulb dangling on a flex from the ceiling. Beneath the light, which the leading gunman had switched on, was a hard upright chair: nothing else.

'You'll stay here,' the man said from behind the hood. 'You won't be harmed, but you'll be locked in and Buffo will be on guard outside.'

'Buffo?'

The gun's movement indicated the big bald man. 'He's strong, as I dare say you've realised.

I repeat, you won't be harmed—that is, just so long as you don't do anything foolish. Right now, I can't say how long you'll be here. Buffo will be informed when the time comes. Anything else you want to know?'

'Nothing,' Shard said sardonically, 'that you're likely to answer.'

There was a laugh. 'Then you're a wise man to save breath.' The man backed away behind his pointed gun. 'By the way, Buffo doesn't know anything. He's a peasant from the Haute Savoie and he's a deaf mute. He'll attend to your needs, food and drink—there's a hatch in the door—but he won't communicate. So once again—save breath.'

The men backed out; Buffo pushed the door to and locked it from the outside. The light remained on. Shard listened to the footsteps climbing the stairs. After that there was silence, an intense silence that seemed almost to muffle thought. Shard paced the cell, backwards and forwards: it was largish, perhaps fifteen feet square. The walls, he found, were solid, repaired in places with new stone well grouted in. The wooden door was solid too, very heavy, and the hatch, which was set at ground level like a cat door, was iron-bound and no more than six inches square. To get out was simply not on. By his watch, which had been left with him, Shard paced for some fifteen minutes before he heard more movement upstairs: footsteps again, more distant than before, presumably coming down from the first-floor level. He fancied he heard them going along the passage that served as a hall, fancied he heard the closing of a door.

Katie Farrell, now bound on her last journey?

Shard, pacing again restlessly and impotently, thought of Katie Farrell: a girl in the flush of her early twenties, attractive, with all to live for, perhaps too much to live for. The real criminals were those persons who had given her her life's interest, her mother and her associates. She had perhaps fallen victim to the romanticism surrounding the Easter Rising: Shard's reading of history had told him that there was a kind of heroism in those earlier days and a genuine passion for liberty. There had been sordid deeds on both sides and Britain had had much to answer for: but in recent years bestiality had taken over and liberty had become a mockery. In his bones Shard was glad that officialdom and its planning for expediency had come unstuck; he could spare little sorrow for Katie Farrell, murderess in her own right. But Hedge's wife was a different kettle of fish...

Sounds outside the door told Shard that Buffo was at hand: clumsy movements and a

67

grunting—it was like an animal. On the heels of heavy breathing, something was pushed through the hatch: a cup of coffee, black as coal.

Shard fetched it. 'Thanks,' he called unheard through the door. There was a shuffle of departure. Shard examined the coffee, smelt it, tasted some on a finger. Innocuous—he hoped! He drank. It was strong and bitter but he felt better for it; he doubted if they would see any point in drugging it anyway. Buffo, the walls and the door were security enough. After drinking, he replaced the empty cup in the hatch and resumed his pacing. Later, though he had heard nothing, he saw that the cup had vanished: Buffo could obviously move silently on occasions. The day dragged by in a damp atmosphere and a stench of drains, as though town sewers were spilling in the nearby earth. Lunch came hatchwise—crunchy bread and cheese and a glass of water. With regret, for he was thirsty, Shard rejected the water, not knowing whence Buffo had drawn it. Later, lunch was repeated in the name of supper. The light remained on, giving Shard a headache till he stood on the chair and removed the bulb. During the night he snatched some restless sleep huddled on the hard chair, which he had shifted into a corner. By his watch, morning came: he was stiff and cold and suffering the aftermath of nightmares during which his mind had raced in circles around the abortion he had made of his assignment, of the fate of Hedge's wife, and around the likely whereabouts of Katie Farrell—or her lifeless body.

Breakfast came: another cup of coffee and a roll. He had run out of cigarettes, but there was no communication with the moronic Buffo. He gasped for a smoke, and the morning passed slowly on towards lunch-time, but no lunch came and the house above was as deathly still and quiet as the cellar. A forgotten feeling came over Shard and after a while, still lunchless, and whether or not there was any point considering his gaoler's deafness, he hammered on the stout door.

To his astonishment, it gave. He opened it wide: so far as he could tell, no hidden Buffo.

Cautiously, he moved out, flesh creeping, all senses on the alert. There was no break in the silence overhead. He reached the foot of the stairs and went up, slow and watchful. The passage was empty; he went to the outer door and tried the handle: free and open! Shard sent a breath whistling out through set teeth. *How long, for God's sake, had that cellar door been unlocked?* Long enough, it seemed, for deaf-and-dumb Buffo to hot-foot out to anonymity!

Shard went back along the passage and up the stairs to the first floor. Outside the death room he fumbled for, and found, the light switch. The brilliance shone on the same scene as before, except that now the quick had gone and only the dead remained in their bloodied silence. And had been joined by an equally silent Paul Legrain.

★ ★ ★ ★

Hedge was shaking like a leaf and his face was a dirty grey. The day before, it seemed, he had been contacted by telephone—a man representing the "private army" interests who didn't want Katie Farrell to be let through to the Middle East: an anonymous man who had said only that Katie Farrell had been intercepted. A metaphorical snook having been thus cocked at the British Government and the Foreign Office, Hedge couldn't wait to impart, but took time off afterwards to reprimand Shard. 'You should have come back sooner. You could have flown from—'

'Not so, Hedge. I didn't want to pull strings over there and jump queues—in the circumstances, security would have been at risk. The delay was minimal in any case, and talking of security, enough seems to have been blown

70

already.' Shard's tone was withering. 'You might inform Messrs Smith, Jones and Brown that someone rumbled their transport right from the start. There hasn't been a smell of those phoney coppers since, so I'm told—'

'All right, all right!' Hedge simmered. 'Don't try to duck. I was talking about Cherbourg. Don't tell me you couldn't—'

'Hedge, listen.' Shard raised his voice. Hedge was verging on hysterics and Shard, not wishing to slap, shouted. 'I got on the first ferry without fuss—they're not running full just now. I decided it was too chancy to leave the car and risk questions. Now, Hedge: when, precisely, did this boy, let's call him the Ulster interest, make contact?'

'With me?' Hedge was only half with it, Shard thought. 'Yesterday afternoon, I told you—'

'*Precisely*, Hedge?'

'Does it matter? I don't know! Oh...a little after three, I think it was.'

'No clues from where—none at all?'

'No. A call-box, obviously—'

'Here at your home, or the FO?'

'The Foreign Office.'

Shard nodded. 'No doubt they'll contact again. If so—'

'If they ring, Heseltine'll be aware. There's

a security tap on the line.'

'Which they'll guess, so in my book they'll find another way.' Shard looked closely at Hedge. He was in a poor way all round; untypically, he'd told Shard to report to Eaton Square when he'd called the FO from Southampton—going home, he'd said, couldn't take any more. And home was already going to seed: with his wife in hostile hands and his butler dead he was coping on his own. Mrs Morton had collapsed with a coronary on hearing of her husband's murder and had been removed to hospital. Not wishing to have poke-noses around, Hedge had telephoned the daily woman not to report for duty. There was a smell of sardines—Hedge had just made himself supper, and already there was a film of dust on otherwise high polish. Shard said, 'So you brought Heseltine in after all.'

'No option,' Hedge said with extreme bitterness. 'That man hasn't got ears so much as radar. He brought himself in.'

'And?'

Hedge flapped his arms. 'He's spoken to the Home Secretary, over my head. Over the Head's head too. The word's come, we're to take no action.'

'About Katie Farrell?' Shard asked disbelievingly.

'No! About my wife. She's to be left where she is, Shard, and God knows where that is!'

Shard looked at him with sympathy. 'Has there been any news of her? Any word at all from the other side?' As he said it, he was grimly conscious of a poor choice of words. Hedge's answer indicated no contact with the representatives of the oil interest, even though the assumption was being made that these people would know by now that Katie Farrell had been hooked clean off the blood run.

'The official view is,' Hedge said, 'that for the time being she's safe. My wife, I mean.'

'I go along with that, Hedge.'

'Do you?' Hedge's tone was glum, doom-laden.

'Yes. She's the hostage, Hedge, the lever. She's only of use alive—'

'But the lever's been pulled now, hasn't it?'

'Insofar as Katie Farrell's gone for now, yes, I agree. But you mustn't lose hope, Hedge. I don't believe that whoever's got Katie will be taking final actions just yet.'

'Why not?'

'For one thing, she's been in the hands of the British Government. I guess they'll want to ask some questions.'

'It wouldn't be like them, Shard. Those Ulster militants?' Hedge trembled. 'They shoot first, don't they?'

'Not always, and for my money, not this time. Katie Farrell's no longer an ordinary bomb-throwing terrorist: she's got big backing, right? She's been projected bang into the big time and they may see a use for her. Don't neglect that aspect.'

'Another lever?'

'A bargaining counter—who knows, Hedge, what they may dream up? And while she lives, so does the hostage.' Shard paused, scanning Hedge's white, strained face. 'We have to get Katie back, that's all.'

'All!' Hedge gave a bitter laugh. 'That's good, coming from you! You lost her, didn't you?' He got to his feet and started pacing the room like Shard had paced the Cherbourg cellar the day before. His whole body on the twitch, he swung round. 'Where *is* she, for God's sake? What d'you think? Would they have brought her back into the United Kingdom, or is she still on the continent? We all know it's easy enough to bring people in...deserted beaches, that sort of thing, and every Tom, Dick and Harry seems to own a boat.' He paused. 'That house—no leads, you said. What about the bodies?'

'Not known in my book, but there may be word through soon from Interpol. I told you,

I made contact.'

'It's not going to help much, though, is it?'
Hedge gnawed at his lower lip. 'We don't—'

'It could help. Oh, I know they keep their
tracks well covered and the right hand doesn't
often know what the left hand's doing—that
sort of thing. We must hope for a break-
through, Hedge.'

'The official line'll still be that we take no
action for—for recovery. Of my wife, I mean.'

'Maybe so.' Shard looked at his watch and
got up from the chair. 'Let's see first what
Interpol comes up with, Hedge. If we get a
lead—if we can find out *where* your wife's being
held—at least we can be ready, can't we?'

'Ready for what?'

'Ready to cut her out, Hedge.'

'Well—yes.' Hedge looked a shade brighter,
but it didn't last. 'They won't be holding her
in any one place for long, though. They'll keep
on the move, won't they?'

'That's possible. But maybe they're nicely
holed up somewhere they see as safe. In any
case, we're as mobile as they are.' Shard
glanced again at his watch. 'Hedge, if I may
suggest it...we must keep plugging the main
chance: we must get Katie Farrell back.'

'That's what Heseltine said, blast him!'

'He's right. Face it, Hedge! That's the best

way to put the hostage in the clear—isn't it? As for me, frankly, I don't much care if Katie Farrell gets what she's asked for, but I'm remembering every minute I have a job to do—and so have you.'

'All right, all right!' Spots of high colour showed on Hedge's puffy face, pointing up the dough-like white. Suddenly he lifted his arms and shook clenched fists in the air. 'The faceless people, Shard...not faceless to us, but by God I'm beginning to realise what that phrase means! They're a lot of bastards, Shard, single-minded, no feeling! When a man's wife is involved...how can he stand aside from that, how can he divide his mind? *How*?'

★ ★ ★ ★

Shard walked through from Eaton Square to Victoria for the District Line, reflecting on Hedge's outburst. It had been natural enough and Shard had been sympathetic but unable to give an answer to the question. The answer was, simply, a matter of guts. And there was an irony about it that Shard couldn't help but feel: Hedge was being hoist with his own petard. Not so long ago, Hedge had pitchforked Shard into Russia for an indefinite period at a time when Beth was about to undergo a serious operation, a life and death affair. Appeal against orders had been met with cold adamancy and Shard, faced with an immensely tricky assignment, had had to do a monumental job of mind-dividing. His feelings for Hedge had been precisely similar to Hedge's current feelings for the Whitehall brass: as a result, he could the better understand poor Hedge now. It would be best if Hedge were given leave of absence. Ascending from the District Line at Charing Cross, Shard walked through to Seddon's Way to spend the night on some patient file searching, to see if those dead faces in Cherbourg might after all ring any photographic bells in retrospect; and also to set in motion a few stirrings of the grapevine that might ripple from London's bent and semi-bent circles and, widening, send back an echo of Katie Farrell. But before reaching his office he used a phone box and rang home and this time it was Beth who answered. Shard said, 'Back sooner than expected, darling. Everything all right?'

'I'm fine, Simon,' she said, and her voice sounded a shade less than fine. 'There have been men hanging around, though.'

'Beth, you're not to worry—'

'I don't, not about that.' There was a light laugh. 'I'm married to a policeman, aren't I, and I hope I'm no dumb blonde. What does worry me is why?'

Shard said, 'That's a question that worries us all, for varying reasons. Look, darling, I'm going to be busy most of the night. I'll be home when I can.'

'What about sleep?'

'I'll kip in the office when I'm through. All right?'

'All right, Simon.' There was resignation in Beth's voice: coppers' wives always had the dirty end of the stick, all wait and no excitement. Probably coppers should be celibate: wives were two-edged; they could be a worry and a distraction. Shard, cutting the call, made a mental note to have a word with Assistant Commissioner Hesseltine, whose watchdogs hadn't sounded too clever at concealment. He went on to Seddon's Way and spent a useless couple of hours reading the back files: then he made a phone call and went across to Scotland Yard and spent more time fruitlessly. It was like a jig-saw puzzle, as usual, and also as usual none of the pieces fitted. At last he had his kip and then a canteen breakfast. Back again to Seddon's Way, he reached the door of his office and heard footsteps coming down the stairs from the floor above; he glanced up. Mutton dressed as lamb was on the way down: dyed hair and warpaint and a red blouse heavy with mammary gland.

'Hello, Elsie. Going out for a rest?'

She giggled, taking it in good part. 'You could say.'

'It's early in the day for beating the drum. And risky.'

'Never bin copped yet, have I? Anyway, like anyone else, I have me shopping to do. Look, Mr er.' She usually called him that when they happened to meet. 'There was a man wanting you…in the early hours, too bloody early, or too bloody late depending which way you look at it. I thought he was someone for me, see—'

'A client?'

'Yes. Stopped at the wrong floor—'

'So you came down?'

'I *called* down. He said something about stamps and would I tell you.'

'Uh-huh. Did he leave a name, by any chance, Elsie?'

'Yes. Stanley Gibbons.'

He gave her a sharp look: she wasn't being funny. She was no philatelist herself and the name meant nothing. The joker would have had no difficulty in summing her up. Shard repeated, 'Stanley Gibbons. What did he look like?'

'Small,' she said, sounding vague about it.

'Sort of sandy…wearing a blue anorak. Mind, I was half asleep.'

'Yes, quite,' he said. 'Any message?'

'No.'

Shard nodded. 'Thanks anyway, Elsie.'

'It's a pleasure.' Elsie tripped away on high heels, clickety-click. Shard looked down the stairs at a vigorous behind. Her way of making a living was a damn sight easier and better paid than his, and right now he felt there were other comparisons as well. Katie Farrell left a nasty taste in his mouth. Wondering what ''Stanley Gibbons'' might portend he unlocked the door and went in and as he crossed the threshold there was a shattering roar and his desk fragmented.

CHAPTER FIVE

'I'm all right' Shard said. His face was streaming blood but the wound was superficial: part of his shattered desk, a sliver of metal, had sliced his forehead. There was a sharp smell of explosive. Shard waved at the faces, among them Elsie's veneer, crowding the doorway:

they'd all come—the man from the porn shop below, an off-duty waiter from a flat above Elsie. There was nothing they could do, and Shard told them so. 'Job for the police,' he said, tongue in cheek.

'After your stamps, mate...reckon they meant to blow the safe.'

'Could be. Don't worry, I'm all right. I'll wait for the police.' He caught one of the shocked pairs of eyes. 'Do me a favour, ring the cops?' He gestured at the remains of the desk. 'I'm out of communication, myself.'

'Okay,' the man from the porn shop said, which was big of him: porn and police didn't mix. He went off, taking the others. Shard pushed the door to, and surveyed the damage —caused, no doubt, by "Stanley Gibbons". He grinned: there had been inefficiency, due perhaps to a degree of rush. Elsie must have caught the culprit on his way out, the door-knocking being merely propagandic. Anyway, the device had gone off prematurely, not waiting for him to sit down and activate the mechanism. The office was a shambles. The safe was scarred and pitted like smallpox, so were the walls and ceiling. And the door. Sheets of stamps hung askew. The metalwork of the desk had contained any outbreak of fire, fortunately. Within fifteen minutes, the bomb squad turned up: the DI in charge was an old comrade from the Yard days and he knew discretion was called for the moment he saw Shard. No questions beyond the elicitation of the bare facts: he began a careful search and struck gold fast.

He got up from his knees. 'You were dead lucky, sir. Had you the door between you and the blast?'

'I had.'

The DI nodded. 'You've that to thank, then.'

'What was it?'

'Grenade,' the DI said briefly, holding a twisted piece of metal in his hand. 'Swedish FFV 542. Very effective. Blasts out upwards of five hundred splinters. Yes, you were very lucky. Any ideas who did it, sir?'

'Some,' Shard answered, but didn't elaborate. 'How about you? Any trade marks in your book?'

The DI sucked in a long breath, shaking his head. 'Hard to say. Could be the Provos, but why? Why *you*, I mean? Or shouldn't I ask?'

Shard grinned and said, 'I'd sooner you didn't, Frisby. But you could be right. Except that on the whole the Provos are more efficient, aren't they?'

'Not always, no. Remember Birmingham?

McDade blew himself up, didn't he?' The bomb squad man took a slow look around: his DS was busy scraping up fragments and another man was dusting for prints, a forlorn task Shard fancied. 'What do you want me to do, sir? Lay off, leave it up to you?'

'If I'd wanted that,' Shard answered, 'I wouldn't have brought you in at all. No—carry out your usual routines. There are other tenants here who have to be satisfied, if you get me. It's just a stamp dealer's office—nothing more. All right?'

The DI nodded. 'Fully understood, sir.'

* * * *

In the Charing Cross Road, Shard hailed a taxi and sat back as it took him towards Whitehall. He thought of the forces of terrorism and their various manifestations: Provos, Red Flag 74 and its updated versions, PLO, Al Fatah, Black September, Angry Brigade, plus a lot more who were not exactly terrorists but, in defence of their institutions, behaved as though they were. One sort of terrorism bred another *ad infinitum*: you just couldn't win today. One of the sadnesses was that people grew accustomed to it in a way totally different from the war days. The Coventry and London blitzes, Portsmouth, Plymouth, Glasgow, Liverpool...they had brought good in their bloody train. They had welded the people together into one nation, urgent for victory: now, in the Seventies, that spirit had died the death. Except briefly after some appalling act of savagery against innocent civilians, there was no general sense of outrage; it was impersonal until it happened to you. No cohesion; an ordered society in which each man ploughed his furrow more or less contentedly had yielded place to the squalid disorder in which one group was continually set against another, and the result was that everyone was pre-occupied with increasing his share of the national cake: an uncaring, uncompassionate society had developed, a society of I'm all right Jack, anyway till the next time...Shard gave a sigh as the taxi stopped near the Cenotaph. He jumped out, paid off the driver, and crossed the road towards the Foreign Office. Going straight to the security section, he found Detective Sergeant Kenwood: Kenwood, at Shard's request, had recently been transferred to the section from the Yard.

'Anything new?' Shard asked. 'In regard to Mrs Hedge?'

'Nothing, sir.'

'No leads in his house?'

'I found a blank. I've done all I can there.'

'Anything show in the prints?'

Kenwood shook his head. 'Not a thing, sir. Only family and servants inside—'

'Front door?'

'No help. Postmen, tradesmen—you know the sort of thing.'

'Yes. The villains wore gloves!'

'Yes, sir. And the new processes, they're not all that good yet.'

Shard nodded. Kenwood, who had been staring at the sticking-plaster that Shard had accepted from the porn shop owner, now asked his question: 'What happened to you, sir?'

Shard told him. 'Currently I'm homeless, workwise. I'll use this office if that's all right with you and Mr Hayward,' he added, naming his DI away on leave.

'Of course, sir.' Kenwood looked concerned. 'Sure you don't need stitches?'

'I probably do,' Shard admitted, 'but I haven't had the time. If you'd ring through—' He broke off: on Kenwood's desk, a phone had burred. The DS answered, listened, caught his breath and stared up at Shard. Placing his hand over the mouthpiece he said, 'Surrey Police, sir. The nick at Guildford. They've got who they think is Hedge's wife.'

'How the hell do *they* know?'

'I circulated a description, nationwide.'

Shard nodded, feeling rising excitement. 'Good work! Gimme!' Kenwood passed the handset over. 'Detective Chief Superintendent Shard. Who am I talking to? I see. Yes, that's correct. Yes...*what*?' He listened, eyes staring unseeingly at his detective sergeant, fingers tapping on the desk-top, face registering anxiety. 'Thank you, Superintendent. Not a word to anyone else—I'll be with you soonest possible.' He cut the call, snapped at Kenwood: 'Christ! Plain car at once—no driver. I'll go down alone.'

'What's happened, sir?'

'Surrey Police apprehended a car acting suspiciously by some woods between the A-24 and A-281—they used their loafs and called up another mobile. Then they closed. They were fired on, but a woman—Mrs Hedge—threw herself from the suspect car. The car drove off and there was more firing. The woman was hit—'

'Dead?'

'Just not, I gather. Time's short. Get that car.'

Kenwood picked up an internal phone. Shard said, 'Don't tell Hedge—not yet.'

Kenwood looked up, surprised. 'He'll want to be with her, surely?'

'Maybe. He can't and I'm sorry, but I don't want him around when I question her. I'll need to be brutal, you see.' Shard paused. 'Something unexpected has come up, something that could be too horrible for words: she was able to speak a little…and she's mentioned Porton Down.'

★ ★ ★ ★

Shard drove fast and dangerously: straight for the hospital and a rendezvous in the car park with the Guildford superintendent.

'What's the news, Mr Gotham?'

'Holding her own, they say, but the prognosis is poor.'

'Let's get in there fast. I have to ask questions. Private room, of course.'

'Of course, sir. And a man present outside.'

'Anyone by the bed?'

'Woman PC. The doctors aren't going to like us going in. In fact they've said so already.'

'They'll have to lump it,' Shard said. Moving fast they entered the hospital's lobby: a uniformed constable saluted and accompanied them to a lift. Disembarking two floors up the constable led them to the private wing the unphased-out remnant, last castle of privilege. A sister rose guardianlike from a desk, and

87

from nowhere a white-coated doctor materialised, wafting hospital smells before him.

'Detective Chief Superintendent Shard. I have to see—' He checked himself: he'd been about to use the name Hedge, which in fact was how he always thought of Hedge's wife, naturally enough. As ever, the cloak-and-dagger that meshed the Foreign Office in its coils of bull was getting round his neck. 'I have to see Lady Felicity.' Hedge was plain Mister but his wife was progeny of a belted earl.

'I'm sorry, Mr Shard—'

'So am I. The matter's urgent, Doctor, very urgent.'

'I'm responsible for the patient's life. I consider you'll be putting it in danger.'

'I say again, I'm sorry. I mean that, believe me.' Shard's gaze, steady and determined, held the doctor. 'I'm over-riding you because I *must* over-ride you. There's no option. I have the highest sanction, Doctor.'

'I can't—'

'Listen, Doctor.' Shard's voice snapped, his fingers clenched. 'If necessary I shall use my authority—which derives from Whitehall. Are you with me?'

'With you?' The doctor stared through thick round glasses, looking uncertain in the face of undoubted authority and the set of Shard's lips.

'No, I'm not—'

'I mean this: any refusal will be construed as obstructing the police in the execution of their duty.' Shard's jaw came forward. 'I shall arrest you.'

There was a gasp from the doctor: stalwart at his side, the sister went deep red, outraged from crisp cap to polished shoes: even the superintendent seemed taken aback, started a remonstrance that was brutally cut off by Shard. 'Which is the room?' Shard demanded.

'The constable—'

'Ah—of course.' Shard walked to the door, leaving the other three in a mutinous group. He nodded at the constable on room duty: the officer opened the door quietly. Shard went in, motioning the WPC to remain seated by the head of the bed. A nurse stared in concern: Lady Felicity was under intensive care though not, for security reasons, in the Intensive Care Unit.

'Who are you?' she asked.

Shard identified himself, saw the doctor hovering with a furious face in the doorway. Ordering doctor and nurse to leave him and shut the door, he bent over the still, silent figure in the bed. The face and lips were bloodless: there was no wound to the head, apparently, and the eyes, faded blue, were

89

open, staring at Shard, a known face. Bandaging appeared on the body above the sheets: there was a bullet near the heart and there was lung damage—this much, Shard had been told. The thread of life, the thread of Hedge's happiness, was thin. Shard, thinking his own thoughts of Beth, was desperately sorry, but the probe had to be made in the interests of perhaps millions of people: Porton Down was the embodiment of all things lethal. Bending close to the bloodless skin he said, 'You know me, don't you? Simon Shard. I'm here to ask you to help.' He paused, searching the eyes. 'Do you hear me?'

The lips moved, framing the word yes. He said, 'I'm sorry to do this, but it's vital, absolutely vital. You were kidnapped. Who were they? Have you ever seen them before?'

The eyes closed: a shudder disturbed the ashen, almost transparent face. For a moment Shard believed she had gone: but then the eyes opened again and he caught the faintest touch of breath from the mouth and saw a movement, once again, of the lips. 'Never seen...I don't know.'

'Were any names mentioned?'

'No...'

'Please think hard.' Blood drummed through Shard's head. 'Are you quite certain you'd never, absolutely never, seen any of them? Never...even, perhaps, hanging around outside the house, that sort of thing? Please, try very hard.'

There was a pause, then: 'No...not me, never. Morton...'

'Morton knew them?'

'I think...he said...'

'Try to remember.' Shard sweated: Morton was dead in any case, he could be no help, but maybe his wife—a long shot, that! Meanwhile time was passing and could be passing right to eternity. *Morton, Porton.* Something misheard by the rescuing police patrol? But the word "down" had been used...Porton Down. Shard pressed that way. 'Porton Down. You spoke of Porton Down. What was it? These men— had they said anything about Porton Down?'

The head moved: a nod, made with a supreme effort. Now blood was flecking the lips, frothy and bright. Shard almost felt the prick of tears behind his eyelids. But he had to be a bastard, remembering all that was stored in the Chemical Defence Establishment at Porton Down...He said, 'Please tell me. *What did they say?*'

'They said...'

'Yes? Go on!'

The lips moved again; Shard bent closer till

he was almost touching, feeling her breath like a butterfly's wing on his face. It was no more than a murmur, borne to his ears on a sigh: 'Bomb...blow up.'

He felt deathly cold. 'Blow up—Porton Down?'

'Yes...'

He stayed bent, hoping for more. He heard no door open but felt a hand on his shoulder, pulling. He looked up and saw the doctor's savage face. 'That's enough, Mr Shard. You can arrest me if you like! This will be reported in the highest quarters.'

'Doctor, I—'

'If you go on, you'll kill her. She's almost dead now, don't you *see*?'

Shard shook off the doctor's hand and looked down at the bed: life seemed very brittle now. The mouth hung slack, the eyes were shut. He said quietly, 'Very well, doctor, I doubt if I'll get any more. I hope she's going to be all right.' He passed a hand across his eyes, feeling sick at heart and just about all in physically: the last few minutes had drained him, and God alone knew what it had done to Hedge's wife. He looked the doctor in the eye. 'Meanwhile, you could have heard certain things. You must forget them. Do you fully understand?'

'Really, I—'

'Doctor, I'm quoting the Official Secrets Act at you. If there are leaks, I'll know where to come. But there must be no leaks, and if you think about it you'll see why.' The doctor would: a lot of what went on at Porton Down was unclassified, it had been in the newspapers. It was what might happen now that the public at large must not know about. The avoidance of panic was vital: this doctor would be able to appreciate the potential of the nerve gases, the various disease germs, the bacteriological warfare and the botulinum, a teaspoonful of which in a reservoir could wipe out all life in a town the size of Birmingham.

★ ★ ★ ★

In the hospital the cut on Shard's head had been stitched and properly bandaged: now he was sitting beside the Guildford police chief in a mobile. The pick-up spot was not all that far: off the A-281 Guildford-Horsham road a right-hand turn onto a side road brought them through woodland, nicely off the main tracks. Some half-mile beyond the second turn the superintendent pointed out the spot, and the driver slowed and stopped. Shard and the superintendent got out: there had been rain, and the roadside and undergrowth were damp.

Shard asked, 'Was it raining at the pick-up, Superintendent?'

'No, that's come since.'

Shard walked off the road and into the woods. Men were busy searching; the suspect car had been seen stopped ahead of the first mobile, just after 1030 hours. Unseen themselves, the mobile had pulled off into cover: suspicions had been aroused partly as a result of experience and of hunches that paid off, partly by the fact of Kenwood's nationwide kidnap alert, and partly because there had been some sort of altercation in progress and the car contained an inordinately large number of passengers, currently disembarked...after the close-in, after the shooting, after the attempted murder of the woman, the culprit car had made a clean getaway: both police cars had had their tyres shot up, for one thing. The moment the report had gone in a search had been put in hand over a wide area, plus road blocks. So far, result negative—like the current search. In the woods, there were no clues.

'They won't get away,' the Superintendent said.

Shard smiled tiredly. 'Your net's secure?'

'Yes.'

'You hope, Mr Gotham—you hope!' Without hope himself, he stared up and down the road. 'You'll keep me informed, won't you? About Mrs Hedge as well.'

'I will, sir. Are you going to inform the husband now?'

'As soon as I get back to London, and I'd like to have some good news to tell him. Now, if you don't mind, I'll get back to Guildford and my car.'

★ ★ ★ ★

'I don't know how you could do it, Shard. I really don't!'

'I've said I'm sorry. I am, Hedge, truly. But it was vital. You must see that.' Shard added. 'Anyway, she's none the worse.' Thankfully, that news had come from Guildford before he'd left the Foreign Office for Eaton Square: Mrs Hedge had rallied.

'But why didn't you *tell* me, give me the chance to come with you?'

'I think you know the answer to that, Hedge.'

'But of all people...it's I who could have got her to talk, and more *gently*, Shard.'

Shard didn't respond to that: in the past, he had noticed that Hedge's wife seemed to be, not afraid exactly, but wary of Hedge as though at any moment she might put a verbal foot wrong. That had been very germane to his decision. He said, 'Why not go down and see her now?'

'I'm going to.' Suddenly Hedge seemed to remember that he had a job to do. 'I suppose you didn't get any leads to the Farrell woman, did you?'

'I wasn't after that, not directly. No, no leads to her.'

'Just Porton Down?'

'*Just* Porton Down!' Shard gave a grim laugh. 'Hedge, you do realise the implications, don't you?'

Hedge was getting ready to leave for Guildford. He said, 'Of course I do, but I can't believe they'll do it. I don't see the point. For one thing it's a two-edged weapon—'

'Not once they're out of the country.'

'I still don't see *why*.'

Shard said bitterly, 'I dare say we'll learn, Hedge. In the meantime, what do we do?'

Hedge sat down with a thump, looking ill. Shard could appreciate his feelings, his anxiety: for the moment, Hedge was not functioning well. 'I'm not minimising this, Shard. Far from it. I'll talk to the Head of Department when I get back. But in the meantime, I'd suggest you have a very private word with Henry Carver in the Ministry of Defence.' Hedge added, 'He's a friend of mine and he's the soul of discretion.'

Shard, accompanying Hedge to the front door, knew what was meant by the soul of discretion when it came from Hedge: Hedge was mortally scared of the Press. And this time, not unusually for that matter, Shard was right with him: this was something the man in the street just had not to know about, full stop. Not even after it was all over. Back in Guildford he'd made use of the fact that a lot of what went on in Porton Down was public knowledge: the Press again! They'd been much too forthcoming in the past, for present comfort. And just the smallest whisper that the murderous contents of the Chemical Defence Establishment were under threat of bombing and wholesale scattering, and never again would anyone in Britain sleep soundly in their beds or go to work without the backward look over their shoulders, seeking out the contamination... Shard, as he parted company with Hedge and made for Whitehall, was thinking principally of Beth.

CHAPTER SIX

Shard was a persuasive man and his voice held authority: a telephone call from the Foreign Office secured him an immediate appointment with Henry Carver, who was one of the Assistant Under-Secretaries of State. Carver was a precise and severe-looking man with a stiff white collar and gold-rimmed spectacles: like an American banker, austere, bloodless. He listened in silence, and with careful and courteous attention, to Shard's summary of events, elbows resting on his desk and his fingers held parsonwise, steeple-shaped in front of his square face. The eyes showed shock at what Shard told him, an immediate awareness of all the implications, but the training of a civil servant kept all traces of alarm from his manner. He said, 'You've come to me because of the apparent Porton Down involvement, of course.'

'Yes, sir.'

'How far are you in the picture about Porton?'

'Only a general idea of the potential.'

Carver nodded. 'I see. Then you're not aware it's been largely decentralised?'

'No, sir?'

The Assistant Under-Secretary opened a drawer in his desk and brought out a buff-coloured file with a red classification sticker. 'It's all here, but I'll summarise.' Briefly he scanned a sheet of paper. 'Over the last three to four weeks, stocks have been shifted by road transporter, under an exceptional security cloak I need hardly add, to various points in West Sussex.' Carver looked at Shard over the tops of his spectacles. 'Do you suppose your adversaries know of this?'

'At this moment, I just don't know. Mrs Hedge may be able to help us more later, but that's doubtful apart from a description of the kidnappers.'

'And Katie Farrell?'

'She may be involved, or she may not.'

'H'm.' Carver pursed his lips. 'That's your job, of course, but if I may be permitted a guess, I'd say she's involved up to the hilt!' He went back to his file. 'These dispersal points they're all in the South Downs, behind Worth-ing...' A glimmer of humour appeared in Carver's eye. 'What the medical profession call the Costa Geriatrica, Mr Shard. Full of octogenarians.'

Shard nodded. 'I know.' He had a relative there, and he mentioned the fact.

'What relationship, may I ask?'

'A great aunt-in-law.'

'Remotish,' Carver murmured. 'No real personal involvement?'

'Sir?'

'This must not leak, Mr Shard. Not even by inference. That is to say, your great aunt-in-law must stay put. You understand?'

Shard said, 'I know my job, sir.'

'Yes, I'm sure,' Carver said quickly, pacifically. 'It had to be said, though. You realise I'm taking this very seriously?'

'I'm glad to hear that, sir.'

Carver looked at him shrewdly. 'Hedge? Do I gather—'

'He's preoccupied at the moment.'

'Yes, of course he is.' Carver nodded sympathetically. 'Now, you'll want to know more about the dispersal points—'

'May I ask one thing first, sir: why was the dispersal ordered?'

Carver smiled. 'Yes, a good question in the circumstances. It wasn't due to any lack of storage capacity at Porton Down, I can tell you that. It was thought wiser, in the current climate of world terrorism, which looks like

100

becoming a permanent way of life, to clear Porton out. You can't disguise the Chemical Defence Establishment, Mr Shard! It's big, it's obvious, and no secret has ever been made of what it's there for or what it contains. The dispersal, on the other hand, *has* been secret, as I said. That is, we hope it has.'

'So you've had just this current threat in mind?'

'Well, something similar—yes. The new stowages should not become known for what they are so long as our security holds up. They're all either underground or semi-underground. Basically they've been there *in situ* for a good many years, and the local people have all kinds of theories about them: water reservoirs, which indeed some of them are— or have been—bunkers for use as radio stations, Regional Seats of Government ready for use in the event of all-out nuclear attack, or simply deep air-raid shelters for the general population. Naturally, they're all in country sites somewhat off the beaten track, and all they show to the casual walker or motorist is a grass-covered hummock, square or oblong-shaped, in some cases with air vents protruding, in some cases with radio masts visible. In all cases except, I think, one midway up the slopes of Chanctonbury Ring, they're surrounded with

101

barbed metal stockades and padlocked gates. I repeat, they've been a source of interest and speculation...but in themselves innocuous. Now they're lethal. I suggest you pay them a visit, Mr Shard.'

'I'll do that. And Porton Down? Is it empty now?'

Carver shook his head. 'Not entirely. It's still the experimental base and factory, where the diseases and gases are actually produced in co-operation with the MRE—the Microbiological Research Establishment, which is also at Porton. Don't forget Nancekuke in Cornwall, either. That's where the VX gas was produced, you'll remember. Nasty stuff! It's a nerve gas—a drop the size of a pinhead is lethal when it's in liquid form, it just has to contact the skin. I—'

'Has there been any dispersal from Nancekuke?'

'No—it's so remote it's considered safe, and the security people have a fairly easy time of it.' Carver paused. 'Now of course we shall have urgently to consider the question of extra security around Porton and the South Downs, probably Nancekuke too, and we have an availability both of your people and our own. We don't want divided command and responsibility, do we? Have you any suggestions?'

Shard said diplomatically, 'It's a Defence Ministry commitment, of course. On the other hand, I'm in charge, under my Head of Department, of dealing with Katie Farrell, and her recovery now—and that's strictly *our* commitment. With respect, I'd suggest you continue to physically guard the stowage points and Porton Down itself, whilst leaving my department to cope with the overall security including any involvement of Katie Farrell and either the people who're currently holding her, or the oil interests who want to take possession of her.'

Carver was smiling. 'Nicely put! You should have been a diplomat, not a policeman, Mr Shard. What you're saying really, is that you wish to have the command, isn't it? We provide the dogsbodies, you provide the brains—h'm?'

'I'm sorry, sir.'

'Oh, don't be, you have a vital job to do.' Carver waved a hand. 'This is going to be no time for inter-departmental squabbles. You do realise what could happen?'

'Only too well, sir.'

'So serious it's impossible to overplay.' Carver, his face grim, thumped his desk in emphasis, the veneer of the civil servant cracking just a little. 'If there's the smallest breach—if even a fraction of the contents of just

103

one of the stowages is distributed...then millions in this country face an appalling death. The over-populated south-east sector will take the immediate brunt.' He got to his feet and paced the room. 'The decision as to the allocation of command and responsibility isn't, in fact, ours to make, Shard.'

'A Cabinet decision?'

Carver nodded. 'Just so. I'll be seeing my Minister shortly, you may rely upon it. You'll hear more very soon—meanwhile I suggest you start travelling around the south. I'll give you some ideas as to where to start.'

★ ★ ★ ★

Back to the Foreign Office: Shard contacted his detective sergeant. 'I'm getting car-borne again, Harry. Hold the fort, all right?'

'Yes, sir—'

'If anything comes in about the Farrell woman, or the Guildford villains, pass the word to me via Steyning 812026.'

Kenwood scribbled. 'And that is?'

'Wiston House.'

'Oh yes. FO staff courses?'

Shard nodded. 'They've been using one of these grassy hummocks for the storage of Top Secret files—'

'Grassy hummocks?'

Shard explained. 'Not any more—no more files. Wiston House will be my HQ for the West Sussex area. If I'm not there, I'll be at Porton Down.' Leaving the security section, he went for his car and headed out of London via the South Circular and the A-3, turning onto the A-243 for Worthing at the Hook roundabout. As he drove, he thought about villains and the nastiness of terrorism, the no holds barred aspect that was the characteristic of the latter. All the millions of people sardine-packed, virtually, into the south-east corner... how much *time* was there left now? At the Washington roundabout a left turn took Shard onto the Steyning road for Wiston House. Passing Chanctonbury Ring to his right, he came to the Wiston House entry and turned up a long drive in the depths of lush green country, well wooded. He stopped in front of an elegant house, one that had been a magnificent private house in the spacious days. He looked around briefly: one car was parked, a Rover 3½-litre, brand new.

Shard entered the building, to be stopped by a uniformed guard. He submitted to a strict and efficient security check. When he'd passed it the man said, 'Major Bentley will be down in a few moments, sir.' A message was passed on an internal line and Shard was not kept waiting any time: almost on the heels of the okay, Bentley appeared, a spare man not unlike Colonel Smith back in the Hans Crescent flat: very military, and currently very anxious, with a nervy twitch that kept his right eye on the blink as he spoke, and a somewhat disconcerting habit of sniffing. He had, it seemed, been briefed on the security telephone by Carver.

'You're a fast mover,' he said. 'I like that.'

'I felt it couldn't wait!'

'You're damn right,' Bentley lifted an eyebrow. 'Your car or mine?'

Shard stared. 'Car? I understood there was a tunnel?'

'Was, yes. Not any more. It was handy for the files. Now the sealing door's been locked. I'm only showing you the outside, the top...and that's half way up to Chanctonbury—'

'This door, Major—'

'Watertight, fireproof, thief proof.' Bentley paused. 'And now germ proof!'

'Sure. But I suppose it does unlock...doesn't it?'

Bentley looked at him and sniffed. 'It does.'

'And the key?'

'Commandant's private safe.'

Shard nodded. Clearly, there had been the not-unusual hiatus in inter-Ministry communications. 'Major, I want in. It's what I've come down for.'

Bentley was firm. 'Not possible. I'm awfully sorry.'

'You'll be sorrier.'

'I beg your pardon?' Bentley flushed red. 'Now look here, I—'

'I'm likely to be the co-ordinator. You know what's in the wind. Right now, there may be a meeting of the Cabinet to consider the position, Major.' Shard's voice was cold. 'I'm delighted to see the security's tight. But I happen to *be* Security. And I say again, I want *in*, not *on*. If you refuse, I'll ask for a line to the Minister.'

Bentley's right eye twitched madly. 'You're a blasted nuisance and I don't care for your tone. But hold on and I'll see the Commandant.' He turned away, back into the building. Shard waited, cursing the delay. Bentley, however, was himself a fast mover: within five minutes he was back with the key. It was no ordinary key: just a straight, slim piece of metal with raised, winding lines like a meat skewer. Bentley said, 'This way,' and led Shard to the back of the hall and down some stairs into a basement. With another key held ready, an ordinary one, he unlocked a wooden door leading off what had once been a wine cellar, and pushed it open. Shard walked through into darkness: Bentley flicked on a light overhead. Shard saw brick walls, damp-looking, leading to yet another door, again of wood. Bentley did his unlocking again: this time Shard moved into a cement-faced tunnel, low enough for him to have to walk along with head bent. There were lights overhead at intervals, leading on for what seemed to be an immense distance. For a while the tunnel took a downward slant, then levelled off. It was close, airless, smelly, though there was a faint whirr of fans coming from somewhere. Shard, over Bentley's shoulder, for the Major had pushed past into the lead, asked: 'How about your files?'

'Stowed in the basement temporarily.'

'And the staff? No awkward questions?'

'Yes, but dealt with. Not to worry. The stowage was said to be damp.'

'And was it?'

'Yes. Much mildew, not good for files.' Bentley walked on. Way ahead, the overhead lights ceased their being: they were now approaching the watertight firescreen door, its heavy dull metal reflecting a few gleams from the remaining lights. The place felt spooky, dead and deadening. Reaching the door, Bentley pushed back a metal slide and inserted his strange key in a slot beneath. There was a curious humming sound, and a crackle. Bentley spoke, but not to Shard. He said as if to the empty air, 'S2. With authorised visitor. God be with you, and with thy spirit.' At that the hum was cut off and Bentley sniffed and said, 'Oh, bugger. That was yesterday's, would you believe it? God be in thy peace, and in thy understanding. That's it, hey presto.'

The hum returned; then, silently, the heavy door moved aside, hauled by some remote-control apparatus into a deep groove cut into the earth. Ahead, the tunnel was metal-lined, and brilliantly lit. It began now to take an upward incline. Some twenty yards ahead a blue-uniformed man wearing the Department of the Environment's gilded crowns on his lapels stood outside a glass-fronted cubby-hole. As Bentley approached the custodian saluted: knowing Bentley, he nevertheless scrutinised the pass that the Major held out.

'And the other gentleman, sir?'

Shard produced his FO identification, glad once again to note good security. Bentley moved on. Shard followed him towards a steep flight of steps that terminated the tunnel proper. They climbed into a small square lobby into which a lift-well descended: the lift was waiting with open doors. Bentley went in, followed by Shard, and pressed a button. Swiftly the lift rose, leaving Shard's stomach way behind: it had the speed of a New York elevator. As it stopped the doors opened soundlessly. They walked out into another lobby with two doors opening off it, and were met by another man, a man in his early fifties: not, Shard judged from his white coat, another custodian but a scientist, a man of Porton Down.

'Dr Lavington,' Bentley said by way of introduction. He lifted an eyebrow at Shard, who nodded back. 'This is Detective Chief Superintendent Shard of Security.'

Lavington held out a hand and smiled. He was, Shard thought, a cold fish; the smile was not a warm one. The doctor asked, 'May I know the purpose of your visit, Mr Shard?'

'Interest, Doctor. Just interest.'

'But more in security than research?'

'You could say that.'

Another smile. 'Oh, you'll find we're very security conscious. We learned that at Porton, I do assure you.'

'Quite. You've settled in here all right?'

The scientist glanced with a touch of malevolence at Bentley and said, 'We're on sufferance, of course. The Foreign Office is the élite...dispossession's a dirty word, Mr Shard.

If you ask Major Bentley, he'll tell you that what we're doing is dirty too—right, Bentley?'

'Yes,' Bentley snapped.

'It isn't really. Defence, not offence, that's our watchword. Other countries are doing it, so we must too.' Lavington turned back to Shard. 'How much do you want to see, now you're here?'

'I'd like to see everything, if that's possible, Doctor.'

'As you wish,' Lavington said. 'I'll explain as we go. You're not squeamish, I hope?'

★ ★ ★ ★

Until now, Shard had believed he had a fair idea of what was manufactured, tested and stored away at Porton Down. He had also believed, and believed firmly, that his stomach was a strong one. He had been wrong both times. Dr Lavington, a man dedicated to death as it seemed, had opened his eyes wide. Leading the small procession through one of the doors off that upper lobby he had, in a succession of metal-lined compartments large and small and in two long galleries with glass-fronted recesses at intervals, paraded his wares with pride in achievement and a well-developed sense of the dramatic. There had been the nerve

111

gases that brought about instant paralysis upon either inhalation or skin touch; there had been aerosols that, when pumped out under powerful pressure from mobile machines akin to flame throwers, produced in humans results precisely similar to those produced in flies and other insects by aerosol cans to be found in any housewife's kitchen: Lavington had detailed the effects. Blinding of the eyes, shrivelling of the lungs and air passages to induce strangulation, dehydration of flesh, fat and tissue so that the human body became a dry husk. Whole armies, whole populations, could be quickly killed, converted into burned-out corpses. There were the things that were not so secret, the toxic chemicals intended for use in agriculture: Parathion, TEPP, HETP, Shradan. Death, said Lavington, could occur from a single exposure to any one of these. The symptoms were tightness of the chest; twitching of eyelids and tongue muscles and contraction of the pupils; headache, anorexia, nausea aggravated by smoking, giddiness, general uneasiness, anxiety, restlessness. These progressed towards respiratory disturbance, sweating, salivation, vomiting and abdominal cramps; and the final stage envisaged great distress in breathing, pinpointing of the pupils, muscular twitching, incontinence, coma, death. Successive small doses could progressively lower the choli-nesterase level without the production of symp-toms but would render a person more and more susceptible to further dosage. There were gases that unhinged the mind, and anti-military psychedelic gases that rendered the victim totally unable to obey a command. There were the other things, the botulinum and allied poisons for the water supplies, the disease germs that could be dropped from aircraft in the form of impact bombs without warheads or dispersed from low-flying planes by cloud-sprays. The diseases were frightful ones that few doctors, in private practice or in the hospitals, would have any idea how to combat: they would be right outside their collective experience. They would be swift in action, had been selected and carefully nurtured for their infectious and contagious qualities. There would be, literally, positively, no defence except the one: the brains and know-how of the men of the Chemical Defence Establishment itself. In every case, and this was some com-fort to Shard in the present circumstances, Por-ton Down or its new satellite establishments, the store-houses, had the antidote. It was no wonder that Dr Lavington, not himself a doc-tor of medicine, paraded his stocks as though he were very God. In certain situations, he could be considered as just that.

Shard couldn't get away fast enough. Walking back along the tunnel his mind was filled with terrible images: the tanks and retorts, the test-tubes, the glass-screened forcing grounds of filth, the invisible crawling horrors that lurked in the cultures, torturous, revolting death in glass bottles. And the results of uncontrolled dissemination, as described by Lavington: the cities of the dead, men, women and children falling in the streets as the plague came down, or as they drank from the taps in their houses. Shard had asked a basic question, even though he could guess the answer well enough: 'Suppose, just suppose, there was ever a breach, Doctor?'

'Of security?'

'No. I realise the security's good. A physical breach...say by a bomb.'

Lavington shrugged. 'We're well down in the earth here...I wouldn't say the same of the other stowages—not *so* deep as us. Of course if it did happen at all it would depend on the penetration, the dispersal, even the weather conditions. It wouldn't be the same as a direct target attack, you see. The wind direction would be important as regards the effectiveness initially.'

'Initially?'

114

'The speed of spread.'

'But it *would* spread?'

'Of course it would!' Lavington had laughed with a long-suffering tolerance, the expert instructing the layman. 'Just a question of time, that's all. These diseases are *deadly*, and as I've said, only we have the antidotes. And even we couldn't possibly hope to control it once it was out. It would begin locally—that's obvious—and spread.'

'How far?'

Lavington said, 'Even with no wind at all, I dare say ten days or so would see the whole country affected, from Land's End to John O'Groats.'

★ ★ ★ ★

The fresh air was more than welcome: Shard felt physically unclean, as though he must have brought out some of the horror upon his body: he had a strong urge towards a bath. Bentley seemed to understand.

'Frightening isn't it?'

'An understatement, Major. I don't suppose I need to say this—but I hope to God your people are keeping right on the top line!'

'They are, and will be. Not that it's easy, and I'm not making excuses. It's a question of

115

divided responsibility to some extent.'

'But I'm told you're in charge?'

'Yes, indeed.' Bentley, standing with Shard outside the front door of Wiston House, took a deep breath. 'I'm OC Security, but Lavington's the inside boss if you follow. Two Ministries virtually under one roof—that dump still belongs to us, to the FO. Porton Down's the bloody tenant and can't be evicted!' He hesitated. 'It's a damn good strong-point lost to us. I don't know if you knew, but it was intended as an RSG—Regional Seat of Government. They're slightly old hat now, though—no-one really expects a nuclear war any more. So it was hooked off us.' He looked up at Shard. 'Care to see the topside of it now?'

Shard nodded. 'Thanks, I would.'

'It's quite a climb. I can drive so far but no farther. But come on.' He led the way towards the Rover that Shard had seen parked earlier. Driving back to the main road, he turned left and then left again along a narrow lane between high hedges sprouting into spring. Soon Shard could see the heights of Chanctonbury Ring ahead in a climbing mantle of big trees, a high peak in the South Downs with its age-old links from a pagan past: suitable ground, Shard thought, for a pagan present, a suitable birthplace for the works of the new Messiah, Jesus

116

Lavington...

Bentley pulled the Rover into a car park and picnic spot: there were a handful of other cars around but no picnicking: this was the Costa Geriatrica, and the tourist season was not yet in its swing. The cars contained the elderly, sitting inert behind glass for their country air and looking as dead as Lavington's products might soon make them. Bentley saw Shard's expression and laughed.

'Out from Worthing. They cluster there from all over, just to die.'

'Why?'

'It's flat the other side of the Downs. So in fact they don't die. They linger and proliferate—I don't mean sexually, of course! They get added to from year to year—quite a problem, they say.'

Shard followed him out of the car park and along a muddy, rutted track climbing Ringwards. He said, 'I have a great-aunt of my wife's there.'

Bentley laughed again. 'My God, who hasn't! I ask you! I've travelled the world...and I've never been *anywhere* that you don't find an Englishman who has, or has had, an elderly relative living in Worthing. It's almost a conversation starter...' For his part, Bentley had come to the end of conversation; he began to puff. The climb was steep, all right, even for Shard who was a good deal younger. After some twenty minutes, Bentley uttered again: 'There. See it?' He waved an arm ahead at a flattish concrete-slabbed structure, overgrown and with two of the slabs smashed in. Bentley was livid. 'Vandals!' he said bitterly. 'Security-wise it's not important, but...' He looked aside. In some trees nearby was indication that not all the area was geriatric: a couple sat in oblivious fondle, long-haired and in jeans, doing everything but the sex act itself. Bentley gave a sniff and said, 'Damn! We'll have to keep our voices down.'

'They'll never, never notice! All the same, I'm with you.'

They closed the crummy structure's broken-down concrete, incongruous cover for what was breeding below. Leaning over the gap in the roof, Bentley said, 'Water-tank. It's deep. Not used now, of course.'

'Relative position?'

'Smack on top of the upper lobby.'

'Secure?'

'Yes. Lavington won't have his damn germs drowned if that's what you mean. It's been reinforced from below.'

Shard nodded. 'Positively no way in?'

'One can never quite say that, but they'd

have to cut through metal.'

'A bomb?'

Bentley shrugged. 'Oh, a really sizeable one would go through anything—you know that! A typical terrorist bomb would hardly cut much ice, I'd think. I'm not unduly worried.' He paused, gave an exclamation, peered closer, then put a hand on Shard's shoulder, and Shard felt a tension coming through from him. 'I say, Shard...we're not alone, I rather think! D'you see?'

'They're paying no attention to us, Major—'

'No, no! Not those uninhibited louts. Down *there*.' He pointed through the shattered roof. 'There's a body!'

'What!'

'Look for yourself.' Bentley moved aside, and Shard peered down, focussing through gloom and a rising smell of putrid water. After a while he saw it: something floating, face down he fancied, clothing bagged out, ballooned with air—or decomposition gas. Staring intently, he saw an arm.

'It's a body right enough,' he said.

'Do we get it out?'

'It's very dead. It'll keep a little longer.' He inclined his head back towards the concupiscent couple in the trees. 'If we bring it out now, it'll register even with them—perhaps. I'd sooner not risk it.'

Bentley glanced at his face. 'See a connexion with you-know-what, do you?'

'I don't know, but there just could be, couldn't there? We'll leave it, Major. I'll have a word with the local police and get it brought up after dark.'

'As you say, Shard. In the meantime, what?'

'Back to Wiston House. I'll call my chief from there, if I may.'

'Of course.'

Shard stood up straight. 'In the midst of life...' he murmured half to himself, but Bentley heard.

'There's always replacements coming along,' he said in a tone of disgust. 'Just look at that!' Shard looked: the loving couple had been unable to wait and were deep in copulation. Bentley nodded towards the thing in the water-tank. 'Some conception ground,' he remarked witheringly, 'for some poor little bastard to look back on in years to come!'

★ ★ ★ ★

At full dark Shard and Bentley accompanied Sussex Police on their macabre journey, squelching through greasy, slippery mud made worse by rain in the interval, rain that was still falling. The police Land-Rover had made it higher up than Bentley's car, but it was still a longish haul behind the torches, and a weird one as the light flickered through the trees, throwing trunks and branches into silver relief. At the water-tank a frogman went in with a line: his job was quickly done. The corpse was hauled up: it was bloated and horrible. A good deal of the clothing had gone and in the torch-light there was a full frontal view: Shard, even though his mind had begun to work along certain lines that had their origins more in fantasy and a vivid imagination than in strict reasoning, had a considerable shock: the corpse was female and the damaged, bloated face held a familiarity...and when the police surgeon moved the lower clothing a little more he saw scarring and a birthmark that were still recognisable.

In a voice he scarcely knew as his own he asked, 'How long, Doctor? How long dead?'

'That's very hard to say with any accuracy. My first impression is that death wasn't due to drowning anyway. There are indications... but I don't know, I don't know at all.' He looked up. 'A snap opinion, Mr Shard: she's been dead for more than a week, maybe much more. Will that do?'

'But—' Shard broke off, biting his lip.

'Yes?'

'Never mind, Doctor. Let's get her away. I want to get her to Wiston House—but that's not to be talked about afterwards. I'd like everybody to come with me, including you, Doctor.'

Amid a curious tension, and in growing fear on Shard's part, the corpse was wrapped first in a polythene bag and then in heavy canvas and placed on a stretcher: Shard, obeying his instincts, had restricted the handling of the body to the police surgeon, the frogman and the two constables who had hauled it up from the tank. The bearers trudged down through the mud to the Land-Rover, slipping dangerously from time to time. In the light from the torches the bundle was put into the back of the Land-Rover; the policemen clambered in, those who had not been in contact keeping clear, to Shard's repeated order, of the canvas. The Land-Rover was reversed down the track, turned, and driven fast for Wiston House. No-one seemed inclined to speak. On arrival Shard ordered the men to get down and muster clear of the vehicle and await his orders. Then he turned to Bentley. 'A word in your ear,' he said. They walked a little apart, and Shard said in a low, tense voice, 'I identify the corpse, Major. Timewise it can't possibly be—but it *is*!

The operation scars and the birthmark on the fringe of the pubic hairs. I've seen them before.'

Bentley's tone was dry. He sniffed. 'Really?'

'I'd rather say no more for the moment. I'll be in touch with the FO right away, but first there's something else, Major.'

'Well?'

'The time factor. What the doctor said—and you've seen the body for yourself. Even the doctor was stymied for what killed her, but I have a pretty fair idea myself—'

'What, Shard?'

Shard said, 'You'll have to send for Lavington and any more of his team you can muster. We'll *all* have to be checked out now. Don't go inside—ring a bell or something. And have it disinfected after.'

His face like that of another corpse as realisation came to him, Bentley gave a gasp of horror and ran for the front door.

CHAPTER SEVEN

Lavington turned up in his car: behind him two more of the scientific staff arrived, followed closely by the establishment medical officer. Lavington kept his headlights on, beamed towards the group of policemen and the canvas-shrouded corpse in the back of the Land-Rover.

'What's happened?' he asked.

Bentley gestured towards the corpse. 'We found her in the water-tank—you know where I mean. She didn't die from drowning. Or from gunshot. Or anything else like that.'

'What are you saying, Major?' In the glare of light, Shard watched Lavington's face: there was caution in it rather than fear or worry. Natural, perhaps; he was, as Bentley had said, the inside boss and he would need to be cautious in all he said in front of outsiders, even policemen. 'Are you suggesting...'

Bentley nodded. 'Shard seems to think so.'

Lavington said, 'My God, no!' For a moment he seemed irresolute, then moved aside with the medical officer and held a hurried consultation. Coming back towards Shard he said, 'We'd like you to wait here. Keep everyone just where they are now. Have they all been in contact with the body?'

Shard said, 'The frogman, the police surgeon, and two constables touched the body. That's all. The rest of the men are clear.'

The medical officer asked. 'And you?'

'No contact.'

The doctor nodded. Lavington asked, 'Why do you suspect—'

'A question of time. I happen to know the woman.' Shard felt positive enough to say that with assurance: though the face had been unrecognisable, the evidence of the scarring and the peculiar birthmark was in his book conclusive. 'I know she was alive the day before yesterday.' He paused. 'You'd never think so now.'

Again Lavington nodded. 'Hold on. I'll go and scrub up.' He turned away and went inside the building at the run, followed by the other new arrivals. Shard waited with Bentley and the police party: no-one spoke. Although the PCs didn't know the score, had no knowledge of the facts of likely disease, they couldn't fail to be aware of something way out of the ordinary about the death that lay shrouded in the Land-Rover. As they waited, more rain began to fall, blown into their faces by a rising wind. Shard's thoughts rioted: why had Katie Farrell been brought here to die? Her killing he could understand, though it had happened much sooner than he would have predicted—than he *had* so confidently predicted to Hedge. But why here? And why, and how, the apparent disease? If his theories were confirmed by the experts, from where had the leak occurred, and how? He walked up and down in the blaze of Lavington's headlights, trying to think things through, disregarding Bentley, oblivious of the cold rain and the wind sighing with eerie persistence through the trees. If the creeping filth was out into the world, in public circulation, where was it going to end?

Lavington and his team came back: they hadn't wasted time. They looked now like something from space, clad from head to foot in rubber overalls, with goggle-eyed helmets on their heads, and wearing long rubber surgical gloves. Lavington led them to the Land-Rover and they lifted the body out, laid it on the ground, and very carefully removed the canvas outer cover and the polythene bag. Lavington and the medical officer, Dr Andrews, made an examination, conferring together in whispers, probing the body entries, pressing the distended stomach, making much use of instruments, taking swabs that were sealed carefully in glass bottles and, finally, taking two samples by means of hypodermics, drawing off liquid from needles inserted at a flat angle into the stomach-lining.

Andrews stood up with his samples, and gestured to Major Bentley. 'That's all for now, Major,' he said. 'She'll be wrapped up again while I make some lab tests. I'll not keep you long.'

'Any idea what it is?' Bentley asked in a hoarse voice.

'Not yet. When I've done some work, I'll know.' Andrews paused. 'Did *you* touch the body at all?'

Bentley said, 'No, I didn't.'

'Positive?'

'Positive. Shard, too. Does that mean we're in the clear?'

Andrews said, 'It may. I don't know that yet either. You'll have to wait.' He moved towards the door into the building, then turned. 'The body. What do we do with it?'

Bentley glanced at Shard. Shard said, 'I'd like it kept here. Have you the facilities, Doctor?'

'Yes, we have, but I'm not too sure of the legal position.'

'Just leave that to me,' Shard said. 'All I ask of you is safe stowage and total silence.'

Again they waited as Andrews and Lavington went back inside, waited with the rain falling along the wings of the restless wind: one of the worst waits of Shard's life.

* * * *

From Hedge, Shard, back in London, accepted a large whisky, neat. It went down fast. Hedge refilled the tumbler; Shard took the second more slowly, beginning to feel better. Sitting in a comfortable chair, he said, 'It had some dreamed-up Latin name, but colloquially it's known as the bloating sickness. The victims just—swell.'

'And that causes death.'

'The skin bursts, Hedge. Everything comes out. Yes, it causes death. It can be arrested by immersion.'

'That was what happened, was it? To Katie Farrell?'

Shard shrugged. 'Apparently. I asked myself why they immersed her, why they bothered if she was meant to die anyway. Why undo their own work?'

'But they didn't undo it, since she *did* die anyway.'

128

'I know. The mystery deepened. I came up with two theories, and they're only guesswork really: one, they threw her in and stood around to observe the reactions—just an added bit of nastiness, of sadism. Or two, she was left up there to die, managed to move around, saw the water-tank, and dropped in to try to save herself, and died in the act.'

'Pre-supposing she knew the facts?'

'Yes. They could have told her...just for the gloat.' Shard blew out a long breath. 'None of this explains why they did it there—sort of drawing attention to the area—or how they acquired the disease germs. It explains the initial assumption of the police surgeon that death had taken place a week ago, which I knew was impossible even though there was all the appearance of the body having been dead that long.'

'These germs...they're strictly Porton?'

'Very! It's one of Lavington's cultures. Not, as it happens, the most persistent, though—'

'But always lethal?'

'Unless immersion takes place quickly, and even then it leaves its filthy traces behind— what's been ravaged stays ravaged. Once caught you're never the same again—that is, once it gets a grip. An injection, a painful one, within three hours of exposure is totally effective.'

Hedge grimaced. 'I trust you're in the clear, Shard?'

'You needn't start feeling for bloat, Hedge. I didn't touch the body. I was in the clear from the start, but I insisted on the injection just to make it one hundred per cent positive. That's how I can vouch for the pain, which is bloody.'

'And the water—the tank on Chanctonbury Ring?'

'That's okay too. Water doesn't conduct it, or whatever the medical term may be. On the contrary, as I said, it inhibits it.'

'Ah, yes, yes. So climbers, picnic parties—they're quite safe?'

'Yes. For now anyway.'

Hedge raised an eyebrow. 'For now?'

'I think the whole area may be at risk, Hedge. There's been an obvious leak and we don't know how far it went. Other things may have leaked at the same time, mightn't they?'

Hedge's face whitened. 'I presume you had a check made?'

'Yes, I did. Lavington reports no tampering, no shortfall that he can see, but you can't see shortfalls with cultures and what-not that are self-proliferating, can you? Lavington's checking the other stowages around the South Downs—he's OC the lot. He'll be working through the night and has promised a report first thing in the morning—*this* morning, now.' Shard looked at the clock on Hedge's chimney-piece—French, all gilt and blue enamel and faintly pansy, like the one he had in his room at the FO. 'I can't do any more now, Hedge. I'm for home and bed unless there's anything else you want to know.'

'No.' Hedge got up and gloomed around the drawing-room, looking lonely: he'd told Shard his wife was showing signs of some improvement but it was clearly going to be a long while before she was allowed home. In the meantime her description of her kidnappers had been too vague to be useful and although she had been able to talk she had no further information about the threat to Porton Down and its products: just a snatch of overheard talk about a bombing, no details, no times or dates. Hedge had said, rather pathetically, 'You were wrong, Shard. She *did* talk to me.' When Shard had pressed, he'd said his wife had positively no more to give and he didn't want her bothered again. Now, Hedge, from the depths of his gloom, said, 'When you hear from Lavington, we'll talk again.'

'Right.' Shard got to his feet. 'We'll have to consider protection for the general Worthing area, I think.'

'Won't that depend on what Lavington says?'

'Yes, up to a point. I still think even Lavington can't be *sure*. What we *know* is that the bloating sickness has been on the loose. We have to reckon with that, Hedge.'

'Security still has to be preserved. We have to catch these people.'

Shard gave a harsh laugh. 'Don't I know it! We still need to be—humane, Hedge.'

'Well, it won't be up to us, will it? All I can do is make recommendations.' Hedge took up the whisky decanter. 'Another before you go?'

'No.' Shard gave a humourless smile. 'It's sleep I need above all else.'

★ ★ ★ ★

The Ealing house was in darkness, all long gone to bed: Shard, opening his gate, was approached by a long-haired young man in flared trousers.

'Just a moment. What do you want in this house?'

'Bed, just bed.'

'Your name, sir?'

Shard gave it, briefly palmed his official identification.

A small torch came out, was flashed in

Shard's eyes: the okay was given, with apologies. 'It's all right,' Shard said, 'I'm delighted you're alert. Goodnight, and thanks for your trouble.'

'A pleasure, sir.'

Shard went up the path and put his key in the lock. Inside, he crept upstairs. When he got to the bedroom, Beth was awake. 'Simon!' she said, not surprised: she was used to his movements.

He grinned and bent to kiss her: but remembering, he held back just before their lips met. He felt unclean, and never mind Lavington's assurances, so positively uttered. Looking down at Beth, he saw Katie Farrell in the water-tank: a brief image, but unutterably horrible. He drew away.

'I've got a cold coming, darling.'

'Are you sure that's all?'

'Of course,' he said, laughing. Quickly he undressed and got into bed. She hugged him with a kind of hunger, and he knew why: senior security men spent a lot of time away from home, and they often met attractive women at very close quarters: Beth, he was well aware, had always been worried, even before his secondment from the Yard. There was a basic insecurity in her, due entirely to his life as a copper: always the chances were there—death and injury and stolen love. Tonight it was really bad: already Porton Down was casting its shadow. He had been too close to that dreadful, ravaged corpse and try as he would he could not relax into his wife's arms. In the morning, when he awoke after only some four hours' sleep with his mind on Lavington's expected report, he got the reaction from Beth. She was hurt. He was in no position to give explanations, to calm her fears. He kissed the unresponsive top of her head, ruffled the long fair hair and felt totally inadequate. Trying to make conversation he made a passing reference to Mrs Micklam and then Beth dropped the bombshell.

'You needn't get uptight about Mother any more. She's leaving today.'

That surprised him. 'Today? I thought she was staying a week?'

'Well,' Beth said flatly, not meeting his eye, 'she's not. Aunt Edith—'

'What about Aunt Edith?' He sat up sharp in bed, looking down at her, guessing the rest of it and starting to worry badly. 'Well, Beth?'

'She isn't well, that's all. Mother's going down.'

'To Worthing?'

'Yes.' She gave him a wide-eyed look now. 'Why the odd tone, Simon?'

134

'I'm sorry, it wasn't meant to be.' He got out of bed and stood in pyjama trousers, tousle-haired, staring down out of the window. Mothers-in-law...surely top coppers had a right not to have to be bothered with them? Music-hall jokes, perennial trials and tribulations of young married PCs and jacks. Somehow you didn't associate detective chief superintendents with mothers-in-law, not until, young for your rank, you found yourself stuck with one of them. Shard turned glowering from the window and banged into the bathroom: and while shaving, and later over coffee and a cigarette, worried with a degree of real despair about Beth's bombshell. Worthing he considered to be at some positive risk right now; and if and when the blow-up threat materialised against the germ and gas dumps no-one would survive, surely, down there in the south-east. But he couldn't warn Beth, couldn't give her so much as a hint. It would be totally uncharacteristic for him to urge Mrs Micklam to stay on when she had announced what would normally have been heaven-sent departure. Mother-in-law would go down to Worthing, right into the heart of the horror that might come, and if it did come, she would die. Shard had never been noted for any warmness towards Mrs Micklam: she was the sort who interfered and wouldn't be told. Once, returning from absence on a case, Shard had found she had been to stay and had shifted the sitting-room furniture around: it had gone back double fast within minutes of his arrival, and there had been a monumental scene from which she had never fully recovered. Shard had said a lot he didn't mean; the scar had remained with Beth. Now, if Mrs Micklam should die when a word from Shard could have saved her, he was going to be accused virtually of murder, and even of remaining silent with deliberate intent.

Breakfast finished, he kissed Beth goodbye, a remote kiss on the top of her head, a safe kiss. He called up the stairs to Mrs Micklam, feeling his voice like a summons to the grave.

★ ★ ★ ★

He had just reached his temporary office when the security line burred. He snatched at the handset. 'Shard.'

'Lavington—'

'Yes?'

'All correct, Mr Shard. No leaks that I can detect.'

'Security okay?'

'Absolutely, yes.'

Shard sent a breath hissing out. In a sense

this was relief, but only in a sense. It would weaken his case for extra precautions, and he felt in his bones that worse was soon to come. 'Then where the hell *did* it come from, Dr Lavington?'

'I've no idea. We could try Porton, the main establishment.'

'Can you go over right away?'

'Yes, I'll do that. Or phone.'

'I'd rather you went in person. You've been in on this from the start.' Shard paused. 'The road transporters. Could anything have happened there?'

'No, no. They all came in intact, no trouble reported and loads precision-checked with Porton's lists.'

'No more on the way, or delivered in the last few days?'

'No. The last came in before the weekend. Anyway, they were all checked—I told you—'

'Yes, indeed. Thank you, Dr Lavington. Call in again when you've been to Porton, will you?' He cut the call and sat back, worried sick. No leads, just deaths: Hedge's man, Katie Farrell, the five nameless bodies plus Paul Legrain across the Channel in Cherbourg. Hedge's wife still on the danger list. If only a lead would come in to the car-borne villains who had shot up Mrs Hedge and the Guildford mobile, then

137

they might get somewhere. In the meantime, all he could do was to follow the slim clue given by Mrs Hedge and talk to the manservant's widow, Mrs Morton. He was about to call Hedge and ask about Morton's widow's availability when his internal line went: the Head of Department.

'Ah, Shard.'

'Yes, Head?'

'I've talked to Hedge. I'm in the picture. I gather you're asking for special precautions in the Worthing general area?'

'I am, sir. From, say, Horsham to the sea, and Brighton to Chichester. That's for a start—'

'I'm sorry.'

'Sir?'

The Head of Department had the coldest voice Shard had ever known. 'The answer's no. Full security holds and is incompatible with precautions at this stage. Too many people would be involved. Come up with something specific to point to imminent attack, and I'll authorise the lot. Until then—no.'

'Sir,' Shard said, matching coldness with coldness, 'a body's been found with—'

'I'm fully aware—'

'Then you shouldn't take the risk, sir—with respect.'

'With equal respect, Shard, I have no intention at this moment of advising the Cabinet to order special precautions.' The tone hardened even more. 'Now there's something else: it's come to my knowledge that you're personally involved. A relative by marriage is not—'

'I'm afraid it's gone beyond a great-aunt by marriage now, sir.'

'What's that, Shard?'

'My mother-in-law, sir.' Shard did his best to explain, but his explanations cut no ice with the brass. He listened with fists clenched as the Head of Department firmly put him down.

'I pay you the courtesy of knowing that personal considerations would never affect the performance of your duty, Chief Superintendent.' There was more in similar vein: equally, Shard must not allow personal considerations sub-consciously to affect his judgment, blah, blah, blah...Shard seethed. His mother-in-law must go to Worthing unless he could find other reasons, first to be submitted to the Head of Department in person, to stop her. 'That's all, Shard. Except for one thing.'

'Yes, Sir?'

'The Cabinet has met and has given us the responsibility for co-ordination. That means you.'

139

CHAPTER EIGHT

Mother-in-law, it seemed, was now a vital link: strange but true! Her movements were of national importance... Shard cursed savagely. He shouldn't have opened his big mouth to the Head of Department, perhaps: one could be over-conscientious. The trouble was the basic friction between himself and Mrs Micklam; Beth's sensitive antennae would have detected something amiss without any difficulty had he tried to circumvent her mother's journey, and Mrs Micklam, circumvented, could not have been trusted to remain silent. She had friends in Ealing and parts adjacent. Yet of all people, Beth herself could be relied upon implicitly: he should have taken that into account.

Too late now? A rush of blood to the head put him in the frame of mind to disobey orders and disregard the Head of Department. He took up his outside telephone and dialled his home number.

'Beth, your mother—'

'What about her, Simon?'

He took a deep breath. 'She doesn't feel...unwelcome? I wouldn't like that. Is Aunt Edith really bad?'

Beth said, 'Yes. Mother's gone already. She caught...What's the matter, Simon?'

'Nothing,' he answered. 'See you when I can, darling.' He rang off. One way out would have been for Beth herself to plead illness, and Mother-in-law would have come rushing back, aunt or no aunt. But, at this point, that would have taken too much explanation and a rat would have smelt very strong indeed. The matter was out of his hands and must be pushed to the back of his mind. Using his security line he called Hedge in Eaton Square and asked about Mrs Morton: she was better, Hedge said, but still in the Intensive Care Unit at the Westminster Hospital. Certain visitors would be allowed: he was going round himself.

'When, Hedge?'

'Now.'

'I'll see you there, then.'

Shard left the Foreign Office and walked past St James's Park into Storey's Gate and on for Great Smith Street and Marsham Street. He walked fast, faster than a taxi would have taken him through the crawling, fume-enveloped traffic. In the foyer of the hospital he met Hedge. Hedge, pompous as ever but looking hungry, was making a fuss about something, harassing a thin woman behind a desk. Seeing Shard from the corner of his eye, he turned.

'Ah, Shard. It's doctor's rounds, I'm told. Confounded nuisance.'

'She's not in a private room, Hedge?'

'No!'

Shard lifted an eyebrow. 'They're not *all* phased out, and when there's a security aspect—'

Hedge danced. 'Ssh!'

'And a retainer of long standing, Hedge.' Shard sounded reproachful.

'Not all that long—but I *would* have paid, of course. Coronaries, however, go into the Intensive Care Unit. And there's no real security aspect in regard to *Mrs* Morton!' Hedge, rejecting the accusation of meanness, fumed frustratedly. He hated being treated like an ordinary member of the non-paying public: he was clearly bursting to say who he was but knew he couldn't. Shard almost laughed: the bowler hat, black coat and striped trousers plus slimly rolled umbrella didn't, even in the post-Castle-ised days—and never mind that the Westminster's catchment area was largely still opulent and classy—fit the aura of the public ward. The thin woman broke into Hedge's anti-democratic rumblings.

142

'The Intensive Care Unit is a very special place, you don't seem to realise. As it is, I'm stretching hospital rules—'

'Very good of you,' Hedge said frigidly, caught Shard's eye and turned his pupils heavenward. He and Shard drifted up and down, waiting upon the convenience of the medical profession. Hedge asked, 'How long have you?'

'Not too long. I've a lot to do.'

'Is Mrs Morton important?'

'She could be. I told you, Mrs Hedge—'

'Yes, yes. She said the same to me. It didn't help. *I* don't know the people the Mortons know, after all. And if Morton was up to any jiggery-pokery, there's no guarantee *Mrs* Morton knew anything about it.'

'D'you think he was...up to any jiggery-pokery?'

'No,' Hedge answered crossly. 'I don't, not for a moment.'

Nor, somehow, did Shard: he recalled Morton as a typical family butler from the old days, a grave, reserved man born to service and, as such, born out of his time. He wouldn't be bent and wouldn't act against his master and mistress: for the 1970s, a freak. With Hedge, Shard continued perambulating, cursing the wasted minutes. Eventually, however, the thin

143

woman summoned them.

'You can go up now, but it's still up to Sister ICU.'

Hedge gaped. 'Sister I see...oh yes—I follow.' His face slightly red, he turned away in obedience to the thin woman's directions. Outside the Intensive Care Unit he and Shard were met by a girl in sister's uniform, looking absurdly young for her accolade. Hedge stated, 'We wish to see Mrs Morton.'

'Well, I'm—'

'A woman downstairs said we could come up. It's vital. I'm her employer—you know what happened, of course.' Hedge indicated Shard. 'This is a police officer.'

The sister nodded. 'Yes, of course, I understand. Follow me, please, and be as quiet as you can.'

They went into high polish, medical smells, and past very sick people mostly as still as death. Mrs Morton was at the far end, propped on pillows and wearing a bright pink woollen bed-jacket. Hedge looked down at her and spoke sombrely. 'Well, well, Mrs Morton, I hear you've made progress. I must say you look very fit considering the shock and your—ah—attack. I'm more sorry than I can say about Morton.' Hedge coughed, glared, gestured peremptorily at the sister. 'Screens, Sister. And

144

I'd like the adjacent beds moved farther away.'

Sister ICU's mouth opened, as did her eyes: she was having difficulty in holding her tongue, stopping herself asking what the hell speciality Hedge was consultant in; Shard moved towards her and pressed her arm and gave her a wink. She grimaced but understood: beckoning a nurse she gave her orders and then moved away, warily, out of Hedge's immediate orbit. With the screens in place and the patients on either side shoved carefully on their wheeled beds out of hearing, Hedge sat on a hard upright chair and loomed forward over the bed. 'You know Mr Shard. He hàs some questions, Mrs Morton.'

'Very well, sir.'

Hedge glanced at Shard, who took over. 'Mrs Morton,' he said, then stopped. She was doing her best not to cry. 'I'm terribly sorry,' he said. 'Your husband was a good man. But you may be able to help. Will you try?'

Dumbly, she nodded.

'The people—men or women, we don't know for sure—the people he let into the house...the other night. We believe he may have known them. I say *them*, because we believe there would have been more than one to do what they did. Do you understand, Mrs Morton?'

'Oh yes, sir, I do.'

'Then have you any ideas as to who they may have been?' Shard paused. 'I'll give you some leads: we suspect they may have been either Irish or from the Middle East but we can't be positive. That they're bent of course we do know, and we know that Mrs—Lady Felicity didn't know them.'

'Why do you think my husband did, Mr Shard?' High colour showed in her cheeks. 'He wasn't crooked, never!'

'We know that too. That's not in question. The fact is he let them in—in all innocence, of course. We think, if he hadn't known them, he wouldn't have admitted them during the night hours.' Shard, sitting on the side opposite Hedge, leaned forward urgently. 'Please think hard, Mrs Morton. Was there anybody to your knowledge who could fit, however loosely?'

She didn't respond right away: she closed her eyes. From beneath the lids tears rolled. She was fighting for control, Shard saw. In a low voice she said, 'There was a man, but I don't know as it helps.'

'Tell me. Just tell me. Anything could help, believe me.'

She moistened her lips a little. 'A dark-skinned gentleman. I don't know about the what was it, Middle East. That means Arabs, doesn't it? Or Jews.'

146

'Broadly, yes,' Shard said. 'But go on in your own words, Mrs Morton.'

She said, 'He was from one of the embassies in Kensington Palace Gardens. Some sort of clerk, I think, but I don't really know for sure like...'

'Yes?'

She swallowed and moved a hand on the bedspread in a nervous gesture. 'My husband used to talk to him over a drink.'

'Where?'

'In the Catherine Wheel. That's a public house on the corner of Kensington Church Street and—'

'I know it. Did you meet him there yourself?'

She shook her head. 'No, I never. I don't go to public houses, sir. My husband...he brought him back once, to Eaton Square.' She looked at Hedge, looked away again. 'The mistress knew, sir. My husband asked permission.'

Hedge's heavy face reddened. 'My wife—did she see this man?'

'No, sir, she didn't meet him. My husband just asked her, that's all.'

The eyes of Hedge and Shard met: there was a feeling in the air of gold having been struck. Shard asked, 'Do you know his name, Mrs Morton? Or which embassy he was from?'

'No, sir, that I don't. I heard the name, mind, but it didn't register if you know what I mean. One of them foreign names...' She was frowning, doing her best. 'I couldn't even get anywhere near it, nor the embassy either, not now.'

'No idea at all?' Shard asked.

'Not really. It could have been...Iranian, Iraqian...or Arabian, but I can't say. He didn't look Arab anyway, not to me. Dark, but not hook-nosed or *hawky*, see?'

She was being honest, Shard had no doubt of that: genuinely she didn't remember. A passing acquaintance of her husband's, a man who had been just the once to Eaton Square...she probably hadn't paid much attention. The downstairs brigade in Hedge's house would be kept pretty much on the hop workwise, if Shard knew Hedge, and it was a big house for two servants to cope with. Once, there would have been half-a-dozen in the servants' hall. Shard made another attempt: 'Mrs Morton, can you think of any reason why this man might have called during the night, and if so why your husband should have let him in?'

'Not really, sir, I can't. Except that my husband did know him.'

Hedge came in on that, brutally. 'Or—any reason why he should have killed your husband

148

and abducted Lady Felicity?'

She shook her head but she couldn't answer in words; soon after that, they left her alone, crying still. Hedge said he would look in again. Once outside Shard said, 'That last question of yours wasn't fair, Hedge.'

'It had to be asked,' Hedge snapped.

'But differently put. Your way, it kind of sounded as if you were blaming her. Maybe it was your tone.'

'I'm sorry!'

They walked on, heading back for the Foreign Office: a score of times Hedge nearly lost his life in the traffic: he always crossed roads as though one wave of his umbrella would bring London to a halt. Shard said, 'A little progress but in effect leading to another dead end. No names, only a vague description that could fit anyone from Tunis to Mecca via Port Said, and a clutch of possible embassies.'

'We do have a positive link now, though.'

'With the Middle East—sure! We pretty well had that already, hadn't we?'

* * * *

On arrival back at his desk, Shard was given word by Detective Sergeant Kenwood: the Cabinet was meeting at 1430 hours in Downing

Street and his presence as co-ordinator was ordered. The brass wanted a report. Shard took a pub lunch in the Sherlock Holmes off Northumberland Avenue, wishing he were half as good a sleuth: Holmes would have had this lot sewn up in one tailwag of a Baskerville hound. At 1415 he was receiving the salute of the copper outside Number Ten. The meeting started a little late as the brass finished its after-lunch brandy, and it started with post-prandial bonhomie—too much bonhomie, Shard thought, feeling sour at an overall lack of real, basic concern. They were all there, with sundry co-options, under the lowering eye of the Prime Minister: Home Secretary, Foreign Secretary, Secretary for the Environment, Secretary for Health and Social Security...Commissioner of Metropolitan Police who greeted Shard as an old member of staff, Minister of Defence together with his acolytes for Navy, Army and Air Force. A very full muster: Shard felt flattered as he gave his report to a largely attentive audience. But the attention wandered when he moved into speculation as to what might happen if the malevolent stockpiles of the Chemical Defence Establishment should be breached. They just didn't believe him, mostly; except for the Defence Minister, who had clearly been briefed by Henry Carver, they tended to jeer. Maybe it *was* the brandy's afterglow; but Shard, growing angrier, thought them a bunch of fools with their heads firmly in the sand. The Chemical Defence Establishment, according to the Home Secretary, was watertight.

'Against a bomb?' This was the Defence Minister, in reference to his own department: if anyone carried weight, he should.

'The *size* of bomb is important, is it not?'

'Of course. How do we know these people haven't big stuff at their disposal?'

A laugh: 'My dear chap, we don't even know who "these people" are, yet! We really can't have the country panicked—have you any conception of the interference to life that would be caused?' Home Secretarial eyes rolled to the ornate work of the ceiling. 'Hospital services, police, social services, the armed forces to back the civil power—we certainly haven't enough civil police to cope with all the enforcement of the regulations that would become necessary. Believe me, it's just not on.'

'But look here—'

'I repeat—whatever *you* say—'

Shard caught the eye of the Prime Minister across the barneying table: there was a shrewd glint, half of amusement, half of anger, in that eye, and Shard took what he fancied might be

151

a hint. He got to his feet. 'Gentlemen,' he said loudly. 'Gentlemen, please.' One by one the voices subsided: silence reigned. Shard said, 'I'm not asking for anything like full precautions yet. I have a lot to do, a lot to find out—though meantime I would like some awareness in the Worthing area. At least I think the hospital and local doctors should be warned, though I understand my own chief doesn't agree.' He glanced towards the FO's Head of Security, who looked down at his blotter and doodled with a Biro. 'Also I think some excuse could and should be manufactured for moving troops into the South Downs. As for Porton, Salisbury Plain can do some troop shifting too—it's in their area. The general public needn't know the reason. All that apart, what I'm most positively asking for now is this: that all concerned ministries and departments should plan at once for a possible national emergency...involving not thousands, not hundreds of thousands, but *millions* of casualties!' He thumped a fist into his palm, raised his voice louder to the assembled brass: 'When it comes, it'll be sudden, that's obvious. It'll be too late then. We have to be ready *now*.'

★ ★ ★ ★

Walking back through to the Foreign Office, Shard looked at his watch: Mrs Micklam would by now be ensconced in Worthing. Her aged aunt, saved by Mrs Micklam's samaritan act from becoming a statistic in the geriatric department, lived in—where was it?—Heene Road. Close to the sea...if the bloating sickness should reach Heene Road, the old lady could be wheeled in for a dip, which might also save Mrs Micklam. But never mind Mrs Micklam: in Worthing itself there were upwards of 65,000 people, and a lot more in the adjacent areas. So far, not one of them knew a thing. In a sense that was just as well: Shard had to recognise the opposing point of view. Lavington hadn't seemed inclined to panic, and he should know. But the line was a thin one and the limits had to be recognised in the very moment that they thinned even more. Time could be short or long: right now there was no knowing. Shard reported to Hedge, who had just returned from a monumental lunch at the Athenaeum in compensation for self-fending at home. He said, 'I don't know how much ice I cut, Hedge, but the feeling was against me.'

'We'll be told soon. In the meantime, what are you doing?'

'I'm going to find that non-Arab Arab. Or try to.'

Hedge said, 'A needle in a haystack. Isn't there *anything* else?' His internal line burred and he answered, looked up. 'For you, Shard. Your detective sergeant.'

Shard took the receiver. 'Yes, Harry?'

'Two reports, sir. One from Dr Lavington. Porton Down's okay, nothing known to be missing and security tight. The other's more kind of operative, sir.'

'Let's have it, then, for God's sake—'

'Yes, sir. Surrey Police, Guildford nick. They have word that one of the villains who shot up the mobile has been arrested at Gatwick—anyway, they think it could be him. He's being taken to Guildford now. Any orders, sir?'

'I'll be right down. Thanks, Harry.' Shard returned the receiver to its rest. 'Action, Hedge. You wanted something else—maybe we have it now.'

He left the room, feeling a surge of excitement and anticipation.

CHAPTER NINE

'How,' Shard asked in the Guildford police headquarters, 'did they latch onto this villain, Mr Gotham?'

'Arrested on suspicion, under the 1974 act.'

'What, precisely, aroused this suspicion?'

The superintendent blew smoke. 'Initially, it was a matter of luck. There was a passport irregularity—'

'Irregularity?'

'It appeared to be forged, Mr Shard. The man was questioned and then searched. He became unco-operative and violent. They found this.' Gotham reached into a drawer of his desk and produced a certificate of AA membership which he handed to Shard: it was made out in the name of a Mr K.P.L. Carmichael.

Shard asked, 'Well?'

'Our villain was fairly obviously no Carmichael. We've been given details of the passport... Saudi Arabian, issued by their London embassy in the name of Ibrahim Azzam. That may or may not be a false name, but we can check—'

'You haven't done so?'

'No, sir. I advised Gatwick to wait instructions from you. I thought you'd wish that.'

'You thought right, Superintendent. I'll deal with that after I've seen the man.' Shard waved the AA membership certificate. 'This Carmichael. Does that name mean anything at all?'

The superintendent was smiling. 'It does indeed. The vehicle that got away—the one Mrs Hedge was in—we traced it via Stolen and Suspect Vehicle Index at C.R.O. As expected, it had been stolen, and it—'

'Belonged to a Mr K.P.L. Carmichael?'

'Right, sir.'

Shard grinned. 'Well done, Superintendent! Now I'd like to see Mr Azzam.'

★ ★ ★ ★

Chance, as ever, played a big part in detection: it had been careless of the owner to leave his AA certificate in the car, but for the fact that he had done so Shard was deeply grateful. From the fact that the villains had evidently seen a use for it, Shard made the deduction that one at least had been of white complexion; though why it had finally turned up in Azzam's possession was currently a mystery. The answer to that as well as other matters might shortly be dug out. On the way to the cells Gotham told Shard that Azzam was still violent: there had been fireworks when he was being taken to the police car at Gatwick, again en route, and again on his way to the cells. He was being guarded now by four constables in spite of being handcuffed.

'I think,' Shard said, 'I'll take the cuffs as sufficient security, Superintendent.'

'I wouldn't advise it, sir.'

'I can take care of myself. You'll agree, I'm sure, that questioning is best done without an audience.'

'That's as maybe, sir.'

Shard stopped and faced Gotham. 'You sound unhappy. We have a good lead, a positive one. For reasons that may soon become all too clear, I aim to follow it up all the way through and I may have to become unkind. D'you follow?'

Gotham nodded. 'I think I do, sir. With respect, I must remind you this is my nick. I don't want—'

'Never mind what you want, Superintendent. I shall take all the responsibility and the less you know the better. Now: the PCs to be removed, please.'

'As you wish, sir.' Gotham was being formal;

he didn't like this but, as the gaoler opened up the cell door to admit Shard, he gave the order. The four constables withdrew. Shard went in and the cell was again locked. In one corner a thickset Arab stood, glowering with his back to the wall and his hands in the steel cuffs in front of his body. Shard looked at him in silence for a few moments: he saw red-flecked eyes, watchful eyes, full red lips in a clean-shaven face. The man was keeping very still but there was an inherent threat, the threat of a desire to kill, in the very way he was holding his hands with the fingers open and the cuffs stretched as far apart as they would go.

Remaining by the locked door, Shard said, 'You're Ibrahim Azzam?'

There was no answer.

'If you're not, we shall know soon. But I doubt if your identity's of particular importance. We have your body, and that's what counts.' He paused, watching the Arab closely. 'Vulnerable things—bodies. Do you agree?'

The Arab's lips bunched and a stream of saliva shot out, the head striking forward like a snake. Shard laughed. 'That breaks no bones. Have you anything you wish to tell me...in order to avoid trouble, perhaps?'

The Arab glared, an almost mad look of naked hate. 'I have complaints. I know, I think, your laws. I have been improperly treated.'

'In what way, Mr Azzam?'

The handcuffs rattled. 'I am in a cell, but not charged with any crime. I have committed no crime. I should be in the charge room, not a cell.'

'That's for your own protection. You might damage police property!' Shard grinned, icily. 'We do the same with drunks. In the meantime, I'm not having you charged formally. This is a time for questions—and answers, Mr Azzam. Those answers I mean to get, so—'

'Who are you?'

'Detective Chief Superintendent Shard— from London. Just to forestall your next question, I have the authority to hold you without charge and incommunicado for five days under current anti-terrorist regulations. I propose to use my authority, Mr Azzam, and do not propose to inform the Saudi Arabian Embassy in the meantime. I hope that's quite clear. A lot can happen in five days, and believe me, it will. Is that clear too?'

The eyes blazed more than ever. 'These are threats?'

'These are certainly threats,' Shard said evenly. 'Having digested that, you can digest the questions. First, I want to know what you and your associates intend doing with the lady you kidnapped—'

'I know of no kidnap.'

'Don't give me that,' Shard said. 'We *know*. Remember Mr Carmichael? And don't lose sight of the fact that you may be charged with the murder of a man in Eaton Square. If your associates don't drop into the bag, Mr Azzam, you'll stand the rap for that on your tod... whether or not you're the one who actually killed him. There are other matters that I'll be going into soon, but for now I want to know about the kidnap. Along with that, I want to know the name of your organisation and the names of all your associates and contacts in this country—*all* of them.'

'I have nothing to say.'

'I'd advise you, strongly, to have second thoughts. Now we have your body, Mr Azzam, we can find out plenty by patient checking. But that takes time, and time's short. And I have a funny feeling, Mr Azzam, that you know just what I mean by that. I'm asking you, in your own interest as well as ours, to shorten the proceedings. I—'

He broke off sharp: Azzam was a fast mover. Without a flicker in his expression, he had launched himself as it were into space, straight at Shard. Just in time Shard dodged left;

Azzam, who had seemed as though he must crash into the cell door, landed lightly in a crouching stance like a wild animal at bay, breathing heavily through his over-red lips. From the corner of his eye Shard was aware of Gotham peering through the spy-hole from outside, and then, in a flash, Azzam was on the move again. This time, Shard was not quite fast enough: the Arab came down on him heavily, his sheer weight bringing Shard to the floor with a crash. The Arab's fingers went round his throat, squeezing powerfully. With every last ounce of his strength, Shard brought his knees up into the thick chest and forced upwards. The arms began to straighten but the grip on Shard's throat failed to slacken: just in time, the cell door banged back against the wall and men poured in.

★ ★ ★ ★

'I did warn you,' Gotham said, not without a certain grim irony. 'Feeling better, are you?'

'Yes.' Black coffee and a shot of Scotch had helped. 'The man's stark, staring mad—must be!'

'Aren't they all?' Gotham said gloomily.

'It was so bloody pointless!'

'Not to him, Mr Shard. It's all pointless

really—all the killing of the innocents. Don't forget, I've had it right here in my patch!'

'I know, Superintendent.' Shard rubbed at the back of his neck: there would be bruising there soon. Meanwhile it felt half broken. 'Well, I'm wasting time right now. Part Two's due to begin!'

Gotham cocked an eye at him. 'What's that to be, then?'

'I'm taking over custody of Azzam as of now, that's what. Personal custody. I have to get my answers—it's vital. I'll want your help, Super-intendent, and here's how: I've taken your point about violence...I'm asking you for an escort of six PCs under a sergeant. Your best men—best in the sense of discretion, of not being liable to open their mouths afterwards. All right?'

'To go where?' Gotham asked.

'Into West Sussex.'

'You know as well as I do, my fiat doesn't run there.'

'But mine does. Rustle up those men pronto, if you please, Superintendent.' Shard's tone was brisk and authoritative. 'And I'll want a van, a closed van—*not* a police van, a plain one. If you have to hire, hire. Give no reasons. Just do it fast—time is of the essence, as I keep on saying.' Shard paused. 'One more thing.'

'Yes?'

'The coppers, all of them, to be in plain clothes. And armed.'

Gotham stared. 'Armed, sir? I—'

'Have no authority without the Chief Constable's say-so? There's not the time, Mr Gotham, for explanations to the Chief Constable. I'm your authority, and if you doubt that, get in touch with Downing Street—afterwards!'

★ ★ ★ ★

They drove fast into West Sussex, heading for Wiston House: before leaving Shard had made contact by telephone with Major Bentley and had received from him certain promises. In the closed van Azzam sat in his handcuffs against the front partition, his legs stretched out on the steel floor: facing him were the armed policemen, ready to bring out their revolvers. Up front Shard sat beside the driver, not speaking, occupied with his thoughts. He was sticking his neck out and he knew it, knew that the consequences could be the chop, but he was very much aware that Ibrahim Azzam was all he had and that he had to make the best use of him. Of the Arab's involvement there was no shadow of a doubt: but involvement—the actual kidnap of Mrs Hedge apart—*in what?*

163

That remained to be found out; Shard, playing his strong hunches, keeping Katie Farrell's grisly end in mind, meant to do the finding out and never mind Hedge or the Head of Department, who were not going to like it. Shard had been handed the job of co-ordinator: he had to have something to co-ordinate against and currently he was suffering a nasty sense of failure. It seemed that everything, the executive order to mount all the possible counter-measures for the protection of life, was waiting for him to produce. Like the conjuror whose white rabbit gets left behind, Shard was faced with professional ignominy.

The van stopped outside Wiston House: Shard got down and banged on the rear door. The sergeant opened up. 'Blindfold,' Shard said. A piece of black material was secured over the Arab's still mad-looking eyes and a coat was thrown over his head for good measure; then he was helped down under strong guard. As he came out, Bentley appeared, sniffing and twitching.

'Well, Shard. This is all very irregular, you know.'

'I do know, Major. I'm deeply grateful for your co-operation.'

Bentley grunted, looking unhappy. 'Very well,' he said. 'Come along, then.' He lowered his voice, and slowed so that the prisoner and escort, heading for the front door of the house, drew a little ahead. 'Suppose he's innocent, Shard?'

'He's not, that I can state positively.'

'Surely there's always a doubt? And once he's seen—'

'Seen, Major? He's blindfolded, isn't he? Not that it makes much difference, since I've a feeling your secrets are very much blown already—but it's a reasonable precaution all the same and I don't quarrel with it. And this time there is *no* doubt.'

Bentley was still dubious. 'Well,' he said, 'on your head be it, my dear chap!'

'I have a strongish head...even if the supports feel as if they've been pole-axed.' Shard moved on: down once again into the basement and along the first part of the passage to the steel sealing door and its strange method of unlocking: along to the lift, and up: Dr Lavington met them as the lift doors opened. His reaction on greeting Shard was similar to Bentley's: 'I don't like this, Mr Shard. We've always been so careful about admissions.'

Shard smiled. 'Very right and proper. But I do know what I'm doing, Doctor.'

'One hopes so, indeed.'

'The proof of the pudding...' Shard murmured. 'Where to, Doctor?'

'Along here.' Lavington moved off left, through one of the doors leading from the lobby. The procession followed him along another steel-lined passage humming with forced-draught ventilation. It was a claustrophobic place, narrower than the rest of the underground complex, with doors opening off at intervals. Lavington went right to the end and opened the last of the doors, one that in fact terminated the passage. The door opened outwards; inside it was another door, a close-sealing door of glass that when closed bedded hard against a continuous strip of heavy rubber. The room to which these doors gave access was small: no more than six feet square. It contained four articles only: a chair, a table, and on the table a bowl, like a goldfish bowl, filled with water and sealed at its top; near it, a brass hand-bell. Shard looked round at Azzam, in the grip of four of the police officers.

'In with him,' he said. 'And for God's sake...be careful!'

The Arab was brought to the entrance and pushed inside with a gun in his back. Eyeing the glass bowl, he went in without violence, then turned and faced the police guns, now all of them drawn. Shard licked at his lips. 'Here you stay,' he said harshly, 'until you've made up your mind to talk. When you have, ring the bell. It'll be picked up by sensors and an alarm will be given. I wouldn't advise you to hold on too long. When your friends do what I believe they're going to do, then because of what's in that glass bowl you'll be the first to suffer.' He caught Lavington's eye. 'Like to explain to him, Doctor?'

Lavington, put in the picture now about the possibility of an explosion, was looking nervous and unhappy. He said, 'Very well.' Turning to the Arab he went on, 'The bowl—it's more fragile than it looks. Very little is needed to shatter it. The mere reverberations of an explosion...when the liquid meets the air, it vapourises instantly. It becomes a lethal gas. It's a nerve gas.' He looked at Shard. 'Do you want me to go on?'

'Yes.'

'Oh...very well. The gas first paralyses, then destroys, the whole nervous system. Not quickly...when the paralysis wears away towards the destructive element, there's pain. Then the body juices dehydrate. The body becomes a husk.' He turned to Shard again. 'That's all.'

Shard nodded. 'Shut the door,' he said. The glass door was shut firmly against its rubber and locked. Before the second door was shut, Shard caught the Arab's eye: there was still the red fleck, still the mad look of anger...but to Shard there was something missing and that was what he would have considered a natural fear.

No-one spoke as the procession went back along towards the lift: Shard felt unpopular.

★ ★ ★ ★

He had been right: Hedge was livid. 'You've done it this time. My God, you have!'

'Not at all. He's merely being held in-communicado—very, till he rings that bell!'

'It's diabolical cruelty, Shard. It's not just the security aspect that bothers me.' Hedge sat at his desk, pink and puffy, agitated in a very high degree. 'It's not good enough simply to say he's a terrorist.'

'It's up to him. He has only to talk and he's out from under.' Shard grinned without humour. 'No sleep—that'll help to rattle him. If he dozes off in a chair he may fall against the table and upset the golfish bowl. The very thought of that should act like a tonic, shouldn't it?'

'There'll be trouble when it gets about.'

'Questions in the House? Come off it, Hedge! Terrorism's made the public lose its soft centre. Try to lose yours. This isn't like

168

you. Do I have to remind you what that man did to your wife, Hedge? Or are you simply bothered about what people will say...like old ladies living behind net curtains? Is that it?'

'You're very impertinent sometimes, Shard.'

'Sometimes I find people trying, Hedge. This is one of them. This man *has* to be made to talk, and you know why!' Shard moved away from Hedge's desk, crossed the room to one of the big windows and stood looking across St James's Park. Crowds of ordinary people going about their business, Londoners, tourists, all nationalities, old and young, none of them aware of what might be waiting for them, what might spread inexorably up from the south coast. Hedge's wife had been explicit even though her knowledge was limited: there was to be a bomb. In Shard's book that and its implications over-rode all, repeat all, other considerations: terrorism had rejected its own human rights. He turned from the window, smiled acidly at Hedge's back. Casually he said, 'It's only water, after all.'

'*What*?'

'Water, plain water. In the bowl. Imagination is an effective weapon, Hedge!'

Hedge gaped, mopped at his face with a linen handkerchief. He seemed relieved. Shard left him to his ponderings and went down to his own temporary office, pondering himself on certain matters: notably, that unlikely lack of fear that had been so evident in the closeted Arab's face and bearing. *Why?* Beyond any doubt he would not have known the bowl's contents were innocuous. The whole thing had been very nicely stage managed by Bentley: all the trappings of drama had been present. It must have been convincing. Dedication to a cause, often enough, lent courage and induced noble self-sacrifice, but Shard would have bet his last penny that even Joan of Arc had shown a touch of fear towards the end. Fear and courage were by no means incompatible: the courage if high enough merely overlaid the fear that human nature would not allow to be entirely subdued. Lack of fear in this case could mean two things, perhaps: bravery and dedication to the point of insensitive stupidity, or an overweening confidence that his skin was safe. Shard's personal impression had been in favour of the latter notion: so again—why?

★ ★ ★ ★

Shard felt the constrictions and the mass of detail close in on him: co-ordination involved a good deal of desk work—too much for his liking. People came and went; patient plod on detection, the exhaustive check-out on Azzam, the microscopic examination of files and dossiers, all this was interrupted constantly by the urgent ring of telephones: for much of the night and all next morning those telephones seemed never to stop. But at last in the early afternoon something came through with point, with the promise of action. The voice on the phone held a hint of the Irish: 'Is that Mr Shard?'

'Speaking.'

'You're interested in stamps, Mr Shard.'

Shard gestured at Detective Sergeant Kenwood, who understood: he took up another line, gave quiet orders for a check. To his caller Shard said, 'Yes, could be. Who's that?'

'Stanley Gibbons.'

Shard's eyes flickered. 'I see. Go on.'

'You don't know me—'

'I have cause to know *of* you.'

'Sure. But that's all.' This was true: the bomb squad had got nowhere, Shard's office and the grenade fragments had been clear of prints. 'I'd like to see you, Mr Shard.'

Shard gave a hollow laugh. 'You'll be lucky.'

'You can't afford to pass it up, Mr Shard.'

Shard said, 'Look, you're talking to me now. If you've anything to say, say it.'

'No way. I'm on a public line—call-box. I'm

not risking a long conversation. You must make your choice, Mr Shard. This is important, very important.' The voice paused. 'Listen, now. King's Cross—the buffet. I'll be there in an hour from now. I'll know you, don't worry. Be on your own or I'll not show. No funny tricks if you don't mind or a lot of people will get hurt. Goodbye now.'

The line went dead. Shard put down his receiver and looked at Kenwood. Kenwood said, 'They won't have had time to check, but I don't suppose it would have helped.' He hesitated. 'Are you going, sir?'

Shard nodded. 'No choice really.'

'He tried to get you once, sir. Don't forget that.'

'I'm not forgetting anything, Harry. But I believe this is sincere.'

'I wouldn't bet on it. It's a bit of a *volte face*, isn't it?'

'We'll know the answers, Harry, after I've met him—not before. Meanwhile, no funny tricks like the man said, but sensible precautions that won't alarm him or lead to wholesale slaughter.'

'Sir?'

'He's Irish, Harry. It's likely he has a bomb in his briefcase...and King's Cross buffet is a crowded place. So we use caution. I'll want six

172

DCs, picked men and armed. They're not to be seen with me, they're to go independently and mingle in the crowd—four inside, one on each door. All right?'

'Yes, sir. Do I come along?'

Shard shook his head. 'No. He knows me, he just may know you. No risks. And Harry …warn Assistant Commissioner Hesseltine— bomb squad and ambulances on stand-by to come in pronto if required.' He brought out his automatic, checked the slide, pushed the weapon back into his shoulder holster, and got to his feet. 'Wish me luck,' he said as he went for the door. Before he shut it behind him, he looked back: Kenwood was staring as though taking his last glimpse. It wasn't reassuring.

CHAPTER TEN

Up from the underground into the gloomy cavern of King's Cross station: there were milling crowds, diesel fumes, trains waiting to pull out for Edinburgh and the north, others coming in. Noise and smell, people and baggage

173

everywhere, a bomber's paradise. Shard looked at his watch: ten minutes to go. He headed for the buffet, recognised the DC hanging around the door from the platform side, long hair, cigarette dangling, electric guitar in a case at his feet. Disregarding him, Shard moved in and went to the self-service counter, queuing for a cup of coffee. Without appearing to do so, he watched closely. He had Elsie's description in his mind but it was unhelpful, too vague. There was small point in watching out for a blue anorak, for instance. Progressing in his queue, Shard bought his coffee, glancing again at his watch as he paid. The time was now. He moved away from the pay desk, aware of another of his DCs, also with coffee cup, at a table shared with a soldier in uniform, a middle-aged man in a business suit reading a newspaper, and a young mother with two small children trying stickily to climb onto the DC's knees: impediments to swift action but the DC, with a fixed grin, was doing his best.

Shard felt slight pressure on his right arm: he looked round and down. A small man with sandy hair and a chubby face—cherubic, almost. Blue eyes and a happy smile. Terrorism came in many guises and he knew instinctively that this was the ubiquitous Stanley Gibbons.

'Bang on time,' the small man said. 'That's

174

nice. There's a shelf by the windows over there.' He pointed. 'Let's stand, shall we?'

'As you like.' Shard looked down again. The man wasn't carrying anything: in that fact lay some earnest of safety after all. They pushed through to the shelf and deposited their cups: Stanley Gibbons had chosen tea. They stood together, with the small man's head on a level with Shard's shoulder. Shard started the conversational ball. 'The other day...that wasn't friendly.'

'Wasn't meant to be, Mr Shard. The idea was to kill you.' He smiled up, cheerily. 'I failed—we can't all be perfect all the time. Now, I'm glad.'

Shard said, 'Check. So am I.' His eyes wandered: another DC had closed in, casually, munching a chocolate biscuit, was now two men, three women and a child distant. It seemed weird to be talking so openly about attempted murder, but no-one had noticed a thing. Shard said, 'Tell me why you're glad.'

'Sure. Times have changed.'

'In a matter of forty-eight hours, little more?'

'That's right. Rome wasn't built in a day, was it, Mr Shard, but a hell of a lot can be destroyed in less. Destruction and building, they're different.'

Shard drank coffee. 'Am I getting there?'

'Could be, Mr Shard. Getting *down* to it...if you get my meaning.'

'Yes, I get it. Tell me more.'

'I will, Mr Shard. But not here, oh no.'

'No? Then why the rendezvous?'

The small man shrugged. 'Seeing it from your viewpoint, Mr Shard, it sounded safe. A public place...' He waved a hand around. 'Nothing much could happen, could it?'

'A trap?'

'Not a trap, oh no. Bait, if you like. Not a trap. I want to help. I don't like nastiness.'

'Nastiness that could spread...across the sea to Ireland?'

'Something like that. Now, you'll want to know more. If you come with me, I'll tell you.'

Shard said coldly, 'Get lost. I'm not shifting.'

'Speak now,' the man said, smiling, 'or for ever hold my peace?'

'Right!'

'I think not,' the man said. He looked at his watch. 'You have just under two minutes, Mr Shard. It's not long, is it?'

'What do you mean?' Shard stared, feeling like ice.

'By the door there's a case which I don't pro-pose to describe—it's one of many. The public never learns, does it? There's a small device in it, jelly based, and an alarm clock. You'll

176

maybe have heard the old jingle, Mr Shard... the IRA man who was sent to Dartmoor back in 1939: *I'd long ago have left the place if only I had got Me couple o' sticks o' gelignite and me ould alarm clock.* Well, now? One minute, Mr Shard. We'll be all right over here. A word from you and *everyone*'ll be all right.'

Shard's breath hissed out: over by the door two of his DCs would get it, as would the small kids at that table—and so many others. Again, he had no choice. He said, 'All right, damn you! Let's move.' He led the way, fast, aware of yet another danger: his DCs, who might move if they should get the idea he was under duress; or might follow. He had a strong urge to be followed but he felt that it could militate against any genuine help from the small man, who had a while longer to be given the benefit of the doubt. Even if Stanley Gibbons hadn't smelled out the DCs already, he would surely be fly enough to spot an actual tail. Shard, catching the eye of the DC at the table with the children, gave his head a fractional shake and saw the reaction with some relief. He made all speed for the door after that, feeling deathly cold as he passed upwards of a dozen assorted cases just inside the door against the wall. The small man kept close and made no attempt to open any of the cases, but urged Shard on through the door.

Shard stopped. 'You said—'

'I know, I know. I've a man there. Two minutes was a little bit of a lie. We need a little more margin yet. Walk straight ahead, Mr Shard, where we can still be seen from the buffet. You'll see what I mean in a moment.' He paused. 'Quick, now.'

Shard moved on. He did as he was told, going straight ahead past the line of ticket barriers. Near a sweet-and-cigarette kiosk were six men. Casually, they moved in; Shard knew them at once for what they were. Before the banning of uniforms they would have been in dark glasses and black berets. They had the grim, silent look that went with all that. The men surrounded Shard and the small man, at the same time, merging with the crowds. The small man said, 'Look back now, Mr Shard.' Shard did so: the small man lifted a hand and waved: from by the door of the buffet another man waved back, then went inside. 'All safe now, Mr Shard,' the small man said. Safe for the people in the vicinity, unsafe for Shard: he felt the hard pressure of revolver-muzzles in his side. They moved in a body out of King's Cross station. You were never so much alone as you were in a crowd, Shard thought bitterly. He was right out on a limb now.

★ ★ ★ ★

There had been a van waiting; the small man and three others had got in with him, the rest had walked on, still looking as if they were shouldering a coffin, grim and silent. The van was a closed one, and Shard had no idea where they drove, except that it was a longish way though experience told him that they could for reasons of extra cover have been circling. When he was brought out he was in a yard, brick walled and anonymous. He was hustled through a back door into a passage, thence up some stairs and into a kitchen, bright with tiles and laminated plastic working surfaces; and currently with electric light—the window was obliterated with a closed slatted blind. There was a table in the middle of the room, with chairs.

Shard was told to sit. The others also sat, keeping their guns handy. One of them, a man who seemed to be deferred to by the others, leaned across the table, his arms folded but fingers not far from his gun-butt. 'You'll want to know who we are. I shall not tell you. I shall only tell you who we are not. We are not the IRA.' He smiled, not an unfriendly smile.

'That surprises you, I see.'

'It does. That bomb at King's Cross—'

'There wasn't one. We don't ape the Provos all along the line, Mr Shard.'

'I'm glad to hear it!' Shard stared acidly at what he took to be the forces of reaction, of backlash against the Provos and their supporters; then waved a hand towards Stanley Gibbons. 'In that case, why did chummy here try to blow *me* up?'

'He didn't.'

'He said he did.'

'I know.' With a trace of weariness, the spokesman smiled again. 'He wasn't authorised to say this. I am. The bomb was set to go off as the door opened. That put you in the clear. It was a warning, that's all.'

'About what?'

'I don't think you need to ask, do you?'

Shard said, 'No, perhaps I don't after all. You didn't like what I was doing with Katie Farrell.'

'An understatement. It was dirty, was that. She was wanted here and in Northern Ireland— the Republic too. The British Government had no moral right...her place was here, in the British Isles, Mr Shard.'

'Which is where she's fetched up in the end, isn't it? I hate to confess ignorance...but wasn't

180

it your lot who hooked her away from me in Cherbourg?' He paused, scanning the faces. 'I detected an Ulster accent. I saw no faces, but I heard voices.'

'So maybe you did.' There was an exchange of glances and a decision was arrived at. 'All right, we hooked her off you, then she made monkeys of us. She took a chance...we crossed back by motor-launch and she went overboard near the English coast, in the dark. Pitch bloody dark...we didn't get a smell of her, but word came through the grapevine afterwards that she'd made it ashore.' Fingers tightened on the spokesman's gun. 'We want to know if you've picked her up, Mr Shard.'

'Not I,' Shard said. His mind raced: these men struck him as amateurs and as such more tricky to deal with than professionals: so often the amateur was the more dangerous simply because he didn't follow the rules. Meanwhile Shard could make a fair guess who these people were, or rather to what organisation they belonged. It didn't make their actions any the more legal, and the Cherbourg police would no doubt like a word with them; and for now, much care was called for: the news of Katie's murder was better kept hidden. 'I promise you she's not in custody. But you tell *me* something, gentlemen: who's behind the threat to Porton

Down? I'm beginning to get the idea it isn't you.'

'Not us, no.'

'Then who, for God's sake?'

The spokesman laughed. 'I wish we knew that. You can be sure of one thing, Mr Shard: if we knew, we'd tell you.'

'It's for real, then?'

'It's for real, all right. It's for real! I don't think you're in much doubt yourself, Chief Superintendent.'

'Check! But you could help. Give me some ideas—tell me who *you* think could be behind it, for a start. Is it the IRA, or is this the Middle Eastern boys set on another collision course with the West? I take your point that you don't *know*. But you must have some theories.'

'None that you won't have for yourself,' the man said dourly. He glanced around the table at his companions. 'We could always compare notes, of course. We don't see the hand of the Provos in this, not at all. Look at the facts: Ireland's too close. It's doubtful if the ports and the land frontier with Ulster could be effectively sealed, and in any case you can't forbid access to the wind. Besides, this country's full of Irish from the south, and even the Provos don't go in for wholesale killing of their own people.' He lifted a hand, waved it. 'You'd do better

182

to look to the East, Chief Superintendent. I don't think I need say more than that.'

Shard nodded: for his money too, this was Eastern, taking into account such scant leads as he had. But he pressed: 'It's a wide area of suspicion. The Middle East is a hot-bed...can't you be precise, gentlemen?'

'No. PLO, Black September who're still around don't forget, even a consortium of oil producers wouldn't be beyond suspicion. Or even one of the illegal Israeli groups—'

'Why them?'

The spokesman shrugged. 'Use your imagination, Mr Shard. Pressure on the West to do more for their national aspirations, their security against their neighbours. Or revenge, perhaps, for having let them down in the past?'

'I find that hard to take seriously.'

'It's a possibility. You asked for suggestions. I have another one to make.'

'Well?'

The man said quietly, forcefully. 'Find Katie Farrell, Mr Shard. She's the key. I believe you when you say you don't know where she is. You were brought here to be persuaded that in the national interest she should remain in custody in Britain—well, that's out of court for now. But get her back. It's vital.'

★   ★   ★   ★

Hedge prowled his office, eyes darting as if seeking out bugging devices everywhere. Shard had reported immediately on arrival back via the closed van and a handy tube station—Tufnel Park, after a long ride.

'You say you wouldn't be able to find them again, Shard.'

'Wouldn't is an embracing word. But it's doubtful and too time-consuming. In any case, they'll have shifted berth for my money, just to be sure. I'll be checking through the rogues' gallery, but they didn't register at the time. I don't think they knew any more, either.'

'Why the Farrell woman?'

'What d'you mean, why the Farrell woman?' Hedge fumed. 'Why did they want her, considering—'

'*They* didn't. They wanted the authorities to hold her for onward transmission to Belfast, to answer for her crimes there.'

'Yes—we knew that was the *original* demand!' Hedge paced on, a puffy pink-faced panther. 'I just don't understand. Perhaps I'm dense. These people point the finger at the Middle East, insist that Katie Farrell is the key to safeguard Porton Down, and then say she mustn't be handed over to—where she was going in your charge! It doesn't make sense.'

184

'No, it doesn't, Hedge.'

'Well, then!'

'I'll be working on it, don't worry. and don't draw too many traditional conclusions in the meantime, Hedge. We're not faced with the orthodox this time.'

'What does that mean?'

Shard said, 'It means this: intrigue is a spider's-web, to us a cliché. Some of the spiders have crossed their webs, interwoven them. There are so many splinter groups, Hedge, half heading one way, half the other, but internally in their halves they don't communicate. There's no co-ordination. They rush hither and thither.' He paused. 'Do you get me?'

'No, I don't!' Hedge snapped. 'Shard, why do they insist Katie Farrell is the key to safety?'

'As of this moment, I don't know. But some other group—say an Arab one—could have plans of its own, couldn't it?'

'Plans to do down some other Middle Eastern interest?'

Shard nodded. 'Exactly. It would be perfectly consistent with what we've learned to expect of the Middle East, Hedge.'

Hedge groaned, put his head in his hands as he ceased pacing and thumped into a chair. 'God! Where does that leave us, for heaven's sake?'

'Up the creek,' Shard answered, sounding savage. 'But I'll be looking for the paddles.' He left Hedge to it and went down to his office, disliking the Foreign Office feel as ever, wishful for the crumminess and obscurity of Seddon's Way where he was not so immediately available, except telephonically, to Hedge. As he went his mind was occupied with paddles: the whole thing was as yet wrapped in a blanket, thick and heavy, but there was no escaping the one thing that Hedge had failed to stress: the key was as dead as a doornail, would never again open any locks. Porton Down and its satellites of filth were on a knife-edge. When he reached his office, Hedge came on the internal line: something of Shard's thoughts had entered his head also.

'Shard, if anybody finds out she's dead—'

'Quite!'

'Well, make damn sure it doesn't leak. In the meantime, I'm going to talk to the Head and recommend urgent action precaution-wise, along the lines you yourself suggested to the Cabinet. I think that's only sensible now.' He rang off before Shard could comment. No sooner had Hedge cut his call than the outside security line burred.

Shard answered: it was Bentley, from Wiston House. 'Shard, there's been a development. I

186

don't know what to make of it.' Along the line the voice sounded strained, anxious. 'That Arab of yours. He's knocked the fish-bowl over—I know it's only water, but...'

'But what, Major?'

'Well, it's hard to say if it was accidental or if he meant to kill himself—not knowing, of course, that it was only water.'

'It wouldn't have been accidental—or it shouldn't have been. Damn it, he'd surely have watched his personal clumsiness! Has anyone been in to him?'

'No,' Bentley said. 'Grounds of security. He knocked over his bell at the same time and the guards opened up the outer door and saw the broken bowl. They shut the door again, fast—I don't blame them. As you know, no-one knew the facts about the water—'

'How about Lavington? *He* knows, doesn't he, he set it up—'

'Yes.' There was a curious note in Bentley's voice. 'That's the funny thing. Lavington can't be found.'

'Can't be found?'

'He seems to have disappeared. He's not been seen and doesn't answer his bleep.' Bentley was starting to flap. 'What do I do, Shard? Will—'

Shard said, 'Hold everything till I get there.

187

I'm on my way. Leave Azzam right where he is.' He slammed the phone down, noting the time as just after five p.m., his mind racing over that earlier nagging thought that Azzam's face, when he had been shut in that death chamber, had held no fear; yet only Lavington should have known the bowl held plain water.

CHAPTER ELEVEN

Shard came out of his car almost on the move. Driving down, speed limits hadn't bothered him. Bentley, his face full of bad news, ran out to meet him.

'Well, Major? Now what's up?'

Bentley's eyes were glassy. 'I've seen it in animals—that was bad enough. Never humans.'

'Tell me, for Christ's sake!'

'That Arab. He's dead now, all burned up. *It wasn't water, Shard!*'

Shard stared, flesh crawling. 'When did this happen? That stuff's supposed to be almost instantaneous, isn't it?'

'Yes. I thought I should go up and take a look after I'd rung you. When I called again,

188

you'd already left.' Bentley was shaking, almost babbling.

'Lavington?'

'Clean gone. Not at home. His wife hasn't seen him since he left for work this morning.'

'So much,' Shard said in a hard, flat voice, 'for our security checks!'

'What?'

'Didn't you ever suspect anything?'

Bentley stared. 'Lavington? Absolutely not! Are you saying—'

'You know what I'm saying, Major—'

'He's a first-class man in his field—the fact I didn't *like* him makes no odds—he was very highly thought of at the Ministry and at Porton Down. He'd spent almost all his working life there till he came to Wiston House, from the immediate post-war years—'

'All at Porton?'

'And the Ministry, as I said. He was never at Nancekuke, just Porton. I don't see why you're quite so definite about him, Shard.'

'He had charge of that fish-bowl—he meant to stop Azzam talking after he'd scarpered. The word that Azzam was being brought in could have sent him over the top, panicked him. Take me up, will you, Major?'

Bentley nodded and led the way inside. When they were in the first section of the entry

189

tunnel he asked, sniffing and twitching, 'If you're right, how did Lavington get him to knock the bowl over?'

'Another bloody mystery!' Shard said. 'He didn't go inside—Lavington, I mean?'

'Not according to the security guards.'

They walked on fast, through the check system, up in the lift, along the passage to the double-doored room at the end. The outer steel door was open and the security men were white around the gills: one had thrown up. The result lay spread from wall to wall: Shard stepped over it and looked through the glass. His own stomach revolted, but he held back on rising bile. Of the Arab there was virtually nothing left: just a husk, even the bone structure, the skeleton, blackened and twisted into the rough shape of a sphere. It was utterly horrible, utterly appalling. Shard forced his mind off the implications for the whole country if this thing should be breached and spread. Without a word he turned away, followed by Bentley, who asked in an unnatural-sounding voice, 'What do you want done?'

'With that?' Shard jerked his head backwards. 'I suggest we leave it. Just leave it sealed—that's all! No risks with personnel, however remote.'

Bentley nodded, seeming relieved. They

190

went back, down in the lift and along the tunnel. Shard said, 'That's my lead gone—as Lavington wanted, I suppose! I've been too damn clever...and hoist with my own petard!'

Bentley coughed. 'I suppose it's going to take some explaining.'

'That can wait. There's more vital things now. First is Lavington.'

'Are you going to put out a call?'

'Nationwide, yes. I'll use your line to the FO, if I may. Then some questioning, right here and now. Everyone in the place.'

'I'll lay it on,' Bentley said.

* * * *

After passing through his call for a search nationwide with all the stops right out, Shard spoke to Hedge and asked for immediate implementation of the precautionary programme: Lavington, he said, could have vanished with some of his stock, and it didn't take a lot. Hedge gave a sound like a whinny and promised the earth: Shard thought of him haring for the medicine-chest and the First Aid. In a high voice Hedge asked, 'Why Lavington? What's in it for him?'

'Money or power—he could have begun to see himself like God, with all that death in his hands. We'll be finding out.'

Shard rang off. After that, the local questioning: it took much time and yielded nothing that seemed of immediate value. Lavington was something of a solitary, a dedicated man immersed in his work, and his personal contacts had been few. Not many of the staff had been to his home in Steyning, where he had recently moved into rented accommodation on secondment from Porton Down. Nobody doubted his loyalty: not surprisingly, since the security check itself had produced no doubts either! The consensus of opinion was in fact the opposite: that he was an unusually patriotic man for the day and age in which he lived, with almost a mission to work for Britain—making it, Shard thought wryly, great again via death. Shard went to talk to the wife, Violet Lavington, alone in the small bungalow: no children, just her. She was pale and upset and frightened. She was also, Shard noted, sexless: maybe, married to a dedicated death-dealer, she had to be. No-one else would have stuck it, for Lavington had not, in the statements of his colleagues, come across as a man with much blood in his veins. Violet Lavington was not of much help, although, staring red-eyed at Shard from above a breastless bosom and from behind thick glasses, she gave her opinion as to where he

192

might have gone: his mother, a widow, lived in Croydon; there was a sister in Halifax in Yorkshire. Lavington himself, said his wife, had always loved walking in the Yorkshire Dales, going off by himself to air his mind as he used to put it, and centring himself on Leyburn on the fringe of Wensleydale. Would he have gone off now, without telling her? Not like him, she said, not like him at all...

Shard considered she had just given him the three places where Lavington was most likely *not* to be found; but nevertheless, on returning to Wiston House, passed the word through for routine check-out. In his office Bentley produced whisky: Shard took his neat, in urgent need of it every time he thought about that burned-up corpse deep below Chanctonbury. While he drank, a report came in for Bentley: all stocks had been checked and there was nothing missing.

Shard cocked an eye at Bentley. 'Mean much?'

'Not necessarily. Lavington could have produced some excess of his own.'

'What I was thinking.' Shard put his glass down. 'That would be subject to check too, though, wouldn't it? Basic quantities—you know what I mean—signatures and that?'

Bentley nodded. 'True, but to a man in

Lavington's position it wouldn't be hard to get around.'

'What could he have taken?'

Bentley shrugged. 'Almost anything. It'd be safe for him, barring accidents. Sealed glass containers, but maybe we're worrying unnecessarily, you know. The big bang's the thing—isn't it? He may not bother, pending that!' He smiled bleakly. 'Cold comfort, I realise! What's your next step, Shard?'

'Back to London. There's nothing more I can do here.' Coming back from Steyning, Shard had already passed through a cordon of troops: Hedge had been as good as his word, and Aldershot had been put on a red alert. Infantry had been lifted in pronto by helicopters and at a road block Shard was told that Royal Marine Commandos were on their way from Portsmouth to back up the army in their task of sealing off all the germ stowages in the South Downs area.

'What do you want me to do?' Bentley asked.

'Just be on your guard, Major, and keep in touch with me at the FO.' Shard left Bentley's office and went out to his car. He had got in and was about to drive off when Bentley came out of the front door at the rush, waving his arms and calling. Shard switched off his engine. 'What is it?'

'Police at Steyning…' Bentley was out of breath and panting. 'They have a report…persons dead in the street.'

'Dead?'

'Swollen bodies.'

Shard felt cold. 'The bloating sickness?'

'It sounds like it, Shard.'

'Where?'

Bentley gestured towards the south. 'Findon valley. Outskirts of Worthing.'

'What sort of area?'

'Bungalows, shops. Fairly closely populated. There's going to be a bloody panic now! What do we do, Shard?'

Shard switched on again. 'Your job's still the security of Wiston House. I'm going to have a word with the police.'

'Steyning?'

'No. I'll go into Worthing, talk to the brass.'

'Then I suggest you miss out Findon. There's another way in. Turn right out of here, through Steyning and over the Downs. It's all signposted.'

Shard nodded. 'Thanks, Major.' He decided to take Bentley's advice: it was sound enough. As the co-ordinator he had no right to take undue risks. He turned out of the drive for Steyning, moving fast, came into the village. It was approaching dark now, and not too many people about. Lights showed in the public houses and there were cars parked. A police car came up ahead and Shard slowed: there was not time now for talking himself out of a cop for speeding. He found the turn to take him over the Downs, and increased speed again, making a long climb out of Steyning. Up on the heights, on a narrow road, he looked back at the clusters of lit windows, people going to bed all unsuspecting of what was loose in the area. Later, reaching the seaward side of the Downs, he came past a school—a boarding school which, like all close communities, would be particularly at risk in the developing situation. Just past the school, a church: Shard gave a shiver. Soon, the parson was going to be a very busy man...*what would be done about the bodies?* Worthing had its crematorium, but it would never cope, maybe shouldn't be asked to. Of course, it was a Department of Health decision—not his; but he recalled, as he turned right onto a dual carriageway for the centre of Worthing, a job that had once taken him to North Africa in the middle of a typhus epidemic. The death rate amongst the village dwellers and in the poorer quarters of the cities, the kasbahs, had been immense: driving from Bizerta to Tunis he had seen huge stacks of corpses, stacks of up to twenty feet in height, all burning and producing the most nauseating smell. That had left a lasting impression: he didn't want to see it again, in England.

In Worthing, following signs for the town centre, he stopped and asked for the police station.

'Union Place. First left after the next set of lights.' The man he'd asked looked ghastly in the yellow overhead lights: a bloated face. Shard shook himself free of negative thoughts and fancies: it was probably just a beer bloat; the trouble was, disease made everything feel unclean. You couldn't fight bugs with normal police methods, they were not susceptible! He parked in Union Place and went into the police headquarters at the run. Opposite, a crowd of young people were coming out of the Conservative Party offices, laughing and joking, in high spirits that were due for a damper by morning. At the front office counter Shard demanded the Superintendent and within the minute was talking to him.

'Findon,' Shard said. 'People dead in the street.'

'Findon *valley*,' the Superintendent said correctingly. 'It's different, Mr Shard—'

'Never mind that. How much do you know?'

'I know the score,' the Superintendent said briefly. 'The Met's been in touch.'

'Assistant Commissioner Hesseltine?'

'Right. So what do we do, sir?'

Shard hissed through his teeth: everyone was asking him what they did—but naturally, since he was the co-ordinator. He said, 'Locally it's up to you, Superintendent. This is just the beginning. How do you propose to cope?'

'It's a big question. I have the CHP coming in any minute, if you—'

'CHP?'

'Community Health Physician, Mr Shard, formerly called Medical Officer of Health. He's—' The police chief broke off as a telephone rang: he answered, spoke monosyllabically and glanced at Shard. 'Not coming—Dr Ferraby. There have been more deaths.'

'Where?'

'Findon valley again, and Worthing Golf Club. Some late drinkers. Ferraby's making arrangements for collection and isolation. He has his hands full—'

'The golf club—where's that?'

'Closer in than Findon valley.'

Shard drummed his fingers. 'It's moving in, then. Look, Superintendent. Leave the medical side. There's plenty of positive action your people can take outside of that. It won't be popular, but what I'm asking is this: mobiles to patrol all areas with broadcast orders—everyone to remain in their homes until they're given an all clear. All people off the streets as fast as they can get home. Public houses to be cleared and shut—likewise theatres, cinemas, bingo halls and what-have-you. It's all we can do.'

The Superintendent looked dubious. 'Over-reacting, isn't it, Mr Shard?'

Shard gave a hard laugh. 'Wait till you see for yourself. No, it's not over-reacting. If you have any difficulty with the Town Hall, quote a directive from Whitehall—you have full authority pending what I shall recommend as the next step, which is a state of emergency that may lead to Martial Law.'

'Troops?'

Shard nodded. 'You'll need them in any case—you won't have enough men to cope. Just as soon as you feel that need, ring my office in London and men will be sent from Aldershot or Portsmouth.' He paused. 'Time's short...and I have a personal problem. I don't know if you can help.'

'What is it, Mr Shard?'

'I have a mother-in-law—'

'Haven't we all!'

Shard grinned tightly. 'I'm glad you understand. She's here in Worthing. I want her out.'

Briefly, he explained. 'She's an argumentative old lady and I haven't the time, or I'd bundle her into my car. I know you can't spare a mobile, but I'm asking you just the same. Will you prise her loose from her aunt and drive her up to Ealing?' He added, 'As her son-in-law I'm not taken seriously as a copper. Uniform will help. Arrest her, hijack her, do what you bloody well like—but get her out!'

★ ★ ★ ★

Driving back the way he had come, Shard pondered on his own actions and motivations: he could, and he knew it, have consulted by telephone with Worthing nick. He had come in person because Mrs Micklam, or more precisely Beth, had nagged at his mind. A personal talk with the Superintendent had seemed a better prospect than a phone call when it came to Mrs Micklam. So time had been lost, and now Worthing was to be deprived of a police mobile: Shard tried to console himself with the thought that the army would soon be making up the numbers, but he knew he had acted in a way no top copper should ever act. The Superintendent had demurred, and strongly: Shard had over-ruled him on his own patch, and now the taste of it was bitter. By not too

200

great a stretch of the imagination, more people could die as a result. A jingle came into his mind: *Oh Mother-in-law, oh Mother-in-law, you've a hell of a lot to answer for.*

As he took the roundabout for the road back to Steyning a police patrol came up ahead of him, blue light flashing, moving slowly, loud-hailer passing the orders received from HQ on the car radio: 'May I have your attention, please. This is a police instruction. All persons are to clear the streets, return to their homes immediately, and remain indoors until a further broadcast. I repeat, this is a police instruction...'

The voice faded into Shard's slipstream. He kept a watch out as he drove: there was a handful of people about, maybe making for home but not hurrying. As of now, they just didn't know...it was going to be one hell of a job to give them any reassurance in the morning, to try to keep the knowledge localised. Probably impossible; but before leaving the nick Shard had impressed the need for secrecy still on the police chief. The Press was to be muzzled, was not to give a squeak; the lid was to be put firmly on Radio Brighton's local information-feed. All this, Shard had said, would be confirmed to the Chief Constable from Whitehall. The longer they could hold the news, the longer they could hold Worthing incommunicado, the better the hope of preventing national panic leading to that next stage of emergency and Martial Law. And national panic was not the best of backgrounds against which to seek out Lavington and his brothers in horror.

Looking out for more bodies, Shard found none. But he felt unclean, and kept his windows tightly closed, until he had passed through the roadside straggle of houses that was Ashington on the London road. And all the time he felt the beastliness on the move, creeping up behind him.

★ ★ ★ ★

In the FO the security section was fully manned, even as far as Hedge and, standing by in his own suite, the Head of Department. There was a sense of doom, almost of waiting for fate, for events to take their own course. Full reports, of the Worthing deaths had come in, and Hedge was in a bad way.

'No leads to this man Lavington, Shard?'

'None.'

Hedge shook. 'We'll have the PM on our backs. He's already been through in person, raising Cain.'

'Not surprising! We're doing all we can.

Worthing's sealed in its various homes. What's the top view now, on secrecy?'

'To be maintained as long as possible.'

Shard nodded. 'As I thought. Troop movements?'

'They'll be explained away as security manoeuvres, just routine like Heathrow and Gatwick in the past. There'll be a news item over the BBC first thing, all the early broadcasts.'

'No mention of disease?'

'No,' Hedge said. 'Not that the villains will be fooled, of course—but that's not the point. The point's to avoid—'

'Panic—yes, I know.'

'This Lavington,' Hedge said after a pause. 'No doubt we assume he let loose this—this bloating sickness, but why? Doesn't the mere fact that he did so give a pointer to where he is, or where he's been anyway?'

'Been is the operative word. Worthing police are looking out, but I don't expect much. He only had to go down into Findon and out again—not much time taken—scattering his bloody pepper-pot on the way. My guess is, he's given us a preview. An earnest of what's to come when his friends blow the lot. He'll *want* national panic.'

Hedge flapped his arms, panicking himself.

'I wish to God we knew *why*, knew what they want!'

'It'll come,' Shard said. Hedge's internal line burred, and he answered.

'For you, Shard. Your DS—he wants you in your office. Can't he talk to you over the phone?' Hedge sounded pettish.

'I'll ask,' Shard said, and took over the handset. 'What is it, Harry?' He listened: it seemed that Beth was on the line, and Shard knew why. Knowing this was something he had to bring into the open sooner or later, he told Kenwood to put Beth through to him. When she came on, her voice accused him of naked abduction: Mrs Micklam, yanked from her aunt's house by force, by police in uniform, was livid. In what had taken place, she saw dire action of her son-in-law, and she wanted to know why.

'That,' Shard said, 'is what she can't know. Believe me, it's all for the best. You'll know in time, Beth dear.' He listened impatiently to yacking in the background of his home, to Beth's tight voice over it, and he cut in sharp. 'No good, Beth. She's home and you must be thankful. I don't want to hear any more about it. And here's an order, all official and red taped: you're not to say a word. Nor is your mother. Just this: she found her aunt was all right and she came back to you. Night, Beth.

I'll be home when I can.'

He rang off. Hedge was staring as at a ghost or a lunatic. 'Shard, what was that all about?'

Shard explained. 'I'm sorry, Hedge—'

'Sorry. *Sorry!* Good God, you ought to be shot!'

'I probably will...by my mother-in-law.'

Hedge raved. 'Don't joke! You've behaved abominably!'

'Family matters, Hedge—'

'Policemen don't have families, Shard, when it comes to duty.'

'True. I do take your point. But families happen to *exist* notwithstanding. Some more than others. And I assure you, nothing's been lost. Mrs Micklam doesn't know anything and won't till it's all over. I admit depriving Worthing of a mobile, but I admit nothing else.'

'You'll have to explain to—'

'Shut up, Hedge.'

Hedge stood with his mouth open. 'What was that?'

'You heard,' Shard said briefly. 'What's done is done, and I've had a lousy day. You didn't see what I saw. In spite of it, I still aim to be a good copper—more so, in fact. But I'm in no mood to put up with pinpricks so just button yourself up tight and bake your wrath for another day.'

Hedge was speechless, face mottled and plumply shaking. He waved his arms again, was brought up short like a fat scarecrow by yet another burr of the internal line. He answered. 'For you again,' he said. There was something in his tone and in his eyes that told Shard this was not connected with Mrs Micklam. His voice shook a little with important news. 'Kenwood has Dr Lavington on the line, and he wants you.'

Shard grabbed the phone. 'Harry, I'll be right down. Don't transfer him—hold him and intercept.' He put the phone back. 'You'd better come along, Hedge.' They went down together to Shard's office. Kenwood was holding on; he indicated another line. Shard used it. There was a hush in the room as he spoke. 'Shard here. Where are you, Doctor?'

'Never mind that, Chief Superintendent. Just listen.' There was a pause. 'You've been in Worthing—'

'How do you know that?'

'I don't. It's an assumption, and evidently justified. You know about the deaths—'

'You?'

'Yes, me. I removed some cultures, and some other things. Ready-use viruses, if you like.' The voice was disembodied, telephone-metallic but utterly threatening and inherently lethal, the sound of dedication that had turned the wrong way. 'I'm afraid it'll spread, Mr Shard.'

'How far?'

'All Worthing is at immediate risk. I doubt if you'll be able to contain it there. However, this is just a demonstration. There will be others, in various parts of the country, culminating in a wholesale scattering of what we discussed, if you remember—'

'I remember. But why? Who are you working for, Lavington?'

A laugh came along the line, smote Shard's ear like a knell. There was something crazy in it, an exaltation, and hearing it Shard believed his suggestion to Hedge to have been spot on: Lavington saw himself as power personified, as very God. 'I think you know enough to make a guess, Mr Shard, at who I'm working for...but the whys and wherefores are far beyond your level. They're the concern of government. I—'

'Then why ring me?'

'Ah—you're my intermediary! You've seen for yourself—you'll even have seen Azzam. You precipitated this by bringing him in—'

'How did you do that, Lavington?'

There was a laugh. 'Substitution—you played into my hands! The liquid looked no different from water, did it?'

'I mean the bowl. The knocking over.'

'He didn't knock it over,' Lavington said. 'It had a...built-in shatter if you like. It was easy enough to fix.'

'And Azzam trusted you, of course.'

'Of course! But let's get back to the point, shall we? I say again, you've seen for yourself now. So your job as my intermediary is to tell the authorities exactly what can happen next—what is *going* to happen unless they co-operate. Soften them up, Mr Shard, all ready for when certain people make contact direct with the Prime Minister. You can do it. It's up to you. If you fail...but I think you know the rest, don't you?'

The call was cut. Shard looked across at Kenwood, who also rang off and took up another line. Hedge demanded. 'What was all that, Shard?'

Shard repeated all Lavington had said. Hedge's face lost its hunting pink and he began to gabble about rushing Shard off to Downing Street for a personal Prime Minister-impressment session. Shard soothed him, though he felt sick in the guts himself. After a delay that seemed endless the phone on Kenwood's desk burred. Kenwood answered, looked up at Shard.

'Any luck, Harry?'

Kenwood gestured, listened, rang off. 'I'd call it efficiency, sir. And good co-operation—'

'Come on, for—'

'Yes, sir. I'd half expected this, so I asked for an automatic check on all inward calls. They report place of origin, an AA call-box on the A-31, west of Ringwood—'

'Ringwood! Heading *west*...west for Nancekuke in darkest Cornwall, d'you suppose?'

'Could be a blind, sir. He could go north from there, fast.'

'True. But it's a chance worth taking. Well done, Harry. Now—get Assistant Commissioner Hesseltine, ask for all mobiles in the area—tell him I'm asking him to contact all Chief Constables likely to be concerned—say, from West Sussex westwards to Cornwall and north along that line up as far as Bristol—and along to Oxfordshire. And I want road blocks on all roads in the vicinity of the call-box...all traffic, repeat all traffic, to be stopped and questioned. All right, Harry?'

'Will do, sir.' Kenwood was already on the line to the Yard.

'Now, Hedge.' Shard's face was tight. 'I'm going in myself. I can be contacted on my car radio at any time I'm wanted. In the meantime, Hedge, Lavington spoke of culmination and a wholesale scattering. The way things are shaping, I smell the dropping of bombs. I suggest you make immediate contact with Defence Ministry and get RAF Strike Command in the air from now on out.'

CHAPTER TWELVE

A blind it could well be: Lavington would have known his call could be traced; he'd hung on while Shard and Hedge had gone down to take the call from Kenwood and by so doing had given them extra time. There could have been an intent in that. Currently, Lavington could be heading anywhere. He would have had the time to vanish before Shard's message had gone through. And, despite the efficiency that had produced the tracing of Lavington's phone call, there had been a distinct lack of observation on the part of the mobiles: Lavington had come a long way from Worthing without being spotted, though his car registration had been notified to all police districts. True he could have switched cars; but there had been no report of his own being found abandoned. Shard, as he drove fast out of London on the

M-3 for the A-30 and Salisbury, knew he was taking a long shot, but not too long: Lavington had been in the Ringwood area within the last half-hour and by now the net would be drawing in tight. Shard cursed the traffic as he left the M-3 beyond Basingstoke: even though it was night, there were plenty of cars heading west. The holiday season was getting into its swing, and never mind the price of petrol: during the summer months twenty million people would nose-to-tail it down into Devon and Cornwall. Shard gave a hard smile, a grimace: come morning, if perchance Lavington happened still to be on the road west, he could be picked up at leisure in the ten-mile jam on the Exeter by-pass. Maybe! Lavington was not, in fact, a fool.

★ ★ ★ ★

In the early hours Shard was himself picked up: he was stopped at a road block on the A-338 from Salisbury to Ringwood and never mind that he was coming the wrong way; by now, the police were letting nothing slide. Shard identified himself as the co-ordinator. 'Don't react, laddie,' he said, and the PC stopped his salute in time. 'What's the news?'

'No contact reported yet, sir.'

211

'Armed forces?'

'We have military assistance, sir.' The constable gestured to his left: Shard saw khaki move into his dipped headlights, a corporal of the Light Division with an automatic weapon held across his body.

'How are the public reacting?' Shard asked.

'Some of them don't like the delay, sir—'

'They'll like it still less in the morning! We're going to be popular when the jams start. You're telling them it's an exercise, of course?'

'Yes, sir.'

Shard's offside rear door came open and a soldier started rummaging. Another was busy in the boot. When he was given the okay, Shard drove on past a parked police mobile and a military personnel-carrier. He headed on for Ringwood, made for the police station where the officer in charge, together with a major of the Royal Greenjackets, was making an all-night stand of it. Checking in, Shard was given up-to-the-minute news from Whitehall: the RAF was on an alert, with aircraft of Strike Command at High Wycombe and HQ Allied Maritime Air Force Channel standing by. Screens were airborne over the South Downs and west of Exeter.

'Covering Nancekuke?' Shard asked.

'Among other places, sir. All the West

Country's at risk, or could be. All those holidaymakers...it'd spread around the coastal areas like wildfire.'

Shard nodded: things were moving. But still no sign of Lavington. 'Worthing?' he asked.

'Three more deaths, sir. Golfers. There was a bit of a party at the local golf club—'

'Yes, I know. Are the police there holding the situation?'

'As of now, sir, yes. It'll be a different story after daybreak.'

'When they want to go to work—quite! They'll have to make the best of it.' Shard paused. 'I don't know why Lavington's car hasn't been seen. Have you any theories?'

The Chief Inspector pulled at a neat moustache, shrugged, glanced at the Major. He said, 'For my money, he'll have made a switch— but nothing's been reported stolen yet. We may have better luck in the morning.'

'By which time he'll be well away. I'm making the assumption he's slipped through the mesh somewhere. He's got the brain to talk himself through and maybe some of the PCs feel pressured. The traffic's building up westwards, Chief Inspector. I'd like you, and you, Major, to warn all road blocks in all areas—from me—that national security is paramount and to hell with the carborne masses.

They can rave as much as they like, I don't give a damn how long they're made to wait and I don't give a damn if the roads are jammed right back into London.'

'That'll be passed at once,' the Chief Inspector said. 'But how about you, Mr Shard? You'll be hemmed in with the rest—'

'Not so,' Shard said, grinning. He turned to the army officer. 'Major, I'm asking for a helicopter to be flown in here to pick me up—can you fix that?'

The soldier nodded. 'Right away.' He lifted a perfunctory eyebrow at the Chief Inspector, then took up a telephone. Within twenty minutes a helicopter from Salisbury Plain touched down in Ringwood's car park, night-emptied of vehicles, and Shard was heading west, skimming above the holiday traffic on the roads. Later, a message came in on the radio: Detective Chief Superintendent Shard was to report soonest possible to the police training college on the Exeter by-pass. Soon, not so far off Exeter, Shard looked down at the stop-crawl line of vehicles stretching way back east; then at the strongly-manned road block some distance back from where the by-pass diverged from the route through the city centre. Was Lavington down there? Lavington wasn't working on his own, he would have other avenues...there was all England open to his death-use! Wales, Yorkshire and the northern counties of Cumbria and Northumberland, Scotland—he could get lost until it suited him to reappear, and he could have been north of Salisbury before the net had begun to close. Yet Shard felt in his bones that the die had been cast westwards, that England's tourist play-ground had been selected as the best breeding-ground for a big-scale demonstration, that only after that would be the time for the outside attack on the South Downs storage plants and the wholesale scatter that would cleave through the south-east and spread inexorably over the British Isles.

★ ★ ★ ★

On touchdown in the training college grounds, Shard was met by a chief superintendent of CID. Inside the building he was handed a folded sheet of paper. 'It came in Home Office cipher,' the chief superintendent told him. 'It's in plain language now.'

'And the man who cracked it?'

'Safe as houses. You have my guarantee there'll be no leak. Just you read it! '

Shard glanced at the chief superintendent's face: it was unbelieving. Shard unfolded the sheet of paper: the originator of the message was his own Head of Department in the Foreign Office, but Assistant Commissioner Hesseltine had been the transmission agency. The message itself was simple but horrific. A telephone call demanding the Prime Minister in person had reached Downing Street, made by an unidentified man whose voice had betrayed a Middle Eastern background: and in this and in the threat that had followed Shard read the deep fears of the traditional oil producers for their economic future, and never mind what Hedge had said at the start about the imponderables of North Sea oil—and never mind, too, that on the surface the demands had an Irish context. When the Prime Minister had come on the line, the threat had been uttered: selected areas of Britain, initially localised, would be saturated with all the devices of chemical warfare, including the dissemination of botulinum in the vicinities of certain strategic water reservoirs, unless specific demands were met. Currently there was no time limit indicated but this was to be notified within forty-eight hours of the call, which was timed at 0345 hours that morning. The demands themselves were two in number: firstly, the British Government was to make a positive declaration of intent in support of the status of Northern

216

Ireland, back-tracking from its earlier postures of semi-support for aspirations emanating from dissidents in the Republic; there was to be an unconditional guarantee from the Cabinet acting in concert that there would be no more talk of shared responsibility. The frontier with the Republic was to be garrisoned immediately and strongly by British troops and armour on a permanent basis, and Dublin was to be warned that the actions of any of her nationals against the security of Ulster would lead to armed attack on the Republic. The Prime Minister's response had been firm: he had rejected this demand out of hand. Nevertheless, he anticipated difficulties in Cabinet: the threat was immense, was total and final, and was most eminently possible of execution. On the second demand he had promised consideration: consideration being a euphemism for utter dilemma and a necessary procrastination, since the second demand had been for the handing over of Katie Farrell, now dead and disintegrated.

'Why the Middle East, for God's sake?' the CID man asked in bafflement.

Shard tapped the transcription. 'I go along with the Prime Minister's assessment as given here in the message. They're getting dead scared. Their own fields have a limit, and ours are just starting up.'

'But—'

'It's a nice little method, painless to themselves, of upsetting our apple-cart, isn't it? To produce North Sea oil costs money and manpower and we can't afford hindrances. Look: if Whitehall sticks firm, we're goners anyway. If Whitehall concedes, the Arabs'll make hay while the sun shines bright for them—because the Provos, in a perfectly natural reaction that the rest of the world will support after we're seen to wield the big stick, won't leave a British town unbombed. Maybe they'll be the ones who'll blow up the North Sea oil rigs...acting as the Arabs' catspaws!'

'And the Arabs?'

'Well, they deny the whole thing, don't they? *They* have nice clean hands—and so far *we* have no proof!' His face grim, Shard brought out his lighter, put flame to the paper. It curled up, blackening as the fire rose. He dropped the burning ember into an empty metal wastepaper basket, seeing the symbolism that linked Katie Farrell's death with the likely deaths of them all.

★ ★ ★ ★

The report came in from Worthing police before Shard left for take-off westwards:

218

Lavington's car had been found abandoned deep in scrub a long way up a little-used track off the Washington by-pass sector of the A-24. From there it seemed he may have hoofed it over the Downs into Storrington, from whose outskirts a car parked in a driveway had now been reported missing. This could be coincidence but it could not be neglected; the new car's number had been circulated to all police authorities. It would now be going out to the mobiles and the road blocks—somewhat late for effective action in Shard's view. Lavington had had a fine start. Once caught, all must hinge on getting him to talk. Lavington might be the pivot, the tame expert *in situ* until now, but he was far from being the whole works. If Shard knocked him off, it was true he would be personally inhibited from any more disease-scattering; but the contents of the South Downs dumps, of Porton and the MRE, of Cornwall's Nancekuke and its VX gas among other horrifics remained no less susceptible to being blown sky-high—unless Lavington talked loud. You couldn't go around collecting and arresting germs, cultures and gases. And in the meantime neither could you bring back to viable life for hand-over the husk that had been Katie Farrell...

Beyond the focal point that was Exeter, the

traffic below Shard thinned as it diverged onto its onward holiday routes to Plymouth and district, to Barnstaple, Tiverton, Bodmin and the rest. Still following his hunch about Nancekuke, Shard directed the helicopter pilot to cover the A-30 into Cornwall by way of Okehampton and Launceston. Some choice had to be made and that was his; it might be desirable to come down at Launceston and set up a central headquarters with Devon and Cornwall Police, keeping the helicopter handy for fast movement when required. He had made up his mind to do this when wonderful gold was struck: the radio came up with an urgent message from Exeter. The car, the stolen car said to be in use by Lavington, had not in fact been apprehended as yet, but a road block on the A-386 Okehampton-Tavistock road, set up near the Dartmoor Inn a little east of a secondary road that branched right for the village of Lydford, had arrested a man answering Lavington's description and was holding him pending Shard's arrival.

'I'm coming in now,' Shard said, feeling a surge of excitement and relief. As the pilot altered course towards the A-386 the rain started: black cloud had rolled in from the west and now started dropping its drenching load over the northern fringe of Dartmoor. Coming lower, Shard looked down on huddled sheep massed together for warmth and shelter, some of them on the roadsides; and down on the long line of cars and lorries edging slowly towards the check-point: the check was continuing, in case the police had the wrong bird after all. It was a desolate scene, given added gloom by a rising wind. The police, as Shard's machine dropped to the roadway, looked miserable beyond words after a long, long night. A sergeant approached as Shard clambered down.

'Mr Shard, sir?'

'Right. Where's the man?'

'In a patrol car, sir. If you'll follow me, please.' The sergeant turned away through mud and rain, water bouncing from the crown of his cap. Shard peered through the window of the patrol car, conscious of deep excitement, of satisfaction and anticipation. Devon and Cornwall Police had done a good job of recognition: beyond a doubt the man was Lavington. Shard brought out the heavy police revolver for which, back in London before leaving on the manhunt, he had exchanged his lighter automatic. With the sergeant and two constables behind him and two more men guarding the other side of the car, Shard opened the

221

rear door.

'This is the end of your road, Dr Lavington,' he said. 'Get out quietly, and move for the helicopter. We're heading for Whitehall. There's a string of questions for you to answer—' He broke off suddenly and swung round on the sergeant. 'The car he was using. Where is it?'

The sergeant gestured. 'In the car park of the inn, sir. That one.' He indicated a light blue Ford Escort Estate.

'Watch it but don't disturb the contents. Some of them are lethal.'

'We've been warned, sir.'

'Good.' Shard nodded, turned back to the man in the car. 'Out now,' he said, 'and take it easy. The police are armed and so am I.'

Lavington smiled. 'You spoke of questions. You want me alive, don't you?'

'No-one'll shoot to kill, Doctor. Just to immobilise.'

'I see.' Lavington heaved his body to the edge of the seat, put one foot out into the rain and the boisterous wind, then paused in his movement. 'I say again, you want me alive. I dare say you want to live, too. Sergeant?'

'What is it?' the sergeant asked.

'You want to live too. And your constables. Am I right?'

222

Belligerently Shard said, 'Get on with it, Doctor. We've neither the time nor the inclination for conundrums. Just get out and be dead careful.'

Again Lavington grinned. 'Dead's the word,' he said. For an instant his tongue showed: on it was a small capsule or pill, red with a purple stripe. He brought his tongue back in. 'Touch me not,' he said, 'or I crunch. After I've crunched, it'll be too late. There's an antidote, but it's not here. I'll die. You can't prevent it, none of you. I—'

'You don't want to die, Lavington.'

'No?' Lavington smiled, an icy grimace above which the eyes blazed crazily. 'My dear Shard, many men prefer death to failure. After I've brought this off, as I shall, believe me, then I'll have—'

'Complete power over life and death, sitting in riches alongside a Middle Eastern oil well, Lavington?'

Another smile. 'A fair assumption. Does any man, when he's close to that kind of promise, consider death worse than losing it all?' Lavington shook his head, a mocking look on his face now. 'No, Mr Shard! I'll die if I have to, and when I do, I'll bloat. Very quickly. When fully bloated I'll explode. When I explode, I scatter. I think you understand, don't you?'

223

He eased himself from the patrol car. 'You'll have to hope to catch up with me again,' he said. 'That's your *only* hope, isn't it?'

He stood up straight in the roadway and slammed the car door. There was a curious sound from the police sergeant, who began backing away and looking at Shard. Shard gestured him to continue his withdrawal. 'Lavington's speaking the truth,' Shard said in a low voice. 'I'm sorry, but we're stymied. Too many people around.'

'But millions more elsewhere, sir.'

'Yes, Sergeant. But it hasn't happened yet, and we need him alive. That's over-riding and vital. Like he said—we try again. Next time, maybe I'll catch him on my own and un-prepared.' He raised his voice, calling to the police. 'Keep clear of him, he's worse than dynamite. Stand away—let him go.'

Lavington gave a deep bow of irony: it was gall to Shard. 'Thank you for your co-operation, Mr Shard,' Lavington said, and turned away, walking around the police car and pulling a short motoring greatcoat close around his body. No-one spoke; in silence broken only by the sound of his footsteps, Lavington walked towards his car. Men pressed away from his progress, feeling already the unclean-ness of a terrible death. Still in silence

Lavington got into his car and switched on the ignition. He drove out from the inn and turned down the road for Lydford. They watched him out of sight, down the hill past a petrol station on the corner. The police sergeant said, 'If we shoot to stop him now, sir—'

'No. He means what he says. Dead, he's worse than useless. I have to get him again, and like I said, unprepared. Which is why I'm not even going to follow.'

CHAPTER THIRTEEN

Shard used the radio in one of the mobiles and called Launceston, convinced that events were moving across the Tamar into Cornwall. Taking a chance, hoping none of Lavington's local associates would pick up the police frequency, he passed the registration number and description of Lavington's current car, asking for it to be circulated in the Duchy and to Tavistock. The car, he said, was to be picked up and kept track of but not approached. Extra security forces already detailed for the chemical warfare

225

establishment at Nancekuke were to be given an immediate alert and the army's South-West District Command at Taunton informed to this effect. Shard indicated that he himself would head out for Nancekuke in the helicopter. His message passed, he at once re-embarked, telling the pilot to head over Lydford for Launceston. As the machine lifted and swung to cover the lonely road descending into the fringe-of-moorland village Shard stared down through worsening weather: the wind had dropped but the rain had turned to swirling mist, patchy so that at times he could see the ground and buildings. On the lip of the tourist spot of Lydford Gorge a tall grey house rose castle-like, with turrets surrounding a large expanse of roof. Past this house the roadway turned, leading down to cross the gorge. Shard could just see the rushing water deep between the rock sides, then the helicopter had moved on, keeping above the road into Tavistock until Shard gave the order to swing north towards the A-30 and then head west above it. He had the Tamar just in view when the radio came up: he was to come down in Launceston at a point indicated to the west of the town where a mobile would be waiting: there was an urgent call for him, from Whitehall. A ring of lights would be provided to guide the helicopter in through the mist. As they approached, the town buildings were only just visible: but the loom of the lights came up ahead, strengthening as they came nearer, and the pilot made a good landing.

Shard was met by a uniformed inspector.

'I'm Shard. Who wants me?'

'Foreign Office, sir, a Mr Hedge.'

Shard ground his teeth and hoped the interruption to his flight was justifiable: with Hedge, you could never be sure. With no time wasted, the police car took him through to the station while the helicopter waited further orders. In the nick Shard called Hedge back and a voice high with agitation answered.

'Shard, at last! Thank God! What have you been doing?' Hedge, having asked the question, cut in on the answer. 'Well, never mind that. You're to come back here—'

'Who says?'

'I do. It's an order, Shard, so please don't argue. You're wanted at the centre, you're the co-ordinator, not just another field man. Besides, there's something else.'

'What, Hedge?'

'The police patrol outside Guildford—you remember—the one that was shot up—'

'Yes—Azzam's mates. Well?'

'We've picked up two more. The details can

227

await your arrival, but there's something curious: they appear to check with your description of two of the men who were involved in your conference, the one that originated in the buffet at King's Cross. Get here, Shard, and make it fast.'

Hedge rang off. Angrily, Shard called him back. 'Come I will, but I'm not self-propelled. I'll helicopter into Heathrow. Make sure there's a car waiting for me there.'

★ ★ ★ ★

The Launceston nick provided breakfast from its canteen: fried eggs and bacon, toast and marmalade, hot strong coffee rustled up in double-quick time. In the helicopter Shard, who was used to cat-napping in uncomfortable positions, snatched some urgently needed sleep interspersed with nightmares about disease germs. While breakfasting in the nick he'd listened to a BBC news broadcast: nothing had broken, security held good so far. There were widespread military-cum-police exercises in progress leading to horrible delays on the holiday routes west and the public was irritated but that was all. Nothing about overall house-confinement in Worthing—a miracle of muzzling that couldn't possibly last much longer.

Inside Worthing, of course, it would be a different story already and a leak was utterly unavoidable: for one thing, the inward commuters from the country areas, held off by the police road blocks, were going to buzz like bees at any moment now. For Shard's money, the national panic they all wanted to avoid was about to break and when it did they would be sunk...

On arrival in the Foreign Office Shard found Hedge doing his pink-panther prowl around the room: and on his desk a collection of prophylactics and panaceas, a hypochondriac's delight. Pills and potions, ointments, surgical gauze mouthmasks and a throat spray: Shard hooted; he couldn't contain it. 'What's all this, Hedge?' He picked up a tin of ointment. 'Cures coughs, colds, sore holes, and pimples on the—'

'Oh, put it down!' Hedge snapped furiously, reddening. 'You never know—one *must* be prepared.' He simmered, prowling still. First of all he had to unburden his mind of things that had been pricking at him. 'All this gallivanting!' he said, sounding withering. 'You're not thinking as a top man should, you're still too much the bobby on the beat, which is ridiculous considering—'

'Let's stop considering it for now, Hedge.

There simply isn't time. These men: where are they, where were they picked up, and when, and how?'

'They're in the custody of the airport police at Gatwick, which is where they were picked up early this morning—'

'Why?'

'Acting suspiciously—'

Shard said, 'Oh, my God! That's *really* watertight—'

'Under the anti-terrorist laws, anything's watertight for five days, as well you know, my dear Shard!' Hedge's eyes shone angrily. 'Allow me to explain. They were observed to be nervous at the security check for Orly, which was the flight they were booked on, and they were hooked out for further questioning. That shook them more. Nothing was found on their persons—no guns, no bombs, no disease capsules—nor in their luggage. But a bright lad from the Home Office staff ticked over very smartly—he recalled the circulated descriptions of your King's Cross friends, Shard—and he had them held while he contacted London. This was referred to me via Hesseltine, and I ordered a clamp pending your arrival here.'

'I see. Your bright lad was really bright, and I'm grateful. You've not been down?'

Hedge bridled. 'Not my job. You're the one

who met the King's Cross lot.'

'Sure. But Hedge...why do you connect them with the villains who shot up the Guildford patrol car?'

Hedge smiled. 'My wife. She's a good deal better, I'm thankful to say. She gave us a description yesterday. That was circulated too. And it checks. Get down to Gatwick, will you?'

Shard nodded. 'I'll gallivant right away—'

'I do hate it when you're funny, Shard.'

'My apologies. Before I go, I'd like to stress the need to stop any leaks. Worthing must be on the brink of panic.'

Hedge needed no reminders. He said, 'That's been considered by the Cabinet, of course. Paramountly, or should I say, second only to actual negation of the threat. I—'

'What's been *done*, Hedge?'

'Directives,' Hedge answered pompously, 'to the BBC and ITA, very positive ones. Likewise all newspaper proprietors and editors, national and provincial. The directives are provided with sharp teeth.'

'Well, I just hope it works, that's all! We'll never hold it in the Worthing area, that's for sure.' Shard paused, rubbed at tired eyes. 'What's the news from there?'

'More deaths—forty-three all told. A fast increase.'

'Bloating sickness?'

'Yes. They're making use of their natural resources—the sea. All known contacts have been told to take a dip, although we don't in fact know if seawater acts as a preventive. It may be simply a cure or an arrestor once it's contracted.'

'And the forty-three, Hedge?'

Hedge shrugged. 'They weren't quick enough.'

Shard looked at Hedge's face: there was a whiteness and a tightness, an unhealthy look, a look of deep fear. Worthing was not so far away and there was, or was normally anyway, any amount of traffic and commuting into London. Victoria Station, for one, might in Hedge's eyes be already contaminated. In point of fact it wouldn't be: with everyone in their homes, there was no movement, but Shard could appreciate Hedge's fearfulness and his instinctive withdrawal-wish from filth. Nevertheless, it raised another point; Shard put it into words.

'British Rail, Hedge.'

Hedge looked up. 'What about it?'

'At the Worthing railway station, they'll *know*. Even if the police put a stopper on reports to Victoria and points east-west, the receiving stations are going to wonder rather more than a bit when no passengers come in.'

'Yes. That's been considered too. We're not fools, Shard. Certain people have to be told, naturally.'

'And other people have eyes. Taxi-drivers, bus crews.' Shard shook his head. 'It's going to break any minute. I hope the Home Office is ready, Hedge.'

'As ready as possible. There's so much to consider.' Hedge ticked off some of the considerations on his fingers. 'The hospital services, ambulances, isolation of contacts—impossible, really! Schools—protection of children, evacuation to safe areas—only we don't know where the safe areas are.' He raised his hands, let them drop again. 'Not our worry, of course. Not directly, that is.'

Shard said, 'Personnel in the stock-holding points. Porton and the others. What do we do?'

'That's Defence Ministry—'

'Sure. But I'd like to know. Are they considering an evacuation or not?'

'Not,' Hedge said flatly, wiping at his face with a linen handkerchief. 'No dispersal of personnel *or* stocks. Too risky—it could leave the stocks more vulnerable to some other method of attack, some alternative we don't suspect—'

'Perimeter guards?'

'They're not a hundred per cent security, are

they?' Hedge was shaking; he looked flabbier than ever, soft and badly rattled. Shard left him to his gloomy fears and speculations, and went down to his own office to tell Detective Sergeant Kenwood he was on the move again. 'I can be contacted at Gatwick, Harry.'

'Yes, sir. Like me to come?'

Shard paused with his hand on the door. 'You're needed here. Otherwise—'

'Inspector Hayward's answered his recall from leave, sir. He's back.'

'He is, is he? All right, Harry. Where's Mr Hayward now?'

'With the passport section, sir.'

Shard nodded. 'Leave a note for him, and we'll go.'

'Car?' Kenwood's hand was on the internal telephone.

'No,' Shard said. 'It's quicker by train...or it will be today! And I want to take a look at Victoria.' Going down, they hopped a taxi in Parliament Street and were dropped in the station forecourt. The lack of customers from the Worthing area was not especially noticeable in the forecourt; but once inside the station Shard sensed a difference in the atmosphere. On the arrival and departure indicator boards, Worthing—East, Central and West plus Durrington, Goring-by-Sea and Littlehampton—

234

had been deleted. Trains ran, said the boards, to and from East Croydon, Haywards Heath, Preston Park and Brighton; the mid-Sussex route was open to Littlehampton via Barnham. Crowds stared up at the boards, bewildered, puzzled: as Shard and Kenwood crossed from the ticket hall to the platform for Gatwick, a station announcement came over the Tannoy: 'Once again we apologise for any inconvenience to our passengers...delay on trains to and from Worthing due to power difficulties in the Worthing area...'

Shard grunted. 'Clumsy,' he said to Kenwood.

'Sir?'

'It'd never wash with a self-respecting train-spotter. But I suppose it'll have to do. It's too late anyway. Know something, Harry?'

'What, sir?'

'By tonight, we'll be in a state of Martial Law.' Shard pushed through the barrier, proffering his ticket: the ticket-collector, unless it was only in the imagination, was tense, looking as if he wanted to make a run for it, wishing he was at Euston so he could hop a train into Scotland. In the carriage travelling Gatwick-wards, Shard pondered dourly on Martial Law. Once, it could have worked; today there were not enough troops to enforce it fully. Panic could overwhelm the military power physically. The only safeguard would be to make the penalties so severe that they became a worse prospect than diseases and nerve gases, but such was surely impossible... Shard's mind went back to Imperial Germany, the Kaiser's Germany: the Kaiser had had the power to declare Germany *belagerungszustand*—in a state of siege. He had been required to give no reason, and once he had made his declaration then any citizen, no matter how eminent he might be, could be given a summary sentence of execution by the military power; and against this there was no appeal, the civil courts and civil authority being stripped of their powers. The rifle and the bayonet ruled supreme. But there was a basic difference between the German and the British peoples, and today was two generations on...

The train stopped at Gatwick: less than thirty miles from Worthing...Shard gave an involuntary shiver, braced himself and walked to the airport terminal to report to the police office.

★ ★ ★ ★

'I think,' Shard said in a quiet voice, 'we've met before. Right?'

'Right,' one of the men said, meeting his eye.

Both had refused to give any names beyond what was on their passports: James Henry Turville O'Riordan, and Sean Conroy Stephens. These could be genuine or not, and a check was being made while Shard spoke to them. He spoke to them in a room guarded on the outside, and with Detective-Sergeant Kenwood standing with his back to the inside of the door.

'You were booked for Orly. Why?'

The answer was a shrug.

'To put the Channel between yourself and disease?'

A laugh. 'It'd be a sensible thing to do. I told you, Mr Shard, this is for real. Didn't I tell you that, now?'

'You did. Now I want you to tell me some more, O'Riordan.'

Again the man shrugged. 'I've nothing to say.'

'I think you'll change your mind shortly. You know what's in the balance. There's no time for the niceties. It's going to be a real interrogation, like what happens in Northern Ireland when the extremists catch up with someone who's done them dirt. Do you get me, O'Riordan?'

'Sure I get you,' O'Riordan said. He had a hard face and a determined one, with a massive jaw: the other man, Stephens, was clearly the

237

weaker of the two and might well be concentrated upon.

Shard said, 'I'm taking you to London, gentlemen.'

'What for?'

'Familiar ground for me. What I'm going to do, I don't want the airport police to know about. You'll be held without charges being made, and you're going to talk.' He paused. 'Just a moment, though. I've had another thought.' He looked across at Kenwood. 'Harry?'

'Sir?'

'Two cars, police cars and two PCs plus drivers. Right away, Harry.'

Kenwood turned to open the door and pass the word. He asked, 'To go where, sir?'

Shard said, 'Worthing, Harry.'

There was shock in Kenwood's face: he had guessed already. Shard, watching the reaction from O'Riordan and Stephens, saw that they, too, had an inkling: he found this interesting. He said, 'Go to it, Harry. I want these bastards to see for themselves...and to be handy for a touch of the bloats if they don't use their God-given tongues.' As Kenwood passed the message for the car, Shard swung back on the two prisoners. 'You heard what I said and I've an idea you fully understand. I mean every word. If you don't talk, I'll find a corpse, God

238

help me, and I'll bloody well tie you to it.' His eyes blazed with a kind of madness and his hands shook.

★ ★ ★ ★

O'Riordan and Stephens were each hand-cuffed to a PC and taken out to the cars with Shard and Kenwood in close attendance and with fingers around the butts of their revolvers: on Shard's personal order, the PCs were armed as well, so were the police drivers. As the procession neared the cars, which were ready with their engines idling but blue lamps not yet on, something incredible, something in the circumstances almost lunatic, happened: Shard might never have noticed had not Stephens jerked his head round, and stopped, pulling back on his handcuffed wrist. Shard caught a glimpse of the reaction in O'Riordan's face as he too looked and saw Stephens's expression. O'Riordan was not happy: turning to look where the two men's interest lay, Shard had the feeling he was going off his head: just entering the main hall of the terminal building was the utterly impossible: Katie Farrell, unmistakable even though she had taken pains to alter her appearance, un-mistakable even though she was dead.

The world had gone crazy.

CHAPTER FOURTEEN

'Take over, Harry. I'll be right back.'

Shard went into the building, moving at speed. He caught sight of Katie Farrell, buying a paperback at the bookstall, cool as ice. Dead she was, yet this was her, he would have sworn it. And she hadn't seen him, hadn't appeared to notice the prisoners outside either—they didn't have to be known to her in any case. Shard, about to make a rush for her, checked himself, his mind racing. This could lead somewhere: she might be of more value if she was to be followed. Making his decision, Shard ran back for the police cars and called for Harry Kenwood. 'Katie Farrell,' he said. 'I'll point her out. I don't know where she's going, but I want you to tail her all the way. I'll fix it for you ticketwise etcetera. Come along, Harry.'

They ran back into the main concourse: Katie Farrell was moving away, heading for the stairs leading up to the buffets: Shard pointed her out, and Kenwood nodded, moved away behind her, and climbed. Kenwood did not know she wouldn't be suspicious: there were plenty of people around as usual, much coming and going. Shard left him to it and went for the Home Office section, who contacted airport security: discreet messages went to all departure points. Shard went back for the exit, pondering on Katie Farrell. Substitution of bodies he could take: it happened from time to time—say when someone wanted to collect on an insurance policy maybe, or something similar. Plenty of women had had abdominal operations that left scars. The faking of a birthmark was more difficult, but was far from impossible: the burning end of a cigarette, or a makeshift branding iron might do that. So okay! What Shard did not believe in was coincidence; it was odd to say the least that two shoot-up villains should turn up at Gatwick at the same time as Miss Katie Farrell, alive and kicking. Back in the car, and it was not O'Riordan but Stephens that he chose to travel with, he mentioned the point, casually, after they had moved away onto the A-23 heading south fast.

'Funny,' he said.

'What is, Mr Shard?'

Shard smiled. 'As if you didn't know!'

'Didn't know what, for Christ's sake?'

'People show up in funny places, and at

funny times...don't they?'

Stephens turned to the window and stared out. 'I don't know what you mean,' he said, 'and that's the truth.'

'Is it? I wonder! You had a good look yourself, and your friend Mr O'Riordan didn't like that. He wasn't *surprised*, though. Not like I was.' Shard paused, whistling softly through his teeth. Pleasantly he said, 'I never did tell you—that day after King's Cross—that Katie Farrell was dead, did I? Not that it matters ...what does matter is, who put that body where I found it? Come to that, whose body? That's going to matter to someone when all this lot's over.'

'But not to me or O'Riordan,' Stephens said disagreeably.

'No? We'll have to see, won't we? In the meantime there's something else you can tell me, and it's this: why were you and O'Riordan meeting Miss Farrell at Gatwick, h'm?'

'We were not.' The tone, Shard fancied, was a little defensive and the statement failed to ring true. 'We didn't know she was going to turn up there.'

'This I rather doubt. Let me reconstruct for you: you'd got the information that Katie Farrell was hopping the twig again, and you decided to stop her, for reasons of your own

242

that I think we know about: you and your organisation, whatever that may be, and I shall find out, believe me—you didn't like the hand-over of Katie to the Middle Eastern interests. Maybe you didn't mean to *meet* her at Gatwick. You knew she was heading for Orly airport, and you decided, just in case she had seen you or O'Riordan before and recognised you at Gatwick, to make Orly before her and tail her from the airport. After that, I suppose you might have flown out for Belfast...a happy little party going back to Ulster. Or more likely you had your own means of getting back in unobserved. How's that, Mr Stephens?'

'Ah, shut up,' Stephens said.

Shard grinned. 'I don't believe it's far out. It'll do for me. From now on out till you either bloat in Worthing or return in health to London, you'll not be seeing your friend O'Riordan again—and you can read what you like into that!'

Stephens shrugged indifferently, but there was a wary look in his eyes: he had the message. Shard was going to say he'd coughed; which Shard was. After that, Stephens clammed up, though he became decidedly jittery once the cars had turned off the A-23 at Bolney to head for the Worthing road. Coming down through the Findon valley Shard watched out for any signs of disease: in fact, the streets were deserted except for patrolling mobiles and now and again an ambulance. Coming past the private road to the golf club later on, Shard noted no movement of cars in or out: the greens, the club house would be deserted now. In Union Place after the weirdest drive Shard had ever experienced in a built-up area in daylight, his cars pulled into the parking bay of the police station. Warned ahead by radio, the reception committee was waiting: a Chief Inspector, a sergeant and six PCs.

The Chief Inspector saluted. 'Where do you want them, Mr Shard?'

'This one in a cell.' Shard indicated O'Riordan. 'The other in the charge room. And in both instances, complete privacy. If you have any clients currently in the cells, I want them out.'

* * * *

With Stephens under safe guard in the charge room, Shard followed O'Riordan down the steps to the basement: himself and alone, he would be interrogator and guard. All police officers were told to clear the cell flat: the Superintendent didn't like it and said so, plain and pointed. 'My patch,' he said. 'I like to know what goes on.'

'It would be better if you didn't.'

'That's another thing: I run this station clean, Mr Shard. You know what I mean.'

Shard said, 'I know and I appreciate it. But we're dealing with dirt, and there may not be much more time left. I'm sorry, I'm over-ruling you. As co-ordinator, I have the right …and I shall take the full responsibility. None of it will brush off on you, Superintendent.' He paused, meeting the police chief's angry eye. 'It'll be done efficiently and O'Riordan knows the score—coming from Ulster, he can't help but know that I'll not be bluffing. And he'll never talk under the soft press, that's for sure.'

Shard turned away, nodded at the gaoler, who pushed a key into the lock of a heavy door. The door swung open: Shard walked in, face blank but every part of him alert for trouble. The cell was long and narrow: O'Riordan stood at the far end, alongside a wooden shelf-like platform raised some eighteen inches from the floor to form the basis of a bed. Shard, whose hand had been round the butt of his holstered gun as he entered, now brought it into the open.

'Belfast,' he said. 'Your lot—whoever they may be—don't hesitate to use guns. Nor do all

245

the others. And nor do I—not now.'

'What are you doing with Stephens?'

'If that's his real name—but never mind that for now. He's in the charge room, as you know. Being charged.'

'What with?' O'Riordan's eyes narrowed. 'Now look. You have five days to play with. Why charge him now? That's not the usual form. Cat-and-mouse usually—isn't it?'

Shard smiled. 'What, precisely, are you admitting?'

'Nothing,' O'Riordan said at once. 'Nothing you don't know. We're part of an organisation—all right, so this you knew. That gives you an excuse to hold us. But—'

'But the charges? I'll tell you something, O'Riordan.' Shard moved slowly in from his stance against the door, his gun aimed at O'Riordan's stomach. 'Stephens—he's coughed. Not quite all—but enough.'

O'Riordan waved a hand contemptuously. 'Ah, don't give me that! Jesus...I'm not grass green!'

'Your belief is immaterial. All I'm asking is that you tell me the rest.'

'The rest being?' There was a sneer on O'Riordan's face and in his voice. 'Suppose you start by telling me what it is that Stephens is supposed to have told you?'

'Right, I'll do that. As a result of information received, you knew Katie Farrell was flying out for Orly. You intended to pick her up in France once she was outside the airport. Then you would have smuggled her back into Northern Ireland for your boyos to deal with. She'd have been killed—for the second time.'

O'Riordan looked up sharply. 'What's that?'

'Don't act green with me,' Shard said softly. 'You knew all about that, didn't you, O'Riordan? You probably knew whose the body really was too—right? You may even have fixed the whole thing—'

'I did not—'

'That, you'll have to prove by your answers to my questions, O'Riordan. And just bear this in mind: what's going on is the filthiest thing terrorism's ever faced civilisation with. When you go down, you'll wish we still had the death penalty. Prisons are strange places—maybe you know that. The cons are not going to like you. And I'll be pressing, so far as I can—and so will high legal authority—for the longest possible sentence. Start thinking in terms of thirty, forty years, O'Riordan, and start thinking now.'

'You don't impress me,' O'Riordan said savagely.

'Why not?'

O'Riordan stared. 'Ask a silly question,' he said. 'And—'

'All right, I'll answer it myself: you know what's going to happen. The chances are you know when, too. You knew very well what had hit Worthing. You think prison, all legal processes of trial and sentence, will be in the melting pot when it spreads further. You could well be right—if it happens! I'm here to see it doesn't. I'm here to get every last bit of information out of you, and if you don't start talking fast you're going to face the kind of thing both sides have handed out in Northern Ireland.'

'What's that supposed to mean?'

'As if you didn't know!'

O'Riordan waved a hand in the air, looking cool enough. 'Here in Worthing, in a British nick? Worthing's a respectable place.'

'Tit for tat,' Shard said grimly. 'You're not worried by a prison sentence, which you see as hypothetical. By the same token, my reputation doesn't stand to lose much either! And it won't be here: we'll be going on a little trip to Chanctonbury.'

There was sudden caution in O'Riordan's face, caution tinged with alarm: Shard was convinced the man knew the facts concerning Katie Farrell's supposed death, and the identity of the real victim of that water-tank half way up to Chanctonbury Ring. Nevertheless, O'Riordan seemed prepared to call what in his view could have been Shard's bluff: maybe he just didn't believe that any British copper would behave in the way Shard had suggested; and maybe, Shard thought, no British copper would to date. But no British copper had ever before been faced with what he was faced with, and one could never be certain of what one's reactions were going to be in a new situation until the moment had come...

'Well?' Shard asked.

O'Riordan stuck two fingers in the air. 'Nothing doing,' he said.

Shard moved back towards the door of the cell, which on his orders had been left unlocked, covering his retreat with his gun. He let himself out, locked the door on O'Riordan, and pressed a bell-push: the Superintendent came down followed by the gaoler and two constables.

'Any luck, Mr Shard?'

Shard shook his head. 'None—yet. We move into Stage Two. I'll take one of the cars from Gatwick, with its driver and crew. If you'd be good enough to give them the order, Superintendent, I'd like them to come and get O'Riordan now.'

'Stage Two being?'

Shard smiled, but his face was tight. 'Better not ask,' he said. 'None of your men will be involved and it's not your worry.'

★ ★ ★ ★

Back through the Worthing streets towards Washington: from the car Shard saw things to alarm him. The population was restive now, people were coming out of their homes to where a police mobile had been surrounded, brought to a halt on the Findon side of the Durrington roundabout, alongside the cemetery. Its crew were doing their best, but the crowd, mostly old people, were angry and dead scared: there had been no hard information and rumour was running riot. There could be trouble, especially when the army moved in—so far, the troops were outside the town, helping with the road blocks and standing by for use when required for other duties by the police authority. Shard's mind worried around the possibilities: maybe Worthing should be given the truth straight, but if that were done, would it be possible to hold the news from the rest of the country? Almost certainly not, and never mind the muzzled Press, radio and television. Hard as it might be, Worthing must be left to stew until a final decision had been reached upon the advisability of Martial Law being declared. Farther on, just past the Cissbury public house, a corpse lay huddled, shapeless, a clothes'-bag of burned corruption in the gutter. A dog sniffed at it, whimpering and pawing: his dead master? Shard, about to tell the driver to blast it away with his horn, decided not to. Dogs had feelings too, were susceptible to grief and tragedy. Turning off the London road through Washington, the police car, with O'Riordan under the guns and handcuffed in the back, headed east for the track up to Chanctonbury Ring. Outside a house not far from the Washington-Steyning road, three young children played, oblivious to encroaching death, but Shard read the almost paralysed horror in the face of the mother, watching them from a doorway: she, too, had heard rumours, would be wondering how long the open country would be safe.

Taking the car as far as possible, they walked the rest of the way up the steepening hillside, O'Riordan still between the escort. The sun was going down now, the shades of early evening falling over Chanctonbury and its death-tank and all that lay fallow below the ground. O'Riordan's face was grey, his eyes haunted. Shard felt in his bones that the man would talk before long provided he could be made to

251

believe that the time for bluff had long passed: that was the crux.

The tank came into view. As they came up to it, Shard halted the procession. He told the police escort to withdraw a little way down the slope of the track. 'You,' he said to O'Riordan, 'back up to the tank. Over there. Keep clear of the drop.' He pointed, keeping his gun aimed at the man's stomach. 'Don't try anything or I'll shoot.'

O'Riordan stared at him, then, shrugging, moved for the perimeter of the water-tank. Reaching it, he turned and faced Shard who had taken up a position half-a-dozen yards away from him.

'Well?' he asked.

'Well, what, O'Riordan?'

O'Riordan licked his lips. 'What do you want now?'

'I want talk, O'Riordan. I want answers. I'm going to have them, believe me! I'll start by telling you something: there's a demand that the British Government concede to the sort of aspirations held by the Ulster militants...or isn't that news to you?'

'It's news.'

'Oh, yes? You don't know who's uttered the demand?'

'No.'

'Then start thinking,' Shard said. 'While you're thinking, ponder on this too: I want to know the time and place, or places, where the threat against Britain is to materialise. And I want names—identities of those involved and where they can be picked up. I want to know precisely where Lavington fits, likewise a man called Azzam and his masters in the Middle East. I want the lot, O'Riordan. I'm going to have it.'

O'Riordan swallowed. In the falling sunlight Shard could see the sweat on his face, greasily shining, and the staring look in the eyes. O'Riordan, accustomed in his own country to handing out brutality, could use his imagination to the full and, no doubt, could believe in the reality of the threat that lay in Shard's manner. Shard said quietly, 'I think you understand, don't you, O'Riordan. You have two minutes to make a start.' He shot the cuff back from his left wrist and glanced at his watch. 'I'm counting now. In one hundred and twenty seconds I'll start shooting. Right ankle, left ankle, right shinbone, left...then the knee-caps. You'll be a shattered man. What's left goes in the water-tank. I think you know I mean it more than I've ever meant anything in my life.'

He waited, counting seconds.

★ ★ ★ ★

They carried O'Riordan back down the rough track to the police car. They carried him screaming, blaspheming, sobbing: he had held out well and Shard's threat had been for real. When he'd squeezed the trigger Shard's eyes had seen through a red mist: for a copper he was behaving abominably, but as co-ordinator he realised the basic truth: one worthless man could not be allowed to stand against a nation's life. Shard, trained as a police marksman, laid his bullets clean: first the right ankle splintered, and, yelling, O'Riordan hopped. But he wouldn't talk: the left ankle went. Then both shins. O'Riordan fell to the ground and screamed.

'Not the knees, you bastard, not the knees—'

'Talk, then.' Shard moved forward, his own face pouring sweat now, his basic instincts telling him that bastard was the right term. He stood over O'Riordan, his gun aimed at one knee-cap. Two more bullets and the man would be a cripple for life, short of miraculous surgery—and the water-tank waited. O'Riordan went on screaming: Shard was aware of police consternation down the track. Again he said, 'Talk and it'll stop. But talk now.'

'Christ...' Writhing, O'Riordan sobbed. But he talked. When talking was done, Shard put his gun away, and called up the police constables. They looked shaken, hostile, were barely polite: they hadn't been in Ulster. They lifted O'Riordan's broken body carefully, the legs dangling in sheer agony. In the car the screaming continued: the man wouldn't pass out. Shard said, 'A doctor—the nearest is the MO at Wiston House. Drop me there too. Then stand by to take O'Riordan where the doctor wants, and remain with him till you're relieved. I'll inform Gatwick. Understood?'

'Yes, sir.'

Shard caught the man's eye, saw the dislike. He said, 'I don't usually make excuses, and I'm not going to this time. I know I've been a bastard, full stop. But you'll carry out my orders to the letter and you'll not leave O'Riordan for a second. And now let's get moving.'

★ ★ ★ ★

Wiston House provided transport to London: at the Foreign Office Shard was passed a message from Detective Sergeant Kenwood, sent from Paris and timed at 1928 hours: Katie Farrell had de-planed at Orly and had taken a taxi to the Gare de Lyon: there she had been met by a man and a woman with an Arabic look about them. Kenwood was watching them, would tail, and would report again when possible. Shard, before contacting Hedge, put a call through to Paris and spoke to a senior police officer known to him personally. He passed brief details then said, 'From information received, the Farrell woman is understood to be making for Marseilles and thence to Tunis. We'd like her stopped at Marseilles and held pending a further decision. Can you cope?'

'*Oui*, M'sieur Shard—'

'Thanks a lot. Watch out for my Detective Sergeant—I don't want him caught in the cross-fire!' Shard rang off, sat back for a moment thinking of O'Riordan's screams, then called Hedge's private number and said he would be round right away.

CHAPTER FIFTEEN

'What about that man Lavington?' was the first thing Hedge asked, slopping brandy into a tumbler: he'd just finished his self-got meal, a late supper rather than dinner, and the remains seemed scarcely worthy of the brandy, which Shard knew was a good one.

'Never mind Lavington for now, he'll keep—'

'But I do mind. He's vitally important—you said so yourself. Where is he now?'

'I don't know, Hedge. Look, I—'

'You don't know?' Hedge stared, mouth open, eyes round and accusing. 'What a thing to admit!'

Shard compressed his lips, then said patiently, 'He's somewhere in Devon or Cornwall, with a strong bias towards Cornwall. He's being watched out for and there's nothing more I could do by being there—though that's not to say I shan't be going west again shortly.'

'Why?'

'If you'd just allow me to explain what I came to explain, the rest might well be seen to follow—even by you.'

'There's no need to be impertinent, Shard. Oh—go on, then, explain.' Hedge paused, eyebrows lifted. 'Brandy?'

'Thanks. I was wondering when you were going to ask.'

Hedge frowned. 'It's not cheap these days. I seldom drink it myself since the last tightening of the screw.' With care, he poured a small measure and handed the glass to Shard. 'Now,' he said, all attention.

'I've got names, dates, places. I think I've got nearly the lot.'

'Nearly?' Hedge sat down with a thump. 'Who from?'

Shard told him. 'I'm waiting for a check on the real identity but I doubt if that's important now. The rest is—or had better be, since I stretched the rules in obtaining it—'

'I don't want to know about that.'

'Not unless questions are asked? All right, Hedge, I do understand. Now just listen, will you?' Shard sat down facing Hedge, stared into the puffy face and small eyes. 'As we thought, the Middle East's the villain—not the Ulster militants, though O'Riordan and his lot are involved. They're a break-away group and they've been too clever, Hedge, took on too much by themselves. I regret what I did to O'Riordan...but he's a killer and he's broken the law so he had to suffer even though he hasn't in fact done anything directly against the State—'

'Are you saying he's innocent after all?'

'Hardly that—those corpses in Cherbourg wouldn't have said so, but—'

'But if he hasn't acted against the State as such, why didn't he come clean earlier?'

'Didn't trust us,' Shard answered briefly.

'Scared, too—on account of his own law-breaking. But I'll come back to that, Hedge. Here's the point: O'Riordan's boys were the cat's-paws...they'd come in, got in deep in fact, from an early stage. For one reason: they'd got to hear about the blood run and Katie Farrell and they intended to operate a very, very big double-cross on the terrorists. Later, they got the word about the threat to Porton and its satellites. Being already on the inside as it were, they fancied their chances of putting the stopper on all by themselves. They didn't want the filth to cross the sea to Ireland—they made that very point to me when I was taken to them from King's Cross, though they used a reference to the Provos to make it. If they'd only told me more...but they didn't, Hedge. I say again, we don't inspire trust in the Irish, any of them.'

Hedge nodded. 'The terrorists, the real ones. Do we know who they are?'

Shard said, 'Yes, we do now. They call themselves Power of Islam, Hedge.'

'Power of Islam?' Hedge's voice rose high, squeaking. 'Good gracious, Shard, we've—'

'Met before—yes! The threat to London's underground. You'll remember Nadia Nazzar-razeen died in custody. There's a new boss now, a man. In the movement he's known as the Mullah.'

'A religious significance?'

'Broadly, perhaps. I suppose the Middle East can always give itself a religious justification if it wants to—like the Irish. I'd say, nothing deeper than that.' Shard sipped his brandy, relishing the glow. 'O'Riordan doesn't know his identity, and I accept that as the truth seeing he's out to help now.'

'*Really* out to help?' Hedge sounded bitter. 'Wasn't his lot responsible for the kidnap of my wife?'

'Yes—'

'Yes you say!' Hedge threw up his arms.

'And again, yes. Just listen, Hedge. They wanted to have the charge of any hostage just because that in itself gave them the power to withdraw the hostage-blackmail handle—don't you see? Your wife was never in any real danger until—'

'But they shot at her!'

Shard nodded. 'As I was about to say: at that particular stage, I guess they had to. I did make the point that their hands aren't lilywhite and they've behaved like terrorists themselves...but it was all in a good cause, the way they saw it.' He paused. 'I know it takes some getting used to, and I realise the personal angle—'

'Thank you!' Hedge snapped. He gulped

brandy, shaking all over. Then he took a grip. 'What you've said adds up, does it not, to this: Ireland, either north or south, is not involved?'

'Not directly, no. You can leave them out of it. This is wholly Middle East, from Katie Farrell on. The Arabs want her for what she knows, for the help she can give in the future to further their little schemes of disruption. Which was one reason why O'Riordan was determined she wouldn't stay on the blood run. The other reason was personal to his mob— old scores to be settled—'

'But the *Arabs*, Shard?'

'Serving both sides at once, but all along they've had just the one object in view: never mind Ulster, never mind the Republic, they're simply out to throw Britain into direst bloody confusion, and for why?' Shard slammed a fist into his palm. 'Our oil, Hedge. You underestimated that, though it seems the PM didn't. As producers, Hedge, they're facing the end of the road within a generation. They want to keep their pre-eminence, they want to keep the whip-hand, they want to keep their prices up while it all lasts. We are the big threat, and to stop us they're prepared to wipe us out if they have to. But they'd rather work through cat's-paws, hence they've given us an alternative. A suicidal one.'

Hedge put his head in his hands. 'When you were taken to that house from King's Cross, Shard. Those men! Did they not themselves point the finger at the Middle East?'

'Yes. That was precisely why they wanted to talk to me, to make certain sure we were aware of the reality of the big threat and who was uttering it—that, and to try to find out about Katie Farrell...having made a cock of hooking her off the blood run. They'd lost her again, Hedge.'

'Yes, yes. But about the Middle East...you *believed* them, so why—'

'I believed them, yes. But they didn't in fact add anything to what we had already thought of for ourselves, did they?' Shard added, 'There was just one thing they deliberately fooled me on—I admit that. The body in the water-tank. They knew about that. They knew Katie was supposed to be dead but in fact was very much alive. They hoped to get something out of me so they could catch up with her again themselves—'

'But they told you she was the key. They *urged* you towards her. Why—if *they* wanted her?'

'Hedge, they knew we wanted her anyway, what they said made no difference. Except in this respect: if we got her back, we wouldn't be likely to shove her on the blood run again, not after what they'd told me about the Middle East. And now we know it's Power of Islam—'

Hedge, giving the impression of being out of his depth, pounced on that. 'Yes, Power of Islam. You say O'Riordan didn't know the identity...how was contact made?'

'Through agents. This mullah can never be contacted direct—it's always he, in fact, who initiates any contact, and the meeting place, when a meeting's indicated, varies—but is most often in Kensington.'

'Kensington?'

'It's happened in the public library, in St Mary Abbots' church, in Kensington Gardens by the Round Pond, at the corner of Kensington Palace Gardens, and in the Catherine Wheel public house. Get it, Hedge?'

Hedge gaped, wiped at his pink cheeks with a linen handkerchief. 'Mrs Morton—'

'Exactly. Some sort of clerk, she said, from one of the embassies in Kensington Palace Gardens. That could check—couldn't it, Hedge? I think she told us all she knew, but she could be worth some more effort. I'd like to leave that to you, while I'm busy on other things. All right?'

'Yes, of course,' Hedge said. He blinked,

263

seemed at a temporary loss, as though mention of Mrs Morton had suddenly pointed up his currently wifeless, lonely state, the state in which a top civil servant had to be his own butler, cook and housemaid. He made an effort. 'What other things?'

'The anti-measures, Hedge. I told you—I have dates and places. To be more precise, one date, one time: tomorrow at 2100 hours. Psychologically timed, to coincide with the TV news broadcasts.' Shard smiled bitterly. 'Just a little Middle Eastern twist of the screw!'

Hedge seemed to shrivel. 'God! A shade over twenty-four hours!' His voice dropped to scarcely more than a whisper, as though he feared all sound. 'What's to happen then, Shard, tell me that!'

'Nothing unexpected, except size-wise. The whole of the South of England is to be affected, from a line drawn between the Bristol Channel through London to the Essex coast. From there, of course, it spreads north by natural means—contacts, winds, that sort of thing.'

'And the means?'

'Explosions at Porton Down, the stowages around Wiston House and the South Downs outside Worthing, and at Nancekuke.'

'Explosions, how?'

Shard said, 'That I didn't get. My man

didn't know. Just explosions.'

'Air attack, bombing?'

'I would assume so. That would be the safest way for the villains. If they tried to penetrate...if they did manage to get in they'd be the first victims. But there's another possibility, Hedge: Lavington.'

'How's that?'

'He's had the entrée to all the establishments, and he's recently been inside them all—except Nancekuke. He could have set devices—'

'Blowable by a timing mechanism?'

'Or remote control. It's a theory and a good one in my book, the best—and I intend to follow it.'

'But you said Lavington didn't matter, Shard.'

Shard gave a short, grim laugh and shook his head. 'Oh, no, I didn't, Hedge! I said he'd keep. He will—till 2100 hours tomorrow night. I have till then to get him, and to do that I'm going back into the field. I prefer the field work in any case—it's better than being the spider at the centre of the web. That's more your line, Hedge. Now I'm going to tell you what I want from you—'

'Just a moment—just a moment. What about Katie Farrell?'

'In France, with Kenwood tailing. She'll be

stopped at Marseilles. When she is, we may, just may, get more leads.'

'But the body on Chanctonbury!' Hedge was almost wringing his hands.

'Hedge, it was in Lavington's interest that Katie Farrell shouldn't be picked up by us, and it was in O'Riordan's interest that Lavington should never suspect that his mob weren't right behind the Middle East. Katie Farrell was still the key—to both sides. When she got away from O'Riordan, she just vanished—where to, is still a mystery. O'Riordan believed Lavington when he said *he* didn't know. Anyway, Lavington decided to kill two birds with one stone: it suited him to have us believe Katie was dead—and he wanted a human guinea pig before he went into the final act. He got one: a girl from Belfast—O'Riordan doesn't know the details except for this: she had abdominal scarring similar to Katie Farrell's and the birthmark was impressed with a specially-cast branding iron. Lavington supplied the germs or whatever of the bloating sickness, and he took this girl up towards Chanctonbury with an escort of Arab thugs. The thugs got cold feet about catching the disease themselves, and they scarpered. Lavington stayed to watch the girl die. He didn't stop her when she went into the water-tank looking for the antidote. He knew she was too late. Hedge, much too bloody late! And needless to say, he never reported that the tank had been vandalised.' Shard had broken out in a sticky sweat. 'I'm going to put all my heart and soul into catching up with my friend Lavington! Now—here's what I want done. First requirement is, an inch by inch check of all the stowages, a search for explosive devices—'

'I'm not sure we shouldn't clear them out after all, Shard.' Hedge took up a phone. 'I'll talk to Defence Ministry—'

'I don't advise that, Hedge.'

Hedge looked up. 'Why not?'

'We've discussed it before. You made the point yourself—'

'But now the situation's different.' Hedge went ahead with his call and asked for Henry Carver. When he got him, Carver asked for Shard.

'Your views, please, Mr Shard.'

Shard gave them, forcefully. 'My theories could be wrong. If they are, we're putting the stocks at great risk unnecessarily. To disperse them into open country, even to put them on the road in convoys—they'd be too obvious. And temporary, basically unsuitable stowages raked up at short notice—they'd be much too vulnerable. It's just not on, sir.'

'I think I agree. I'll—'

'I'd like it left to me, sir. Lavington's the fuse. I'll render him harmless.'

There was a humourless laugh along the line. 'I wish you every success, Mr Shard! Do your best. Now give me Hedge, will you?'

Shard passed the phone back: Hedge bridled into it, slammed it down huffily after a short exchange. 'On your head be it, Shard,' he said. 'We must just pray we find the devices, if they exist.'

★ ★ ★ ★

The army's South-West District command at Taunton, already on alert, was given the fresh facts by Whitehall; the Major-General Commanding, London District, was ordered to bring his forces to a state of readiness just short of the actual implementation of Martial Law: he was to be prepared at virtually a moment's notice to reinforce the police authority on the streets of the capital. The Commander-in-Chief, UK Land Forces, was warned to be ready for troop and transport movements and deployment of guns and medical convoys and armour nationwide. Similar warnings went to the various RAF commands: Southern Maritime Air Region at RAF Mount Batten in the

Plymouth area prepared to cover any intrusion across the Channel; 38 Group at Benson in Oxfordshire, 46 Group at Pewsey in Wiltshire, 11 Group at Bentley Priory in Stanmore, were those immediately concerned with air cover for the germ dumps themselves. A directive went out to Devon and Cornwall Police and to the troop commanders operating in the West Country generally, that Lavington was to be found at all costs—but was only distantly to be contained, tracked, watched and not lost again, was not to be put into a position where he would be likely to crunch what he carried in his mouth: this, as Shard stressed to Hedge, was vital. Lavington must be left with a visible and viable way out: it would be a devil of a task for the troops and police to reconcile possible escape with continued surveillance but it was, it had to be, paramount: Shard's theory of a remote-controlled blow-up was just a theory. A live Lavington could yet provide the real answer. When all requirements had been passed via the Head of Department, Shard took over a departmental radio-equipped car and went home to Ealing: he felt guilty about even a small delay, but he was human, and if this thing didn't work out then he wasn't likely to find home much of a place to come back to afterwards; comfort lay in the fact that Ealing was near enough on his way to RAF Northwood whence he would be helicoptered west.

It was midnight when he let himself into the house: Beth hadn't gone to bed, nor had Mrs Micklam. It seemed Beth had been worrying about him and was overjoyed to see him, but Mrs Micklam, prised away from her aunt, attacked.

'I think it's monstrous. We're not a police state yet, are we? Mind you, there are some funny things going on in Worthing, that I don't deny.'

'What things?' Shard asked, all innocence.

'People being taken ill, Simon,' Beth put in. 'I've been worried—the police who brought Mother back said—'

'Said I'd been there?'

She nodded. 'Yes. Anyway, you're back now—'

'Did the police mention the illness?'

'No,' Mrs Micklam said, 'but Aunt Edith did, on the telephone. I rang her when I got back here, and again this evening. People dying like flies was what she said—'

'Oh, Mother!'

Mrs Micklam fluffed a hand around tightly-set white hair. 'It's all very well for you, dear. You're not down there.'

'Nor are you,' Shard said, and at once

realised he'd been stupidly indiscreet: Mother-in-law was as sharp as a needle, and like a needle, she probed.

'So that's why you had me seized,' she said, staring at Shard. 'Well! I must say I'm surprised. I thought you usually wished me dead, Simon.' Beth looked unhappy; Shard, brutally, gave no denial. Mrs Micklam went on, 'I don't know what all this is about and I do think you ought to tell us, Simon. Am I going to come out with this illness, for one thing?'

'No,' Shard said firmly. 'You were never in contact at all, and—'

'And you?'

'Me?' Shard reacted to accusation with a flushed face: he hadn't been in contact either, except in Katie Farrell's case after which he had been decontaminated at Wiston House, but Mrs Micklam would never take that. Nevertheless, he tried. 'Not me. No way! I'm clean.'

'You may not be. How do you know? I think it's abominable, taking a risk with your family.' Her voice shrilled like an out-of-tune bagpipe. 'You're so selfish, Simon. I'm sure that Scotland Yard of yours could have found you a bed—'

'Look, I'm not staying—'

'—and yet back you come, breathing germs, undoing the good work you might have done

271

by having me taken away—oh, yes, I admit that possibility though it was *very* high-handed and you had no right—risking Beth's life and mine and all because you wanted to come and *gloat* over having me manhandled back to London...' Mrs Micklam panted herself to a stop. Shard, driving away for Northwood soon after, had the rattle of her voice in his ears for most of the way. He wondered if any young PC on the beat would believe it possible that a Detective Chief Superintendent, no more than two grades removed from Metropolitan God, could be driven out of his own house by his mother-in-law. Until self-control cut her off like the flick of a tape switch, Shard drove badly, not concentrating, knowing that if things went wrong in the next few hours his last memory of his home and Beth would be totally over-shadowed by Mrs Micklam's tongue.

★ ★ ★ ★

Helicoptered fast through the night, after an infuriating mechanical delay at Northwood, Shard reached Exeter at 0415 hours. He was put down at the Police Training College off the by-pass, preferring to be on the ground at this stage. He was given a plain car, equipped with radio. He drove at speed along the by-pass; it was almost empty at this hour, free and open, and he made good progress westwards, consumed with impatience and his nagging worries, his mental eye constantly on the clock. Clearing the outskirts of Exeter, he headed on for Okehampton, driving under a haze brought by the approaching dawn. The farther west he went, the more activity he found: police, troops, air cover high up, road blocks. For now it was still being done, so far as it could be, discreetly—still a major joint exercise, a general advance preparation against any unformulated acts of terrorism that might occur in the future. Before Shard had left London, the Head of Department had given him the official word from Downing Street: at this stage, no Martial Law. The time of declaration would depend upon his own further report, and if it so happened that nothing was heard from him to the contrary by 1900 hours that evening, then a proclamation would be made and the civil population totally immobilised in their homes throughout the southern half of the country. In the meantime, although full warning had been passed to the various concerned Area Health Authorities who had filtered it down to their districts and consultants and admin staffs, no overt measures to combat the diseases were being taken and the ambulance crews had not

273

yet been put on any special alert. Antidotes were on their way by air and road from Porton and the South Downs to all areas, but everyone knew, as Shard himself did, that even with the medical columns of the RAMC they could be no more than a drop in the ocean and once the thing spread and multiplied there would be positively no holding it. The dead and dying, the bloating, the shrivelled husks, would lie everywhere...

Shard passed through Okehampton on the Launceston road, branching off the A-30 onto the A-386 for Lydford and the road block where, only the day before, he had lost Lavington. At the road block, no fresh information: just in case—however unlikely a thought—the dog should have returned to his vomit, Shard turned right for Lydford once again, driving slow through the straggle of houses and cottages. There were a few people about, mostly gathered in small groups, talking. Wondering what was in the air, no doubt! Shard's heart sank: the West Country he liked, its people too. They were friendly, helpful and smiling, a happy breed and a contented one, all country people at heart, even the town dwellers: and Lydford had a friendly feel about it, the feel of a genuine country community. Maybe it would not survive much longer: the village was on the track east, a little south maybe, from Nancekuke. The weather reports coming in on his car radio spoke of a strong westerly wind expected with the shades of the evening. There would be a wide scatter... Shard's thoughts, with an effort, veered away from Lydford: when all was said and done, it was just one place among many. Not for the first time, Shard wondered how, if his Lavington-controlled blow-up theory was correct, Lavington meant to blow Nancekuke: the answer probably was, an accomplice *in situ,* a man who would have planted a device. His mind was going over and over the possibilities when, at last, his radio bleeped and he answered.

'Field One, over.'

'Control calling Field One. We have a clear in all points.'

Shard flicked his switch. 'Thank you, but keep trying. Out.' A clear in all points meant that none of Lavington's devices had been located: and it meant *just* that, in Shard's view—no more. Lavington would know precisely how to site them where they were not likely to be found even by Bentley and his opposite numbers in the other establishments. The imponderables were legion: Shard cleared his mind, hoping that a vacuum would ask nature for a fill. He made back through the byways for the A-30 into Launceston, past the village war memorial into the narrow lanes. Bypassing Launceston, he headed on west across Bodmin Moor, grey and lonely but brightening as the sun came up behind his speeding car. In Bolventor he passed Jamaica Inn, granite-hard and grey like the moor itself, ancient haunt of Cornwall's smugglers, an isolated place where you could almost smell still the brandy and the tobacco that had found its romantic way past the prosaic clutches of the excisemen. Here on Bodmin Moor with its bog patches and its grotesque tors was the feeling that anything could happen at any moment. Ahead mist was rolling in, increasing the remoteness. Meeting it, Shard dropped his speed and flicked on his windscreen wipers and lights. Other lights came up like searching eyes, moved past and away east. As the mist thickened Shard was left in isolation, in a world of his own, thinking about shortness of time and about Lavington: and about security and the anti-measures. Had they done enough, had there been over-sights anywhere along the line?

The mist was patchy: coming down a hill Shard found the visibility better and he put on more speed. A police motor-cyclist overtook him, going fast; army transport, heavy vehicles bunched in convoy with outriders, passed him heading east. Then into another belt of mist, real fog, thick and clinging. Down through the gears again and, this time, stop: he couldn't see the verge. He cursed and switched off his engine but left his lights on. Maybe it would clear soon, when there was some strength in the sun or a wind to blow it away. For the moment he could do nothing: the swirls of fog slid thick against his windows, sealing him in. The sense of eeriness was immensely strong. Into his private world came once again the bleep of his radio: with relief at even vocal company, Shard reached out and answered.

'Field One, over.'

'Control. It's me.' It was Hedge in person: the voice was unmistakable, as was the rejection of proper procedures. Odd in a way, but Hedge never used the radio in the authorised manner, though Shard would have expected him to wallow in the official jargon of Control Boss Two and whatnot. Hedge went on, 'Where are you, Field One?'

'Bodmin Moor, A-30 west of Bolventor. Stuck in a mist. Over.'

'Stuck in a mist did you say. Too bad.' There was a pause. 'I have news of first contact. Will be returning a.m. Do you wish to interview? Over.'

Shard gritted his teeth: who the hell was first contact? Reason suggested Katie Farrell, about whom Shard had not expected to have news over the car radio. If this was Katie, it would seem she had been apprehended as requested, which was fine; Shard would have preferred Hedge to hold the information off the air, but maybe he'd tried the police stations and couldn't wait. Shard flicked his switch. 'I wish to interview, yes. But I say again, I'm stuck in a zero visibility mist. Over.'

'One must sometimes take risks.'

'Then I suggest you come and look at this one.'

'Oh, God. When's it going to clear?'

'You've just invoked the only authority that can answer. Now listen, Control. First contact to be despatched onward, repeat onward, to await my arrival. Got that? Over.'

'Yes. Received and understood. I trust you'll soon be moving. Over and out.'

Hedge clicked off. As he did so something thumped hard against the offside rear door of the car, which swayed a little on its suspension. Shard's gun was in his hand before he dimly saw the culprit moving in the swirls of mist: a sheep, horned and shaggy, as lonely as Shard himself. Shard grinned, but swore: his nerves were fairly ragged, which wasn't good. The

278

sheep's advent had curdled his stomach. Seething with his impatience, he sat and waited for a clearance. With Katie Farrell back in Britain and held in custody, things might start to happen: at least the girl might prove some sort of bargaining counter. On the information side, it was doubtful if she could tell him any more than O'Riordan, but one could never be sure. Though even if she could, it all boiled down, in Shard's view, to getting hold of Lavington before the deadline expired. They knew the score by now, they knew the demands and the threat. What they had to do was short if not simple: prevent it!

He sat and waited: there was nothing moving now and the silence was as intense as the mist itself. His thoughts were bitter: Britain could go to its doom just on account of its weather if this mist was widespread enough to inhibit the whole area of search. The wind predicted by the meteorologists was not expected until the evening: much too late! Shard prayed for sun, strong sun to melt away the water-particles. Mist could persist for days...all morning might be the very least. Time passed, dragging its heels. He drummed urgent fingers on his steering-wheel and began to sweat. Then after a long interval he heard more sounds from outside, some kind of movement.

Another lost sheep?

Feet on the tarmac, slightly dragging—it didn't sound like a sheep. The rhythm was of two, not four. Shard once again brought out his gun, remained otherwise very still, listening out. The sounds came closer and he heard something scrabbling at the boot of the car, then he heard muttering, a whimpering sound, followed by a groan and the slide of something heavy down the back of the car.

Then silence.

He got out, his gun ready for action, leaving the driving door open. There was no sound, no movement. Carefully, eyes straining through the mist, Shard moved towards the back of the car. Vaguely something came up, a black huddle looming through the dampness, something collapsed behind the car. Shard moved closer and squatted on his haunches, instinct telling him not to touch, not to go too close. He saw the shine of chrome, buttons and shoulder numbers, a policeman. A dead policeman, already starting to bloat. Nauseated, Shard backed away: the instinct now was to run, run like a madman...but reason overrode instinct and he flung himself into the car and crashed the door shut.

CHAPTER SIXTEEN

Shard fought down his stomach's enmity and called Launceston nick: 'Field One calling Hector.'

The response was immediate: 'Hector answering Field One, receiving you loud and clear, over.'

Shard flicked his transmit switch. 'Inform all concerned, fish arrived three miles west of Bolventor on A-30.' Fish: bloaters. This had been pre-arranged and coded. 'My diagnosis: Keyman may be found in vicinity. Could have been approached and acted to protect himself, using perhaps a spray-gun. Ring area as soon as the mist lifts. When this happens I shall proceed and contact Bodmin police. I repeat the general instruction: throw a cordon only, do not approach Keyman. Over and out.'

Shard flicked off and resumed his wait. Out there—unless he was still carborne—Lavington might well be, now lost and stumbling around. The hopes of Britain must not be allowed to sink into a bog. Yet queries still remained: how long since that dead constable had got his dose? The onset was fast; if Lavington, surprised by an equally surprised PC, coming upon him by chance in the mist, was the culprit, then he had to be close whether he was in a car or on foot. The alternative was that the disease was already spreading west from Worthing, and that was highly unlikely: no report had as yet indicated other than that Worthing was still containing its own troubles. That left just one more: Lavington in his travels, which in this case need not necessarily be close at hand, was starting to infect Cornwall, casting out yet another warning that the threat was for real.

Some forty minutes after making his transmission Shard found an improvement in the visibility: he began to see the road verges, then the nearer stretch of moorland to north and south of the A-30. He got on the move thankfully, away at last from the corpse behind; then slowed suddenly as his rear-view mirror showed a police mobile coming up. He stopped and got out, running back and waving his arms. The police car stopped and the driver looked out, saw the object on the ground, and went green: the body had burst and lay on the road like a split haggis, the uniform parted under pressure at the seams.

'Don't touch it,' Shard said, feeling sick again.

'And you are?'

'Detective Chief Superintendent Shard. Considering the visibility, you're here fast.'

'We had your message, sir, and we weren't far behind you as it happened, when the mist cleared. The police driver was staring at the spill on the roadway as if he couldn't look away. 'That, sir. Is...is that the body?'

'I'm afraid it is. Don't let it shake you into any indiscretions if you come up against Lavington—he has to be handled carefully for everyone's sake—you know the orders.'

'Yes, sir. Any special ones for us?'

'What orders do you have currently?'

'To patrol the A-30, sir, ten miles each side of Bolventor, contacting other mobiles each end.'

'I'm over-riding them,' Shard said. 'You stay here and keep all comers away from that body. It's lethal and the sickness can spread fast. Don't approach it—stay in your car with windows closed. Report back to your control by radio. The army's South-West District at Taunton has an availability of decontamination crews, widespread by now. Ask for the nearest to be sent in on my orders, pronto. All right?'

'Understood, sir.'

Shard ran back to his car, skirting the body. He drove fast for Bodmin. On the way in he passed some of the troops and police detailed for the toothcomb, the flushing operation. Men and vehicles, an impressive array. He hoped they understood their orders fully: it was a flush and not a fight and they were moving in as beaters, no more. Lavington was to be treated with blind eyes and when he emerged he was to be reported and not shot at. In Bodmin Shard decided to keep going for Nancekuke; already far too much time had been wasted and it was acceptable to risk missing any messages from London until he got to his final destination.

★ ★ ★ ★

Nancekuke lay on the north Cornish coast about mid-way between Portreath and Porthtowan, a lonely place, wild, not so far from the boom of the Atlantic rollers dividing off Land's End. Shard turned off the A-30 in Redruth, taking the B-3300 to Portreath, thence a right turn onto an unclassified road to Nancekuke village.

The chemical warfare base was strongly guarded, Shard's papers painstakingly checked. Admitted, he drove in past a gate guard of police, troops and domestic security men. Dogs were around, held on leashes as their handlers patrolled the establishment's perimeter. A wind was coming off the sea, a south-westerly—the predicted one that was later going to back to the west? Shard shivered as an armed corporal of the Royal Military Police escorted him from the gate to the admin building: this looked a grim place, comparable only with Princetown and its lonely prison buildings on Dartmoor, a dreadful place to be stationed in. Inside it was grim as well: to Shard, the prison comparison held. He was taken along a bare corridor that echoed to his footsteps, and was ushered into a room the two windows of which looked out distantly over the Atlantic beyond the Cornish North Coast path—grey and turbulent with that rising wind, streaked with the long white gashes of the rollers. Below the windows was a desk: a man sat behind it, a man now rising in greeting, long and thin and yellow-skinned like a man of long service overseas. Another man rose from a chair at the side.

'Mr Shard?' the first man said in a voice as thin as his body.

'Right.'

'I'm Wendlestock—Director.' He gestured towards the other man. 'Smith-Lyneham, Security. *Major* Smith-Lyneham.'

You had to be a major, Shard thought sardonically, even to be given so much as an interview for this sort of security appointment. He shook hands and got down to business. 'Well, gentlemen. I take it you're both fully acquainted with all the facts?'

'Certainly.' Wendlestock coughed, a hollow sound: he was not, poor man, far off being a husk already. 'I hope you come with happier news, Mr Shard?'

'I'm afraid I don't.'

'Then you believe we have just...seven and a bit hours?'

Shard checked his watch. 'Yes. Unless we take Lavington alive.'

'That will solve it?'

'It doesn't have to, but I'm hopeful. Can either of you tell me anything about Lavington as a man...anything his wife might not have told me?'

Wendlestock and Lyneham-Smith exchanged glances. Smith-Lyneham said, 'Actually, we can't. Neither of us knew him.'

'I see. I gathered he'd never been here to Nancekuke?'

'That's correct.'

'How about your staff? The possible planting of a device—have you any suspect, Major?'

Smith-Lyneham spread his hands. 'They're

all clean—they'd have to be, or they wouldn't be here—'

'Lavington was there—at Porton, and Wiston House.'

'Yes, that's true.' Smith-Lyneham gnawed at a finger-nail. He was stoutish, with an indolent look, and a kind of self-indulgency: but a man would scarcely be lazy in the circumstances. Duty would have been done. Smith-Lyneham proceeded to indicate that it had been. 'All personnel have been questioned and every conceivable place searched, visually and with detectors, Mr Shard. I'm convinced there's nothing of the sort that's been suggested. I'd give my guarantee on that.'

'Can you suggest anything else?'

Smith-Lyneham said, 'Only aerial attack, bombing. But that has its problems from the other side's viewpoint.'

'Such as?'

'It's obvious: availability of bases and aircraft, the imponderables of whether or not they can be sure of penetrating our radar defences and fighter screens, the chanciness of *any* air attack hitting the target.'

'How about rockets fired from aircraft? Have they the penetrability?'

'In many cases, yes. Some of the stowages are very deep, though, and heavily protected.

Of course there are the big rocket-launchers, seaborne or land based—'

'But that would call for an availability of bases on the continent—or in Ireland maybe—or ships that'd be spotted in no time. I have my doubts that they'd get away with land based launchers—you can't keep that sort of set-up hidden for long.' Shard got up and paced the room, frowning. 'As a matter of fact all these possibilities have been considered...I stick to my hunch, gentlemen. I have faith in it. Lavington's still the key. I ask again: can neither of you suggest any other way—any way, that is, apart from a time-fused or radio-controlled explosive device—that he could use to blow the dumps?'

'I can't think of any,' Smith-Lyneham said. He lit a cigarette: there was a noticeable shake in his fingers. Shard was about to go into the death-potential of Nancekuke in more detail than his documentary summaries had given him when a red telephone burred on Wendlestock's desk. The Director answered, then handed the instrument to Shard.

'For you, Mr Shard.'

'Thank you. Shard here.'

'Oh, Shard, thank God!' It was Hedge again, sounding put out. 'You've got there. We're coming in shortly—from RAF Pewsey, by

288

helicopter—'

'Who's we, Hedge?'

'Me and you know who. First contact. I know this is a security line, but—'

'Why you, Hedge?'

'I'll explain all that when I see you. It's to do with my wife.' Hedge rang off: Shard put down the receiver with a crash. The last person he would ever have expected to turn up in Nancekuke was Hedge: Hedge did not normally venture into the field; that was not his job. And Hedge's wife? How, for God's sake, did she affect the issue—unless, of course, she had produced some further information about the attack in Eaton Square? Even that would not, presumably, require her personal presence in Nancekuke. Shard, with half his mind now on Hedge's advent and the chances of getting hard information out of Katie Farrell, listened to Smith-Lyneham's catalogue of Nancekuke's stockpile: the VX gas in liquid form, the various disease cultures, the germs and the botulinum. Once enough of the latter to cover a half penny reached any of Cornwall's water reservoirs, you could kiss the West Country goodbye. Smith-Lyneham took Shard on a quick inspection of the stocks: basically, it was the South Downs all over again. It was still difficult to realise just how much death and suffering the various containers held. In toto, here in Nancekuke alone and never mind the other dumps, was more than enough to kill the world's population a hundred times over. But it wouldn't be the world that would suffer when Lavington went into action: the English Channel, the silver sea until now serving as Shakespeare's wall or moat defensive to a house against the envy of less happier lands, would act as Britain's leaden coffin.

Back in the Director's office, loud sounds from the sky announced Hedge, helicoptering in. Shard went out to meet the party: Katie Farrell, looking pale and tired, was under armed military escort. There was no sign of Hedge's wife. One member of the party Shard was glad enough to see: Detective Sergeant Kenwood.

'Well done, Harry,' he said. He lifted his eyebrows in a question, with a jerk of the head towards Katie Farrell: the answer was a shake. No coughs—yet. Shard turned to Hedge, who was being welcomed by the Director. Catching his eye he asked, 'Mrs Hedge?'

Annoyance flickered across Hedge's face. 'A contretemps.' He approached Shard, took his arm conspiratorially and spoke close to his ear. 'The hospital she was in. The damn porters run the show these days. Some sort of strike—they refused to service the private wing. She's convalescing now and she insisted on going to her brother near Plymouth. Damn fool came up and got her and never mind what *I* said!'

'What *did* you say, Hedge?'

'As much as I could,' Hedge snapped, reddening.

'And you came down to say it all again?'

Hedge glared and turned his back. Talking again to Wendlestock, he marched inside the admin building. He hadn't said a word about Katie Farrell or about Mrs Morton. Presumably, and reckonably, Mrs Morton had had nothing more to offer. Behind Hedge's back, Shard caught the eye of Detective Sergeant Kenwood. 'We'll let him cool. With any luck, he'll be off to Plymouth shortly. Tell me about Katie Farrell.'

Kenwood said, 'Not much to tell, sir. I tailed her to Marseilles—'

'And her companions?'

'Yes, sir. One man, one woman, both Arabic by the look of them. At Marseilles, the French police moved in. This Arab pair drew guns and there was a shoot-up. They were both killed. I kept tabs on Miss Farrell. The French police flew us back to Paris and we flew out again from Orly in an RAF jet fixed by Hedge. That's all, sir.'

'Did you interrogate?'

'Yes. Nil result.' Kenwood paused, glancing across to where Katie Farrell was being held by her escort, her thin dress blowing in the wind off the sea. Kenwood had something more on his mind. He said, 'Nil result in what she said, or wouldn't say, sir. All the same...I fancied I got a reaction when I mentioned Dr Lavington.'

Shard's face tightened. 'What did you say about him, Harry?'

'Nothing security-wise, sir. Only to say we'd been in touch with him.'

'I see. All right, Harry. This reaction: what was it?'

Kenwood frowned, pursed his lips. 'Hard to say really. Just a flicker of interest...a *heightened* interest all of a sudden. Enough to make me begin to see a link. It was as though she cared, kind of. Just then I didn't probe.'

'Why not?'

'Seemed too tenuous, sir. And I thought you'd prefer to do it yourself anyway.'

Shard clapped him on the shoulder. 'Good man, Harry, you did right. Anything else?'

'Could be, sir, could be. Again it's no more than a feeling, but I got the impression she knew Porton. You see, I didn't so much interrogate as—well, chat, sir. You know how it is when you chat to someone, things emerge accidentally. She was covering, fending off— but that was what I felt, that she'd been in that part of the country and knew it pretty well.'

There was a gleam in Shard's eye. 'I'll be bearing it all in mind, Harry, when I start the grill cooking,' he said.

★ ★ ★ ★

Smith-Lyneham provided secure accommodation for the grill. Shard set it up personally and with care: a hard chair for Katie, facing a bare table, and himself behind a bright light beamed straight into the girl's face, a spotlight that brought her up stark and left the remainder of the small room in darkness. With their backs to the door stood the military escort, wearing steel helmets and camouflaged uniforms and carrying quick-fire heavy automatic rifles held across their bodies. This escort consisted of a Guards detachment, a corporal and two guardsmen.

When Katie was brought in and seated, Shard's first question was over her head to the shadowy figures in combat dress behind.

'You've served in Northern Ireland, Corporal, I believe?'

'Yes, sir.'

'All of you?'

'That's correct, sir.'

'You'll have heard of Miss Farrell, I'm sure.'

The answer was bitter. 'We have that, sir.'

'Personal experience, Corporal?'

'Not personal, sir, no. Nor the regiment. But lads we knew...brigaded with us, sir. Infantry and sappers—Royal Engineers, sir.'

'Bomb squads?'

'That's right, sir.'

Shard nodded. 'Thank you, Corporal. All that being so, I doubt if any of you are squeamish. You'll have seen interrogations in Belfast—or rather, the results of them. I'm referring to certain unofficial gentry, if you get me, not the proper authorities. Right?'

There was a laugh. '*Right*, sir!'

Shard reached out and angled the spotlight a little more: Katie Farrell's eyes reflected back, diamond hard and bright. Shard studied the face, remaining silent for some while: Katie was growing restive. Shard, though acutely conscious of time passing, time running out too fast, kept all haste out of his voice when he spoke at last, sounding relaxed and easy. He said, 'I want your help, Katie. If you give it...well, there may be things I can do to help you.'

'I'm not asking your help,' she said, and shrugged.

'No? You may change your mind. The alternative to my help is not pleasant. You heard what I said to the escort.'

'You're threatening me, are you?'

He smiled, coldly. 'Yes, Katie. I'm threatening you, all right! Don't make any mistake about that. Once, I was a copper in the Met. They knew me as Iron Shard—'

'Coppers don't threaten. So they say.'

'And they say true, Katie. They don't threaten. I'm not an ordinary copper any more. That makes a big, big difference, as you may be finding out.' Shard's tone hardened as he leaned forward, keeping in shadow still. 'I want to know the names of your associates. I want to know exactly where you yourself link in with what's currently being threatened against this country. I want to know why a body was planted, made up to look like yours.' He paused. 'I want to know what your own connexion is, or was, with the Porton Down area.'

The spotlight showed the flicker, the wary look coming into the eyes: something had sunk home. She said, 'I haven't any connexion there, none at all.'

'Sure, Katie?'

'Quite sure. Try something else, copper.'

'All right,' he said easily. 'I will.' He paused, giving the girl time to reflect a little, to weigh the alternatives in her mind. He was about to put the next question when there was a knock on thé door—loud, urgent. Shard cursed under his breath but gave the order to the corporal to open up. The NCO went outside, came back in and reported, 'Major Smith-Lyneham, sir. He'd like a word. It's important.'

Shard nodded and got up from behind the light. 'Watch the prisoner,' he said. He went outside. Smith-Lyneham was pacing up and down, biting again at a finger-nail. 'Well, Major, what is it? I'm—'

'It's your man Lavington. He's been sighted—'

'Where?'

'Bodmin Moor. South-east of Camelford... between there and Rough Tor. The police have him under distant surveillance and they don't think he's seen them. Have you any orders, Mr Shard?'

Shard said, 'Yes. Tell them to keep it that way and tell them I'm coming in. And tell my Detective Sergeant to join me at the helicopter, will you—and see that my boss is informed. I'll be airborne, hopefully, inside two minutes.' Smith-Lyneham turned away and made off fast along the passage; Shard went back into the interrogation room. About to tell the escort to hold Katie Farrell secure, he changed his mind: true, left in Nancekuke, she might well cough when she saw the hands of her watch ticking away towards her death. But Shard had a theory, born of Harry Kenwood's words earlier; and his hunch was that she could be persuaded to cough with much more point if she was present in person at the hunting down of Lavington.

CHAPTER SEVENTEEN

As Shard reached the helicopter with Katie Farrell and her military accompaniment, he saw Hedge come flying out from the admin building.

'Shard!' Hedge shouted.

'What is it?'

'I'm coming with you.'

'Like hell you are, Hedge.'

Hedge panted up. 'Don't be impertinent, Shard. I've said I'm coming and I'm coming.'

So there, Shard thought to himself. He was furiously angry; Hedge would be an unparalleled encumbrance in the field—the literal field, sheep droppings and all. Bodmin Moor was no picnic and they would in all probability still be there after dark. Hedge scuttled up inside the helicopter's belly, pursued by Shard's question: 'Why, for God's sake?'

'It's my duty, Shard.'

'Oh, balls,' Shard said rudely: then apologised. It was a *fait accompli*: Hedge was already seated and could hardly be ordered out. The rest got in: it was a tight fit but they hadn't far to go, and would survive if the machine could lift off with Shard as an extra to the inward flight. Lift-off was in fact achieved without fuss and the pilot headed out north-east across a wind that, as forecast, was starting to back round to the west. Below, Nancekuke dwindled: beyond it, the sea was turbulent. A nasty night was coming up, nasty for sailors out at sea, for landsmen out on Bodmin Moor. But not so nasty as what might happen to Nancekuke and its staff. Which, of course, was the reason Hedge was currently airborne. Hedge was perhaps not quite a coward, but he was never noticeably swift in coming forward when physical danger threatened: to give him his due, it wasn't exactly expected of a man in his particular position. But undoubtedly, had he not joined the task force in flight, he would have been expected to stand by at Nancekuke rather than load the air traffic with squeals for another helicopter to ferry him to safety. Bodmin Moor, at any rate for Hedge, would look like a safer bet from all points of view.

Shard, sitting behind Katie Farrell, leaned forward and shouted into her ear against the racket of the helicopter. 'Dr Lavington,' he said.

'What about him?'

'We're going in to get him.'

She looked round, eyes wide and scared. Shard grinned, a tight stretch of lips against teeth. The look in the girl's eyes seemed like confirmation. He spoke again: 'He's probably going to die. If I were you, I'd think about that.'

For the present, he said no more.

★ ★ ★ ★

It was only late afternoon—a little under four hours yet to go; but the day had darkened with the heralds of a coming storm: no mist now, but an increasing wind and a nasty lash of rain to meet them as the helicopter touched down to Shard's order a little way short of St Teath on the A-39. Not wanting Lavington worried by any incoming helicopters, he had radioed ahead to the police in Camelford for mobiles to await them by the St Teath turn. No hitches: the transfer to the cars was made, one of them taking Hedge and Kenwood. The police drivers headed in fast for Camelford. Shard, in the other car with Katie Farrell and the escort, was thankful he had not currently to listen to Hedge's moans. Only one response would have sufficed, and that wouldn't have helped harmony. It was tough on Harry Kenwood, but was good training for promotion. Nearing Camelford, they met a police motor-cyclist: Shard had him stopped, then leaned through his wound-down window. 'Detective Chief Superintendent Shard. Anything fresh?'

The PC saluted. 'No, sir. The man's under distant surveillance and won't get away now, though when I left the post he was temporarily out of sight. They think he's lying up behind some boulders on the lower slopes of the tor, sir.'

'He's not suspicious?'

'We think not, sir.' The constable grinned briefly. 'You'll have a job to find our lads yourself, sir.'

Shard smiled back. 'All right, I'll not detain you.' They drove on again. Shard found himself gripped by a looseness of his guts: it was all so much touch-and-go and his whole assessment could be way out. If it was, his head would be on the chopping-block and deservedly so, only there wouldn't be any chopping-blocks operative. Lavington had to be the key, the key had to be broken off smartly, right in the lock...savagely now, he swivelled in his seat and looked back at Katie Farrell sandwiched between the escort.

'I told you to think,' he said through set teeth. 'Have you?'

'Get stuffed,' she said.

He grinned. 'That's crude. You've not been that before. Suggestive, perhaps, when on route for Cherbourg—but not crude. Am I getting through at last?'

No reply.

Shard said, 'I can be just as crude, Katie. Has Lavington?'

'Has Lavington what?'

'Done some stuffing,' he said. 'It's you I have in mind.'

She flared up at him, reaching forward until the soldiers' hands forced her arms down painfully. 'You bastard,' she said. 'What's it to do with you what I do?'

'That,' Shard murmured, 'doesn't sound quite like a denial, somehow. Anyway, it's your funeral. And Lavington's.'

There was a snap in the eyes but no further

speech from Katie. Shard felt his theory was holding up and, given time and a good view, might yet crack Katie and at the same time, with luck, crack Lavington as well. Shard was thinking back to Steyning and his visit to Lavington's wife Violet. He had found her sexless, utterly cold, utterly unresponsive to him as a member of the male sex. There was, he knew, nothing egotistic in the thought: women who were not sexless always responded in their eyes, their manner, their whole reaction; not just him—any man brought it on: it was not a case of forwardness, it was just something glimpsed, something inexplicable, the electric rapport between man and woman. All this had been lacking in Violet Lavington: he recalled that when meeting her he had had the thought that, since she was married to Lavington, this was just as well; his view of Lavington had been that he was just as cold a fish. But in man, as opposed to woman, that could be no more than an exterior: it was possible for passion to be concealed under ice. On occasions this was essential, was part of man's defences in various compartments of his life: jobwise, just to mention one aspect. Kinkiness? That was pure conjecture, but Lavington could have all manner of desires that were better kept under a cloak. Harry Kenwood had spoken of two things:

mention of Lavington had brought out a reaction in Katie Farrell and she had appeared familiar with the Porton district. She could have spent time there prior to her arrest. She could have been the release for Lavington's urges. Maybe it was a long shot to imagine Lavington turning an attractive woman on, but it was better than nothing and might be worth keeping in the forefront of his mind.

They entered the small moorland town of Camelford on the Camel River, drove down an almost empty street, past public houses and cafés to a car park on the north-eastern outskirts just beyond the river: here they found a mobile command post, a radio-equipped van with a Chief Inspector and staff. With the Chief Inspector was a Major of the Royal Artillery.

Shard glanced at the Major. 'Not thinking of using field guns, I hope?'

'Hardly! My battery's assisting your chaps, that's all—'

'Where is he now—Lavington?'

'Still out there so far as we know.' The gunner waved a hand south-eastward, out across the rain-swilled moor.

'As far as you know?'

'He hasn't moved out from cover.'

'You're sure he's still there?'

The Chief Inspector came in on that. 'We're

pretty sure, sir. We have men screening on an extended perimeter and no movement's been seen—'

'And he hasn't seen any of your people, or the troops?'

The police officer shrugged. 'If he has, it can't be helped at this stage, sir. They're using camouflage, the visibility's foul, the ground's rough and they're keeping on their stomachs. And keeping their distance. It's all we can do, sir.'

'If he hasn't seen anyone, why's he in hiding?'

'Waiting his time, most likely, sir.'

Shard nodded. 'That's possible enough, I suppose. I'd like to look at your maps, Mr Welsh.'

'Right here, sir.' The Chief Inspector turned to a table behind him. The wind was freshening fast; the van rocked to a heavy westerly gust as Shard pushed past towards the table and its outspread Ordnance Survey maps.

'Show me where.'

A pencil-tip came down on a spot a little over three kilometres from Camelford and on a south-easterly bearing: Shard did a quick sum; he wasn't fully metricated yet. He arrived at two miles. He scanned the area in the vicinity of Lavington's hiding-place: the 1,312 feet of

Rough Tor lofted another couple of kilometres beyond Lavington. 'Rough Tor,' he said thoughtfully.

'Sir?'

'I believe he's going to transmit a signal and that signal has to go a long way. He won't be able to do it from behind a rock, right down low in the shadow of the tor, Mr Welsh.' Shard tapped a ball-point against his teeth. 'For my money, he'll be aiming to climb Rough Tor.' He looked up at the Chief Inspector. 'You're aware of the facts, I suppose, or what we believe to be the facts?'

'Yes, sir. A radio-controlled blow-up at three points—Porton Down, West Sussex, Nancekuke.' The police officer hesitated. 'Mind if I make a suggestion, sir?'

'Go ahead.'

'A police marksman, sir.'

'To pick him off at long range?'

'Yes.'

Shard smiled. 'I'm a police marksman myself. It could come to that—but not yet, Mr Welsh!'

'I don't understand why, sir.'

'Then I'll tell you: I'm working on theory, nothing else at the moment. The attacks could come from some quite different quarter, something we haven't even begun to suspect yet and so haven't covered for. The one man we have who may be able to tell us is Lavington. Which is why he has to be kid-gloved until I can take him off his guard.'

'It's brinkmanship, sir—isn't it?'

Shard nodded. 'You don't have to tell me.' He glanced along the line of maps on the table, jabbed in three places with the cap of his ball-point. 'Stithians, Drift, Bussow—Cornwall's water, all at risk. Stithians—the biggest—south-east of Nancekuke and right in the windstream. Just a pinch of botulinum...I know! We'll still play it my way. And in the meantime I want you to draw in the net the other side of Rough Tor, all right?'

★ ★ ★ ★

Hedge stuck to Shard like an unwelcome leech as, with Katie Farrell and Detective Sergeant Kenwood, they left the harbourage of the command post, back temporarily in the cars again, heading for the foot-slog operation. They headed out of the town, took a right-hand turn signposted for Rough Tor, drove fast along a narrow road into the rain and the blustering wind. They passed troop concentrations, reserves concealed behind high hedges; in a farmyard was a squadron of heavy tanks, fine last-resort vehicles for the moor so long as they navigated clear of bogs. They came down a long, bleak stretch, down a steep hill and up again, through a gateway with a cattle-grid: the moor stretched, grey, lonely, rain-swept, with Rough Tor itself invisible behind a film of falling water.

'Lower Moor,' Shard's driver said, waving a hand into the rain. 'Do we wait here, sir?'

'Yes,' Shard said. He got out, followed by the rest of the party, which included a PC provided by Welsh as guide. They got on the move at once, no time lost, sliding through mud on a rocky base, slithering downhill to a boulder-filled stream, accompanied by Hedge. Shard had done his best to persuade Hedge that he would be better off by remaining in the Camelford command post, though this suggestion had been clearly unpopular with the Chief Inspector and the gunner Major; they had not been impressed with Hedge's chemist's pack, for one thing. While Shard had been map-reading Hedge had sprayed his throat and had then fussed silently, his manner and expression both very eloquent fussers. In the command post he would be the most monumental liability and the Chief Inspector had clinched his vanishment from the scene by remarking, as it were casually, that he would be glad of the presence of the brass as a complete can-carrier afterwards—a proposition which, Shard was convinced, had already occurred to Hedge. Likewise he had refused to remain in the police cars on the fringe of the moor. It could have been a courageous desire to be in the very front line but Shard had his reservations on the point. Meanwhile, as they trudged along, Hedge kept yacking about his wife: naturally her proximity to one of the threatened areas was a worry to him, but Shard wished he would contain it.

'Why not join her, Hedge?'

'I don't see that it would make any difference.'

'The reassurance of your presence?'

'Well...yes.' Hedge plodded on: they were all muddy now, feet gaining weight with every step. There was worsening visibility, almost solid water in the wind that sliced, slashed and sogged. 'My duty's here, though...the Head of Department would say...and anyway there's no transport to be spared.'

'Back in Camelford, they—'

'No, no.' Hedge halted for a moment, looking round fearfully: Bodmin Moor was a far cry from Eaton Square and taxis. 'I'd only get lost. It's good of you to suggest it, Shard, but no.'

Shard gritted his teeth and silently blasphemed as he trudged on behind the police guide, watching out as closely as was possible

308

in the overall filth. In spite of mackintoshes and Wellingtons provided by Chief Inspector Welsh, they were all wet through: Hedge, who had small feet for his size and had been provided with huge Wellingtons, had kept his town shoes on inside, and the expensive leather was squelching around in water that had come over the top as, at one moment, he had plunged them into the stream. It was getting bloody cold, too, Shard thought. More plod, more mud, and the police constable ahead held up a hand and turned.

'Far enough, sir.'

'In the screen, are we?'

'Yes, sir, part of it, right on the perimeter.'

'Well done! I can't see a damn thing more than—what—twenty yards ahead.'

'I know the ground hereabouts, sir. Brought up on it, I was.'

'I'm relieved to hear it,' Shard said, and meant every word. 'Look, where's the nearest field command outpost?'

'That way, sir, about half a mile.' The constable pointed left. 'The ground's a little marshy both sides of where we are now, so you'd better watch it, sir.'

'I will, don't worry. Can you find that outpost, d'you think, and get back here in one piece?'

'Oh, yes, sir, no difficulty.'

'Then do that, please. Tell whoever's in charge where I am. I don't want to use my radio in case it gets picked up, and I don't want him to use his—except in an emergency when I'm to be contacted at once. And I want to know about any movements Lavington makes. All right?'

'Yes, sir.'

'And tell the officer in charge I'm taking over the command and intend moving forward in twenty-yard hops as soon as you get back here. Give him a time—you'll be the best judge of that.' Shard clapped the PC on the shoulder. 'Off you go, lad—and stay out of the bog!'

When the policeman had faded into the wind-driven sheets of rain Shard said, 'From here, it's a case of slither.'

Hedge shivered. 'Slither, Shard?'

'On our stomachs.'

'My God.' Under Hedge's borrowed police mackintosh was a Savile Row suit, all four hundred guineas of it. 'Is that really necessary, Shard?'

'Yes. Of course, you can still go back—'

'No, no, no.' Clearly, Hedge's mind was filled with thoughts of bogs. 'I'll manage somehow.'

'Great!' Shard swung round on Katie Farrell,

who was somehow contriving to look seductive still: the high collar of the dark blue mackintosh suited her, set off her face and figure wonderfully. If Shard was right, Lavington must have made a lovely meal of her: the contrast with Violet Lavington was almost cruel. Now, Shard decided, was the time for a full probe. Suddenly he asked, 'What are you thinking, Katie?'

'Thinking? Nothing.'

'Your mind's no blank, Katie. Or are you one hundred per cent bitch?'

She stared. 'Meaning what?'

'Meaning this,' he said harshly. 'Lavington's out there, not far off. He hasn't much longer. I'm going to get him, you know. I may have to kill him.'

'So?'

He looked at her intently. 'You don't care?'

'Should I?'

He fancied there was a wariness, and also a brittle quality. It was the brittleness that intrigued him and he pressed to see if it would shatter. 'You've slept with him, Katie. You've been his mistress—'

'Don't be stupid.'

'Am I being?' He laughed. 'I don't think so, Katie! You got into this business first of all in the line of...let's call it, duty. For some dirty

311

reason, your path crossed with his. Then other things started to cross—didn't they? It became an affair. Lavington was an unsatisfied man and dedication to his work didn't compensate for no sex. You came as a godsend.' Looking into her face still, he was aware of her reaction: she had paled, and half shut her eyes, looking dangerous, a snake about to strike, but a bloody attractive snake, he thought: fury heightened her sexiness, made Bodmin Moor feel almost warm and dry like bed. He could do with her himself, forgetting even Beth for the length of time it took. He went on, 'Then things went wrong for you. You were arrested. I can well imagine how *that* put the wind up Lavington! When you were hooked off the blood run, he got really scared—didn't he, Katie?'

'Get stuffed,' she said.

'You could have been the lead-in to what he was doing. He'd have known that sooner or later you'd be picked up. So he made arrangements for you to die. Appear to, that is. At the time it didn't matter to Lavington that the manner of your supposed death linked with the death stocks ex Porton. He was near enough to the off, wasn't he? And it all helped to confuse the issue. Clever! So what have you got to say, Katie?'

She almost spat at him. 'Nothing!'

'Oh, well,' he said, smiling, 'there's time yet. Just so I know where I stand for now. Harry?'

Kenwood moved in closer. 'Sir?'

'Whatever happens, don't let her get away. Use your gun if you have to, but don't kill her.'

'Understood, sir.' Kenwood checked the barrel of his revolver, checked the silencer that, like Shard himself, he had fitted after leaving the Camelford command van. They waited: a moment later Katie Farrell opened her mouth and gave a shout. Kenwood made a grab for her, but the back of Shard's hand got there first, slamming cruelly across her mouth. Her lips split and blood ran, and she cried.

'Shut up!' Shard said in a snarl. 'Do that again and I'll put you on your back.' He was breathing hard. 'A warning—wasn't it? You love the bastard after all. Or maybe you just don't want him to fail!'

He was about to say some more when he heard the suck of footsteps in the mud, and the constable's helmet and mackintosh loomed through the rain, approaching at a makeshift run.

'Mr Shard, sir, that shout—'

'You heard it, did you. Well?'

'Lavington will have heard it, sir.'

'How right you are,' Shard said, sounding bitter. 'Now you're back, we close that twenty yards inward. Any news?'

'No, sir, no further sighting.'

'I don't like it,' Shard said. He was about to get on the move when his radio began bleeping. He answered: the Chief Inspector came through from Camelford.

'There's a report from London, from the Home Office.'

'Well?'

'The Prime Minister. He's sticking, won't meet the demands. He's preparing to speak to the nation at 2100 hours, on all TV and radio channels, and to announce Martial Law and a batch of emergency regulations. Message ends, over.'

Shard said, 'Thank you, control, out,' he caught Kenwood's eye. 'A little late in the day...we just have to make his talk redundant—that's all! Hedge?'

'Yes?'

'Best foot forward, Hedge. We're advancing.'

He turned to face ahead: from beside him, there was a hollow sucking, surging, muddy sound as Hedge got under way.

CHAPTER EIGHTEEN

'Hold on!'

Quietly, hand raised, Shard once again halted the advance. The light was really going now, the filthy weather shortening the day drastically. Shard glanced at his watch for the hundredth time: 1935 hours, just under an hour and a half to go if the time-schedule was kept to. Carefully, watchfully, he stood up. Mud and slime drooled from his mackintosh: behind him now, Hedge was practically in tears. The Bodmin Moor mud had a high penetrative quality and the Savile Row suit was black inside as well as out, and Hedge was conscious of having a nasty smell of sheep too. Shard moved ahead of the others, who remained mud-prone, half sunk. He stumbled over a rock, then again over a big boulder, nearly went headlong. By now they were, after a number of short advances, on the lower slope of Rough Tor itself—the boulders alone told Shard that.

He stopped, listening out. No sounds, no signs of human life. Lavington, he was convinced, had shifted berth unseen, was maybe climbing up the tor already. If so, he was keeping well out of sight—or more likely had got himself beyond the visibility of the ground watchers. Shard cursed, wished with all his being that he had felt able to use the helicopters but knew that his decision not to had been the right one. Turning, he beckoned the others on. He heard them moving up behind him, breathing hard. The wind blew strong, right off the sea, filled with salt, lashing them with rain that found its way into every crevice of clothing: why did people ever come to the West Country for their holidays? They struggled on, beginning to climb, the local man, the policeman, just ahead of Shard, leading the way. They were no longer on their stomachs now; they heaved themselves from boulder to boulder, with Hedge puffing like a steam engine. Once again, Shard called a halt.

'Keep down and keep quiet. Watch the woman, don't let her give tongue.'

'What are you going to do, Shard?' This was Hedge, sounding querulous. In the dimming light, Shard watched him take a pill from his mobile pharmacy, and swallow.

'I'm going in, Hedge. I'll take the guide and Katie Farrell. No escort Harry?'

'Yes, sir?'

'A careful watch. If I miss him—if you see him before me—you know what to do: get him talking, don't move right in.'

★ ★ ★ ★

It was a tricky business, the trickiness revolving around Katie Farrell. He kept her right ahead of his gun but he couldn't be sure of its effects: she was well aware he wanted her to live, and equally well aware that a wounding shot—even should Lavington fail to catch the report of a silenced gun—would turn her into an impediment to climbers. Heavy breathing apart, they went up in silence, along the muddy track between the boulders that scattered the sides of the tor, squeezing through narrow gaps. For all Shard could tell, Lavington was holed up behind any one of the boulders, watching them: if so, the shot in the back could come any moment. That gave Shard a naked and unprotected feeling. Yet Katie was in a sense a protection: when Lavington saw her, he would have something to ponder. Curiosity alone might inhibit both the gunshot and the lethal crunch. They climbed on: Shard's leg muscles began aching and his back felt stiff. The ground was slippery, keeping one's balance was not easy: they lurched against the

317

huge boulders. But at last the ground levelled out, though the going was rough and difficult still. Now they were in amongst the grotesque capping, the high edifices of igneous granite, freaks of nature, immense, impressive, age old —stone upon vast stone perched and balanced in seeming precariousness these last million years as gradually the softer layers had eroded away to leave the hard granite cores.

They had reached the top.

No Lavington in sight—no-one in sight at all. Shard said, 'Move right, get in the lee of the rock piles.' He pushed her ahead of him. Up here, the wind was cruel, tearing at them, billowing the mackintoshes out like tents, almost sending them off their feet. They moved behind the piled heavies and found shelter: to either side the granite loomed, vast and solid. Keeping his gun in Katie's back Shard pushed her along behind the guiding policeman. Cautiously, watchfully, they moved along the summit, listening out, alert for the smallest indication, the smallest movement. It was an eerie business as the wind and the rain swirled about the lonely, rocky top of the tor, gusting around the perched pinnacles as though it must cast them down to start an avalanche of huge stones. The going was terrible, lethal: one slip could mean a broken arm or leg. If Lavington was up here, then he was very well concealed…Shard felt his heart sink as he reached another area of open ground, a rough circle where, set into the rock, lay the war-memorial plate to the army's 43rd Wessex Division, a reminder of death and courage and sacrifice…Shard stared down the other side of the tor, down what appeared to be a sheer drop with the distance lost in the foulness of the rain and the deepening dark. He found no sign of life—no human life: here and there on the side they had climbed, the sloping side, a grey-white splodge indicated a suffering sheep half tucked behind a boulder. Somewhere in the rain below the southern drop Chief Inspector Welsh's men—those ordered by Shard earlier to close the net on the far side—could be presumed to lie hidden, or to be making their way up by means of sloping ground farther to the east. If Lavington was *not* up here, then somewhere along the muddy, treacherous line they had all lost him. If that was the case then things looked bad: Shard's watch said 2005 hours. Fifty-five minutes left to the nine o'clock news broadcast, to the Prime Minster's announcement to the nation, to catastrophe. Once this thing started, it could not be reversed. Shard's head seemed to swell and burst: everyone in the bloody country, he thought, depended on him;

and he was stuck, useless and impotent, on the summit of Rough Tor. Just one thing had jelled: when he caught up with Lavington, the time for the soft approach would long since have gone. Now there would be no time left for Lavington to talk: Shard's guess had to be the right one, and Lavington had after all to die before he transmitted.

Shard looked into Katie Farrell's eyes: he told her his decision. 'Have you anything to say?' he asked.

She shook her head.

'Think, Katie. Think hard. He's going to die.'

'Only if you find him.' She was shivering from the cold and wet.

'If you had anything to tell me now...he might live. Give me the facts, Katie.'

She stayed silent, looking back at him, her face pale and tight. He said, 'He may not have to die, don't you see? If this thing doesn't go into action the way I've assumed it does, if Lavington doesn't have to send out a signal, then there's no point in killing him.'

'You can't kill him anyway,' she said, 'till you find him. I don't know where he is any more than you.'

'All right,' he said, 'that, I accept. But we know he's in the vicinity—that's for sure. So we're going to find him. Half the army's looking, not to mention the police. I say again, he doesn't have to die. Maybe. It's up to you. You can't make it any worse for him now.'

'Worse?'

He said, 'There's a better side, Katie. There always is.'

'What's that supposed to mean, then?'

'Think, Katie. No promises—but you yourself were down for the blood run. You know the authorities do it on occasions.' Shard dashed rain from his face, rain mixed now with sweat despite the cold of the high tor. 'He could be let out, let to run.'

She scoffed at that. 'And take his know-how with him? That's bloody likely!'

'What use is secrecy after a country's died, Katie?'

'You'd still go back on it afterwards.' She tried a quote: ' "Put not your trust in princes." Still less coppers.' She almost spat at him then: 'Go on, try and get him. You haven't much time left, have you? I'm not saying another word.'

'You'll die with the rest of us,' he told her. 'You didn't expect to when you hopped the twig to Orly—but you're going to. Try thinking about that one! I—'

He broke off, sharply: his radio was bleeping

him. He pulled it from his pocket, flicked and answered. 'Field One answering, over.'

He flicked again. Camelford control came up, loud and clear: 'Control to Field One. Object got out from under, is believed back tracking, moving around the tor easterly. Orders, please, over.'

'Where's he heading?' Shard glanced at Katie Farrell: she had heard. Her face was tense, but there was the start of a gloat visible.

The disembodied voice said, 'Not known for sure, but could be Brown Willy. He could have seen our screens—'

'Brown Willy...height?'

'1375 feet.'

'Right, we make the assumption. How far? I'm currently on the summit of Rough Tor, right by the Wessex Division memorial.'

'One mile south as the crow flies, more like five if you follow round easterly. It's all part of the same complex...but if you look down you'll see a precipice. Then there's the De Lanke River and a slow climb if you try the short hop—'

'Okay,' Shard said. He turned to his police guide. 'Got that, have you? You can lead the way?'

'Yes, sir—'

Shard spoke to control again. 'Right, we

follow round. We could be wrong about his destination anyway. In the meantime, just in case, I want the new target taken in advance of arrival, fastest means, I say again, *fastest means*, approach from south, all high points covered. Do you get me? Over.'

The voice came back: 'Understood, Field One, will do.'

Shard switched off, reached out and grabbed Katie Farrell by the shoulder. 'We're going down fast. Get moving. Don't fall. If you break a leg I'll drag you.'

They moved down, dangerously, back the way they had come but leaping from boulder to boulder, a faster progress than was offered by the twisting track, the easy path. It didn't take them long. Where he had been left, they found Hedge, using Detective Sergeant Kenwood and the military escort as shelter from the wind and rain, a sorry sight, bedraggled and shivering.

'Shard, Shard—'

'Yes, Hedge?'

'I shall get a chill.'

'You won't. You'll be moving too fast.'

'Where to?'

Shard explained. 'I'm going in now like a bull in a china shop and to hell with it. Lavington may have picked up Camelford's transmission or he may not—we don't know. What we do know is, time's short. But I'll be banking on him not jumping the gun before the deadline—for all he knows, the Prime Minister may be doing a brinkmanship act right to the end—'

'With the intention of giving in, Shard?'

'Lavington may think so. And it's been done before, hasn't it? It could happen again...if it does, our credibility as a nation goes for good. Meanwhile, I've asked for troops to be helicoptered in to Brown Willy. Get up, Hedge.' Shard bent and yanked unceremoniously. Hedge rose like a surfacing whale.

'Using the open radio like that—'

'Save your breath, Hedge. We have a long run ahead of us, and I mean run.' He passed the pursuit orders to Kenwood and the soldiers; they got moving without more delay, two of the troops manhandling Hedge, one on either arm, lifting and carrying as though he were some grotesque baby doing an assisted hop-walk between doting parents. As they left the lower slopes of the tor the mud was atrocious, sucking and pulling at their booted feet, making progress desperately, dangerously slow and heavy. To run was in fact impossible. Shard was drenched with sweat after twenty yards and breathing heavily: but knew that precisely

324

similar conditions were slowing Lavington. Thanks to the weather, full dark had almost come: behind, the triple peaks of Rough Tor had again vanished, invisibly pointing to the skies. By now the troops should be on their way to Brown Willy, a welcoming committee of steel and lead for Lavington—but Brown Willy, like Rough Tor, was a wide area and he could be missed again. Shard plunged on doggedly behind the guiding policeman. Now they could see, as vaguely moving shapes, the troops and police of the in-closing screen, spread to either side, herding Lavington towards his destination. By now Lavington must be aware... Shard glanced at his wrist-watch: thirty minutes left, not enough ground covered. But Lavington, too, was as yet way off his transmission point. He had to have height: some delay would no doubt be acceptable to the other side. It was even logical to suppose that the 2100 deadline would automatically be put ahead now, to give the Prime Minister a chance to back down on television. Logically, the villains were not likely to blow the moment he came on the screens; Lavington could have had fresh orders radioed to him after the Prime Ministerial broadcast had been announced: the fact that no interception had been reported was not conclusive.

Hope was, as ever, refreshing.

Feet dragged up through mud, moved forward, plunged down again, slid off rocky boulders, the widespread clitter from Rough Tor. This was what the men in the front line trenches had to endure in the First World War: they had endured it, lived, slept, eaten, fought and died in it for four years...Shard gritted his teeth, felt the rain penetrate to his skin. If they had done it, so could he and Hedge, but you wouldn't have thought so to look at poor Hedge, a-swing between the cursing soldiers, heave, flop, plunge, splosh and start again. His weight was bringing the two men down almost to their knee-caps. If ever they came out of this, Shard would never be forgiven. In front of his gun, with the army corporal on her left flank, moved Katie Farrell, lithe and sinuous still under the layers of mud. She had said nothing more: Shard would have given much to know her thoughts. What was she to Lavington, had they been lovers, was she more concerned about the men behind Lavington than about Lavington himself, more concerned with reward beyond the sea, the reward for which she'd tried to get out of Britain on that Orly flight? But not now, surely! As Shard had said, she was going to share in death, not riches. So what did she know? The answer could be:

nothing. She was still a counter to be used, just the same. Whether or not her feelings for Lavington were deep, it had yet to be seen what Lavington's feelings for her might be. After he'd blown the death dumps, after he'd got out ahead of the wind-whirled germs—and he had to have an escape route—maybe his plan for the future had involved a Middle Eastern love nest with Katie Farrell...

One snag: it was all, basically, conjecture.

★ ★ ★ ★

On the move, the reports reached Shard: contact, it seemed, had again been lost. Lavington was assuming the proportions of a will-o'-the-wisp, a bogle, a mere gremlin. To use the idiom of the Irish connexion, a leprechaun. The wider reports also came in: all was quiet at Nancekuke, at Porton Down, at Wiston House and Chanctonbury's wooded slopes. No attack, no aircraft in the vicinities or on the radar screens, though RAF Strike Command was ready and waiting. The Prime Minister was all set to go to the cabinet room for his broadcast to the nation, but there was no availability as to what he was going to say. Behind the scenes, so said some spokesman unknown, the Press was in ferment: they had the story and they were red-hot to go but knew their headlines might be read only by a diminishing public if ever they got printed at all: there were union difficulties, and the Press was not the only employer to face that. The word had spread now and all London was panicking: all the unions were coming out unless the Prime Minister gave way, a general strike against a possible early death, God please take note and agree to negotiate. In these circumstances, could Martial Law cope? To Shard as he listened the answer came clear and unmistakable: no, it could not.

Mud, mud, mud...*where was Lavington?* Three minutes to go, just three minutes apart from any extension, involuntary or otherwise. Two and a half minutes...

The scream came like a banshee, away to the right of the onward-lurching party. Shard halted, shouted to the others to stop. Hedge quavered.

'Shut up, Hedge! *Listen...*'

They all listened, stock-still now. Another scream, then the will-o'-the-wisplike flicker of light, a despairing torch, only just seen. Shard caught it and turned towards it. 'Come on,' he said. 'Someone in trouble and it could be one of ours.' Or it could be Lavington. Hope, excitement, spurred him: he moved faster than before, his very feet feeling lighter even as he lifted and plunged and was sucked at by mud wetter than ever: these were bog conditions. He was holding on to Katie Farrell like a limpet, and she was crying now. Maybe, he thought, something has finally penetrated, maybe when she sees Lavington, if it is Lavington, she'll talk. He went ahead: then the torch died and there was another scream, the most dreadful scream he had ever heard, a long-drawn sound that ripped the very night apart. Sweating, knowing what he had to see, Shard brought out his own torch and beamed it powerfully ahead. A few swings and it hit target: it showed a head, and it was Lavington's, sticking just above the surface of the mud, lashing by wind and rain. The mouth was open in that sustained screaming, and one hand clawed at the air, clawed unbelievably in its duty, reaching maniacally towards some object wrapped in waterproof sheeting just beyond the arm's reach.

CHAPTER NINETEEN

Shard could go no further: only just in time, two men of the military escort grabbed him and pulled him clear of the bog. Mud, clinging and sucking, was above his knees.

The screams had stopped now: Lavington's eyes, clearly seen in the torchlight, stared insanely towards the object in its waterproof sheet: Shard had no doubts that this was the transmitter. He turned to the escort and Kenwood.

'No shooting,' he said. 'Without his box of tricks, he's harmless. And he's going to die anyway.'

Kenwood's voice was little more than a whisper. 'A bullet'd be kinder, wouldn't it?'

'It would be murder, Harry. But if he looks like getting to that waterproof sheet...that'd be different.' Shard looked around, beaming his torch to try to pick out the perimeter of the bog. It seemed fairly well defined: a circular ridge of raised ground, fringing a pond-like area of soft mud. Lavington had been dead unlucky, but in fact he was not too far from the hard perimeter behind him. Shard moved round, followed by the others, watching his step carefully. From behind Lavington he beamed the torch again. Once more the screams had started up, and Lavington was again reaching towards the waterproof sheet. Shard understood why: this was not an act of duty, of dedication. Lavington had panicked utterly and saw the object on the bog as his salvation, something solid to reach for and cling to.

From beside Shard came the voice of Hedge, hoarse, high, badly shaken. 'Why doesn't he use that pill, for God's sake?'

'He wouldn't have it constantly in his mouth, Hedge.'

'Where, then?'

'His pocket.'

'What do we do now?'

Shard said, 'Probably nothing. This thing may be over, Hedge. He can't transmit now—'

'You could have been wrong all along, couldn't you?'

'Yes. But I've another shot left.' He turned. 'Now, Katie. Have you anything to say?' There was no answer: the girl had her hands clapped over her ears, and her eyes were tight shut. Shard caught the sparkle of tears running from below the lids when he swung the torch onto her. Handing the torch to Kenwood, he tried again. He took Katie's hands and wrenched them from her ears. 'You've not got long,' he said harshly. 'Look at him. Soon, he'll submerge. He'll give up. He doesn't need to.'

'What?' She stared back at him dully.

'I said, look at him. He hasn't gone down further since we've been here. I believe his feet are on hard ground. And he's almost within reach. It won't be easy, but he can be got out. *Can be*, Katie. Whether or not...that's up to you. Do you understand me?'

Her body seemed to sag: Kenwood caught her, held her upright. She said, 'You'd let him stay there?'

'Yes, I would. And will! If you've anything to say, say it fast. I want to know the facts—' He broke off: she was struggling in Kenwood's arms, fighting like a tigress, her face contorted, eyes blazing, her whole body reacting to Lavington's continuing screams. She seemed unable to speak: Shard lashed out at her, two stinging back-handers across the cheeks, and she checked suddenly.

'You love him, don't you?' Shard said.

'Love him! God...those things you said earlier! You just have no idea, have you?' Her eyes stared, one glance more at the head on the mud, then away. '*He's my father*. My mother's

dead… his wife never knew. He's all I've got.'
Shard was rocked by what she'd said. Her voice rose, cracking on a hideous high note that seemed to rip right through Shard's sudden compunction. 'Christ, you bastard! Get him out, for pity's sake!'

'He'll keep. First—you talk. That water-proofed package. Does he transmit with it, or is there something else?' He reached out, took her face in both hands and rattled her head like a castanet. 'Talk, Katie!' He stopped the shaking, held her still, staring into her eyes. 'Well?'

'He doesn't transmit to blow,' she said. The words seemed to be forced from her, to come out against her will, slow and reluctant but inevitable. 'He transmits to inhibit—that was the safeguard. And you need his set to do it. You haven't got long. It's timed for nine-thirty.'

For a second Shard felt paralysed: then he swung into action, calling to the search parties, the troops and police who had now closed in. 'Macs, coats, the lot. All of you—spread them out on the mud. Get that transmitter—leave Lavington till we've sent out the safe.' He turned back to Katie Farrell. 'I want the frequency and the code for the safe. When I have that, when I've transmitted, we get him out. Not before.'

★ ★ ★ ★

She hadn't known the transmission details: it was Lavington himself who gave them once the transmitter had been safely brought to firm ground—Lavington with Shard pressing down on his head with the extended butt of a police marksman's rifle. Immediately, Shard sent out the transmission: now they could do nothing more but hope and pray. The transmission made, Lavington was with difficulty heaved clear. Hedge, shaking like a man with St Vitus' Dance, assisted: as the fattest, he was positioned flat on his stomach on the brink of the bog to act as a combined sandbag, lever and firm base. When allowed up, he had been impressed some six inches into the ground. When Lavington was out, Shard asked him one question: where had the charges been placed?

'In VX gas containers...re-sealed afterwards.'

'But not containing VX gas?'

'No. High explosive, enough to shatter the buildings.'

'And the deep stowage?'

'Enough to break the surface.'

Lavington was in no condition for any closer questioning: there would be time for that later, hopefully. Shard used his own transmitter and called Camelford control with urgent messages for onforwarding to Whitehall and the military commands concerned. During their progress back through the mud and rain to base, inward messages came via Camelford: there had been no explosions, no disseminations of lethal stockpiles. The declaration of Martial Law had been avoided by little more than seconds; and a final touch had been nice: the Prime Minister, already launched into his television broadcast to the nation, had been handed the information on a slip of paper together with hastily-constructed hints on how to continue. Smoothly he had calmed national fears: 'All I have just said was not intended to alarm...only to reassure you all that we in Government are always fully alert to protect your interests and those of Britain as a country...I have been speaking to you only as an essential part of the large-scale exercise that has been in progress....'

Clever! It brought a small touch of lightness to the homeward trudge through the darkness of Bodmin Moor. And tonight the great British public would sleep soundly in their beds, unaware of the truth, unaware of brinksmanship that had succeeded against an appalling threat. Come morning, the criticisms would start up, loud and clear: the Establishment had had no right, etcetera, etcetera...

★ ★ ★ ★

No sleep for Simon Shard: in Camelford he picked up his helicopter and was flown direct to Whitehall, touching down on Horse Guards Parade. Hedge was with him, Hedge in a clean suit that didn't fit, provided by courtesy of Devon and Cornwall Police. The Head of Department was waiting: already the reports had come in. Porton Down, Wiston House, Nancekuke: all were safe. The VX gas containers were being removed and opened under safe conditions. Nancekuke was the first to report a finding: in one of the containers, an ingenious detonator and primer with a soundless time-mechanism that had stopped at 2116 hours, just fourteen minutes before the off. All this was packed into enough TNT to do what Lavington had predicted. Shard was released for a snatch of sleep on a shakedown in his office as dawn broke over London. He was still asleep at ten a.m. when Hedge came in and woke him, and he sat up bleary-eyed.

'What is it, Hedge?'

'Lavington.'

'What about him?'

'He's dead. A sudden and massive heart attack. It was too much for him—last night, you know.'

'He's no loss.' Shard rubbed at his eyes: they were stinging with tiredness and reaction. 'Hedge, the fact that he was Katie's father. Security's got a lot to answer for there.'

'Yes indeed,' Hedge said smugly. '*Defence* security—not us! A bad show, of course, but it's happened many times before. Lavington was clever—so was the girl. Even your friend O'Riordan didn't know! Naturally there'll be an enquiry and heads will roll.' Hedge pondered, pulling at his chin. 'As a matter of fact, Shard, Lavington did a little more talking before death supervened. About—'

'About Power of Islam—this Mullah character?'

Hedge nodded, frowned, his *pièce de resistance* spoilt. 'I got it out of him—'

'You, Hedge? On your own?'

Hedge flushed. 'Actually I sent for your friends Smith, Brown and Jones—remember? The flat in Knightsbridge? They were a help. I regret to say the Mullah's safely in the Middle East, but his wings are to be clipped shortly. There will be...intense diplomatic activity, shall we say.' He was full of self-satisfaction now, resilient as ever. 'There's certain work I shall turn over to you—I have names and addresses, meeting points—it was a biggish organisation and we should net a full bag. I do believe I can say the threat will *not* recur, Shard.'

Shard said, 'There's still Katie. We have to think what to do with her.'

'Not our concern, my dear fellow—'

'Ah, but your recommendation will go a good deal of the way! Along the line, I made proposals about her father...if she talked. She did talk, Hedge. She saved the day—remember? I think my proposal should hold good for her, now.'

Hedge fidgeted. 'What are you suggesting?'

'After the questioning, back on the blood run—if she wants to. In the circumstances, she just may not. But she must have the chance. I want you to recommend it, Hedge.'

'Well, I don't know that I shall.' Hedge was frigid, drawing himself up. 'After what's been done—'

'Oh well,' Shard said, sounding casual. 'Let's change the subject, shall we, Hedge?' He paused. 'How about you?'

'Me?'

'I've no doubt you've put a report in already. Have you, by any chance, had any advance reactions—about you personally, I mean?'

'Oh—I follow. Yes.' There was the hint of a smirk, of more preening self-satisfaction and thoughts of glory. 'As a matter of fact, the

338

Head of Department did say...not too *precisely*, of course...something about recognition in due course. An honour. You know the sort of thing.'

Shard nodded. 'Oh, yes. Courage, adherence to duty—conduct *beyond* the call of duty. Heroism, remarkable endurance, an unwilling-ness to admit defeat, thus ensuring the nation's security. Right, Hedge?'

Hedge evidently felt obliged to deprecate. He looked coy. 'Oh, that's going perhaps too far.'

'It is, isn't it.'

'And naturally—in view of my position, my role—it would have to be ascribed to something else.'

'Yes, indeed,' Shard said pleasantly. 'Such as moans about chills and mud...having to be half carried...and you almost had a nasty acci-dent when Lavington started screaming, didn't you, Hedge? Then there was your pharma-ceutical pack. You could become a laughing-stock if people were nasty-minded enough. I was there, remember?' He added, grinning, 'So was Katie Farrell, Hedge.'

Hedge's mouth opened and shut again, his face went from pink to violent orange, and he simmered. He swung away and went out, slam-ming the door behind him, hard. Shard grinned again, stretched and telephoned for a cup of coffee. Later, when he went up to Hedge's office, Hedge was busily making out a claim for a new Savile Row suit, cost four hundred guineas, and a pair of hand-made town shoes from a bootmaker in Jermyn Street.